The WONDER GIRLS
Rebel

SOUTHAMPTON SO15 5DR

Text © J. M. Carr 2024
First published in Great Britain in 2024
This edition published 2024
by
The Cindy Press
Southampton SO15 5DR
United Kingdom
www.thecindypress.com

J.M. Carr has asserted her right,
under the Copyright, Designs and Patents Act 1988
to be identified as the author of this work.

All rights reserved.
No part of this publication may be transmitted,
or used in any form,
or by any means, electronic, mechanical,
photocopying or otherwise
without the prior permission of the publisher.

Cover artist: Anne Glenn,
anneglendesign@gmail.com

By the Same Author
You're Magic Duggie Bones
Bert... so far
Spare
The Wonder Girls
The Wonder Girls Resist

Contents

Prologue: The Naming of Florrie 7
The Story So Far.. 29
1: The Muckraker 31
2: Baby on Patrol.. 39
3: Archie..52
4: Sir Malcolm Taggart 64
5: Ellis Island 73
6: June Under Pressure 80
7: Veronica Arrives in Nettlefield............................. 86
8: The Nettlefield Courier... 99
9: Arnold Coombes 110
10: Miss Oswald & Mister 120
11: It's a Market Economy! 129
12: Muckraking in Nettlefield 141
13: Hewett Island 147
14: In Underwood's Yard... 156
15: Brian's New Assistant 166
16: Veronica's Guilt..178
17: Veronica Confesses..192
18: Burgers & Chips 197
19: Where is Baby? 208
20: Ida Doesn't Steal a Car 216
21: Baby in the Boot...223
22: The Blackshirts' Nest...231

Chapter	Title	Page
23	On the Road	245
24	Frances	251
25	Interviews	260
26	Truth	269
27	Baby's Boat Trip	278
28	History	290
29	Return to Hewett Island	300
30	Memory	309
31	Baby's Last Hour	314
32	Where are the Orphans?	323
33	Reunion, Almost	332
34	Taggart's Persuasion	339
35	Too Late	347
36	Rendezvous	352
37	Bravo, Bravo!	357
38	Goodbye	365
39	Inheritance & Responsibility	370
40	One Year Later	377
	Epilogue	384
	About the Book	389
	Acknowledgements	402
	About the Author	404

*To the Mashed Avenger,
his four tall and talented apprentices
and their wonder-full accomplices.*

Prologue
The Naming of Florrie
London, October 1935

BABY CAUGHT A WHIFF of the lumps of eel that Moll had given them for their tea, on her sister's breath. The two girls, Baby and Florrie, lay together in a nest of rags inside their barrel. It smelled a bit, but to Baby that was the smell of home, and she was used to it.

Florrie could sleep for England, dead as a body dragged out of the river, except she was dry. And breathing. She attracted trouble like wasps to a jam pot. When they were out and about, Baby's worry for her sister churned in her belly. But tucked up together in their barrel, it was calm.

They were sisters only in so much as they grew up together with Moll looking after them from when they were little scraps. Moll told Baby that she came from a country called India, but Florrie was probably born in London.

All Baby knew about India was from a friend of Moll's called Abhi. He was a lascar, a sailor. He sat with them by the river sometimes, chewing and spitting the paan that made his teeth red. 'One day, Baby,' he'd say, 'we sail over much sea, you and me. I show you Mother Ganga, holy river where water flows from heaven and gives life to all it touches.' At this, Moll would suck on her pipe and say nothing. But when he had gone, sometimes for months and months on end, she'd say, 'Don't you believe all Abhi says. His tales are as tall as the masts on them old ships. America's the place for you, my gel.'

The thought of going anywhere with Abhi and his red teeth, always made Baby cling to Moll even closer.

Baby propped herself up so she could see Moll outside, sat against the edge of the barrel. It made Baby feel safe to see Moll there.

Over the clanking of the docks and the lapping of the river, Moll hummed a little song – *Yankee Doodle went to town...* Her pipe bounced on her lip.

Above them, in the dark blue sky, the moon, as round as the barrel, shone. One star twinkled beside it. It was so beautiful up there. How must the sky feel to look down on the docks, on the stink and the smoke and the mud? Baby was used to it, but she guessed that somewhere in the world it wasn't like this. Somewhere, grass was green; trees had leaves and the sun shone on clear water that sparkled with its light. That must be how it was in America.

Folk were still about but not many ventured their way. In the distance, Baby could hear their laughing and chatter spilling out the pub a few streets back. She hummed along to Moll's song... *and called it macaroni...*

'You still awake in there?' Moll turned and Baby caught a puff of her tobacco.

Like the stars, Moll's eyes twinkled too. Somehow no matter how dark it got in the night; they always caught a bit of light.

'What's the time?' asked Baby.

'Time you should be asleep, ducks.'

Baby heard footsteps along the wharf, a tap-tap that turned into the click-click of newly heeled boots.

Moll shuffled on her bottom across the opening of the barrel. Her skirts ballooned but there was still a little gap where the moon looked bigger than ever.

The footsteps stopped.

'I'm looking for my sister,' said a man's voice, a toff's voice, trying to sound in charge.

Baby laid her arm across her sister's chest. She wasn't letting Florrie go anywhere.

'Oh yeah,' said Moll. 'And what makes you think you'd find 'er round 'ere?' Moll didn't let anyone be in charge of her.

'She lost erm... something,' said the young toff, 'and she was anxious to reclaim it.'

'So what was it? Perhaps I seen it... for a reward?'

'It was lost some time ago and I, with my family, am not anxious to reclaim the... item. We are only anxious to find my sister.'

'Well, I ain't seen no lady wandering round these parts. She'd be in a right pickle if she was.'

'I'm sure, madam,' said the toff.

'When did you last see her? I can keep my eye out if you make it worth my while.'

'I very much doubt you'll be keeping an eye out for anyone other than yourself, old woman,' said the toff. 'Take that and be done with you.'

Baby heard the chink of pennies on the cobbles.

Moll stretched forward, scraping up the coins. She tucked them in her skirts then relit her pipe.

Baby was waiting for the footsteps to go away.

Fingers snuffled in her sleep and rolled over.

'What's that you've got inside there?' The toff was still there. His cane poked inside the barrel.

It looked like a sixpence was stuck on the tip of the cane, but it was bigger than that, too big, stuck there like a little saucer. Baby was glad Florrie was asleep. She'd have pulled the coin off.

Carefully, so as not to rock the barrel, Baby pulled the flap of her old silk jacket over both their faces and with her fists curled tight, willed Florrie to stay still.

Through the silk of her old jacket, where it was thin under the arms, Baby could just make out the shape of a man's head and shoulders against the glow of the moon.

'You don't want to go poking about in there – might catch some of me wildlife,' said Moll with a cackle and a smoky cough.

The toff stood up and harrumphed.

At last, Baby heard the footsteps tap-tap tapping away. And soon the clanking of the docks and distant merriment from the pubs was all that disturbed the peace of the night.

Baby whispered, 'Who was 'e, Moll?'

'Just a toff where 'e's no business to be, ducks. Go back to sleep.'

Baby wrapped her arm round her sister again and safe in the knowledge that Moll was always there, looking out for them, she went to sleep.

A few days later, Moll, Baby and Florrie took a trip up west. 'Where the pickin's are rich,' said Moll.

'Where are we?' asked Florrie.

'Up west, I told you.'

'But where?'

'Come on now, gel. What you doin' giving me a geography test for, when that lot's over there, ripe for the pickin'?' Moll pointed to a crowd of all sorts of folk, posh and ordinary, rich and poor, some as poor as Moll, but all bustling up the street, to the theatre, coats flapping. 'Go on, get off with you and bring me back enough for a real fish supper.' It was a joke. Even if they found enough for a fish supper, they couldn't spend it all on one meal. It had to last.

Baby and Florrie joggled along with everyone gathering outside the variety theatre that they called the Palladium. Baby's reading was really coming on. Moll hung back to wait and rubbed her hands together. Perhaps Baby could find Moll a nice pair of gloves.

People stood aside for men in top hats and women leaning on their arms in satiny dresses that rippled like the river and furs so thick you'd think the whole beast was round their necks. Baby and Florrie followed on their heels before the crowd closed in again.

Florrie had no bother dipping her long fingers into the gaping pockets of whoever was careless enough to leave valuables where a small girl might find them. But when Baby saw the coppers' blue uniforms at the front of the crowd, she pulled her sister back. 'Watch out. Don't get caught.'

Florrie shook Baby off. 'I'll be all right. Stop frettin'.'

A red carpet covered the theatre steps and the lights shone bright over them. Baby felt the excitement around her: Is that them? Are they here yet? What do you think Her Majesty will be wearing?

So that was who everyone was waiting for. Moll always said the best time for pickin's was when folk were occupied with something else.

The lady who'd just been let through by one of the coppers had a silk train on her dress that rippled over the steps like water. The train was dirty, and Baby spotted a rip in the hem too. The tall man with her wore bright white gloves and carried a cane; a coin was stuck on the tip like a little saucer.

Could there be more than one like that?

The lady stopped on the top step turned and scanned the crowd. She wore a headband, but it looked a bit old fashioned. Mind you, Baby couldn't judge, considering what her, Florrie and Moll had to wear. Baby's silk jacket might have been fashionable at one time, but it was old and dirty now.

The man's hand went to the lady's back, and he tried to push her through the theatre doors where everything was glitter and sparkle.

But the lady was looking across the crowd as if she was searching for something. Her eyes met Baby's. The lady opened her mouth and pointed but the man grabbed her pointing hand and pulled her through the doors to the theatre. The man was speaking to her but it was impossible to hear over the excitement of the crowds.

Baby didn't really want to pinch anything from the ordinary folks. She was as curious about the King and Queen as they were. So she thought she might hang around to see them. She looked about for Florrie. Baby bent over and tried looking for Florrie's skirt–lots of layers, lots of pockets. Moll made them. She had a friend in the rag trade. She had friends everywhere.

But the forest of legs was too thick. Maybe the coppers had caught her. Baby breathed deep and tried to swallow the sick feeling she got every time Florrie was out of sight for more than a few minutes. She told herself she'd have heard whistles and Florrie would have run anyway. Moll must have her. Florrie was right: Baby shouldn't worry.

Bony old fingers wrapped tight round Baby's arm and pulled her back into the crowd. 'Where's your sister?' asked Moll.

'I dunno,' said Baby. She felt the goose-pimples pop up on her arms 'She were here a minute ago.'

'Oh Gawd, I knew I shouldn't have risked it,' said Moll.

'Risked what?' Baby's stomach churned like she'd swallowed a whole jar of jellied eels in one go. 'Have the coppers got her?'

'No, course not. She's a deal too slippery for them. The King's the problem, him and 'er. They've brought everyone out for a looksee. There are too many of 'em.'

Moll dragged Baby back through the crowd, jostling people out the way. Nobody bothered about them except to complain–you're in my way or to gleefully fill a gap nearer the front.

Her hand tight in Moll's, Baby ran with the older woman, away from the theatre steps and the crowds and the coppers out onto Oxford Street. Baby's eyes widened with the riches of the place. For a moment she even forgot about Florrie.

The gas was lit in the lights down the middle of the street and the shop displays shone like nothing Baby had seen before. Tall thin statues of women in the windows curved elegantly, showing off the latest fashions. Shoppers were still going in and out with bags and parcels of the stuff they'd just bought, not pinched, bought, with money, lots of money. The few pennies that Baby had managed to find jangled in the pockets of her skirt.

The folk who'd been walking along in front of them, suddenly stopped and pointed.

Coming down the street was the biggest, poshest cab Baby had ever seen. Coppers on motorbikes rode on either side. More people on the street stopped to stare.

Through the window of the cab an old lady waved like a wind-up doll Baby had once seen in a toyshop window. Her hair was piled up on her head and a little crown nestled in it. Blimey, that was the Queen! And then an old man's bearded face appeared from behind her with the same slow wave of his hand like they'd got a machine to do it for them. Baby supposed you could get machines to do all sorts if you were royal. You wouldn't have to do anything yourself.

The King and Queen in their big cab with the coppers on motorbikes beside them turned off the main street to where everyone was waiting for them. Moll and Baby turned off into a different side street, where Baby hoped only Florrie was waiting for them.

Baby kept close to Moll's swishing skirts as she hurried up the street. The light from Oxford Street faded the further they went.

Moll stopped where one little lamp glowed with a green haze over a door tucked away where the street turned a corner. ''Ere we are,' she said, opening the door.

Baby tugged on Moll's sleeve. 'What are we doing 'ere? Aren't we finding Florrie?'

'Yes, we are,' said Moll. 'Now ssshhh...' she put her fingers to her lips and crept inside.

Baby smelled paraffin or something like it. Was there a fire somewhere? It wasn't until a lady appeared with next to nothing on and feathers stuck to her backside that Baby knew where they were. 'Come along,' said the lady. 'Are you with the *Round About Regent Street* lot? You're on in the first half. Hurry up now.'

Another lady with feathers joined her. 'Goodness me, that show certainly goes in for realism. Did you smell them?'

Baby heard the women laughing as they disappeared down a long corridor.

'That were lucky,' said Moll. 'Come on this way and stay close.' Moll took Baby down a flight of stairs, where a door was open at the bottom.

'Shouldn't we be looking for Florrie?'

'We are,' said Moll. 'Wait a mo...' Moll felt the wall by the door. With a click, the room brightened. How did Moll know how to do that?

Electric lights strung across the ceiling lit up racks and racks of strange clothes from animal skins to silver suits and helmets. The place was enormous.

The stink of mothballs mixed with the paraffin got up Baby's nose. The floor was hard concrete, dusty but solid. There was nothing underneath them. Boxes were heaped up around the room or propped against the walls – round hat boxes, boxes shaped like violins, trumpets... more feathers, swords and shields, bikes with one wheel, a horse's head... Baby had never seen such an odd collection of stuff in one place.

In the distance, far away in the building she could hear music, the orchestra tuning up for the show. King George and Queen Mary must be in their seats.

But over that far away music, she heard something else, so beautiful, it took her out of the theatre to a place much higher. She heard notes clear and pure, how Baby imagined the stars would sound if they sang to her.

Moll pulled Baby through the racks of coarse uniforms, furs, and silks towards the music. The hangers rattled as they made their way to a darker corner of the room where the costume racks had been pushed aside to make space for a harp.

Baby had seen snatches of Harpo Marx playing one when Moll had snuck them inside a picture house, so she knew what the instrument was. The only other people Baby had seen playing them weren't really people at all. Angels in church windows played harps. Though this harp player had their back towards Baby and Moll, there was no mistaking who they were, and she was far from an angel.

Florrie sat on a stool with her arms stretched across the instrument. She didn't turn round, even when Baby stood where Florrie would be able to see her. Florrie's long fingers travelled backwards and forwards over the strings plucking clear pure notes, then sweeping across them, high to low in rainbows of sound. Was that what her fingers were really for? Not just for dipping into folks' pockets but plucking at the strings of a harp?

The harp was as tall as she was and her arms weren't long enough to reach all the strings but the lower strings that she could reach, made a tune as round as the moon.

Baby was so confused; where did she learn this? 'Did you teach her, Moll?' Baby was desperate to know but didn't want to miss any of the music.

But that was silly; how could Moll have done that?

'No, course not. No one taught 'er, ducks. It's in 'er blood. This was where I found 'er. Well, 'er ma found me, before she scarpered with 'er fella to play music abroad somewhere. Berlin, that was it. She give me some money and said she'd be back one day. But the money didn't last long and I 'ain't seen hide nor 'air of 'er since,' said Moll.

'I don't remember that.'

'No, I left you safe somewhere; while I came and got 'er.' She tapped the side of her nose with her finger, like it was a secret.

Florrie was still playing the harp, in a trance, like she could play forever. Like it was the only thing she was ever meant to do. She was in heaven and had probably forgotten about Baby and Moll altogether. The music was inside Florrie and this was its way out.

Moll laid her hand gently on Florrie's shoulder. 'It's time to stop, ducks.'

But Florrie still played, not noticing Moll at all.

Moll gave Florrie's shoulder a little shake.

As if Florrie had been woken from a dream, a nightmare, she stood up. The stool toppled over. Florrie stepped away from the harp as if the beautiful instrument had turned into a monster.

Her face screwed up in horror at the sight of the thing she'd just been playing.

'It's all right Florrie,' said Moll. 'I knew those fingers were for something special. They're just like yer ma's–

Miss Florence Violetta, she were called, not her real name of course, never knew that. Don't think she did. But they called 'er the Angel of the 'arp. They said you 'ad to feel sorry for the gel. She were young and on 'er own but... well, you got her fingers, Florrie. One day she'll come back and hear you.'

Florrie looked like the weight of the whole world had dropped on her shoulders. 'She wasn't on 'er own, was she? 'E was with 'er,' she said quietly.

'You can't remember that; you was just a little scrap...'

Florrie tugged on Moll's sleeve. 'I don't want her to come back. I want to stay 'ere with you, with both of you.' She let go of Moll's sleeve. 'Florrie. That's short for Florence ain't it?'

'Yeah, it is,' said Moll.

'I don't want to be called that no more, either. Case she hears.'

'How's she gonna hear?'

'I don't know but I don't wanna be called it.'

'All right then... just let me think for a moment...'

'Fingers,' said Baby. 'How about that?' Baby never wanted to forget the beautiful music her sister played. And she knew about things that needed to be kept close and not spoken about.

Footsteps tapped down the stairs, soft taps, not that hammer-on-nail-Blakey sound of newly heeled boots. Steps that could creep cat quiet if they needed to.

'Well, how about it Fingers?' Moll took her hand.

The frown on Baby's sister's face lifted. 'All right Fingers. Call me that.'

The footsteps on the stairs weren't trying to be quiet. They were getting louder.

Moll pulled Baby and Fingers into a tall rack of cloaks. The three of them buried themselves in the fabrics from velvets to sackcloth.

The steps stopped on the stairs. Another set, lighter and tappier joined the first set.

'An old woman and a child you say?' said a man's voice.

Moll breathed out a little whistle through her lips.

'Yes, I thought they were in the show,' said a woman. 'You know the *Round About Regent Street* players? They looked like they were in costume ready to go on.'

The light steps tapped away again.

The door to the underground room was opening. The hinges creaked. Whoever it was, knew they were there because the lights were still on.

Baby pushed herself as far as she could into Moll's skirts and pulled Florrie, no not Florrie, Fingers behind her, then wrapped a cloak around them both with a tiny gap to see.

A man in his shirtsleeves, grey hair greased flat and braces holding up a pair of brown corduroy trousers, stood in the doorway. 'Moll, is that you?'

'Alright Ted, yeah it's me.' Moll stepped out from the cloaks into the light. 'She found her way back. It was a mistake coming up here...' She looked up at the ceiling and pressed her lips together. '...or was it? I dunno. I just didn't think she'd remember. She were only a few year old.'

'You did a good thing that day, Moll.'

The man, Ted, spotted Baby peeking out from the cloaks. 'And who's this? That's not that little one that was asleep, swaddled up on yer back is it?' Ted's smile was kind, like Moll's, his whole face lit up with it.

'She is,' said Moll proudly. 'She's Baby and this 'ere's little Florrie but we's calling her Fingers now.' Moll beckoned Fingers out from the rack. 'For some strange reason she don't want anything to do with a ma who left her for dead. She haven't been back, have she?'

'No, not been a word from her since that evening. She said she was going to Berlin with him. Heaven knows how they've got on over there. If they are still a 'they'. But sounds like you're safe little Flo... sorry Fingers.'

'They sure are,' said Moll, 'both of 'em'. It'll take me a while to get used the new name. But it's a good name that don't remind me of 'er ma but does remind me that 'er ma gave 'er one good thing and it's there for 'er when she's ready for it.'

'NO,' said Fingers like it was the one thing she was completely sure of.

What had happened to her when she was with her ma? One day Fingers might let it out, like she did the music, but Baby had a strong feeling it wouldn't be beautiful. She knew how Fingers felt. Mothers were people that left you behind.

Ted reached into his trouser pocket. 'Look Moll, here's something to see you by. How are you getting by?'

'We're getting by just fine, aren't we gels?'

Baby thought the look on Ted's face said that he had a fair idea how they were getting by but he didn't really want to know any more. He was happy with Moll's answer. 'Look,' he said, 'it's payday soon. Have this an' all.' And he handed a Moll a small handful of coins from his other pocket too. Then perhaps you might leave our audience well alone tonight. You heard we got royalty in I suppose.'

'I 'eard,' said Moll. 'Well, we'll be off. Nice to see you again, Ted.'

She shooed Baby and Fingers up the stairs and out into the little back street. 'Come on, we'll see if that lot in there,' she said, pointing to the theatre where they'd just come from, 'have dropped anything in their excitement to see the King.' She jangled her skirt pocket, where she'd tucked away Ted's coins. 'This little lot won't last forever.' And with Baby and Fingers in tow, she bustled off, back to the bright lights.

Oxford Street was still busy with shoppers and folk just out for a walk. A few coppers were hanging about too, looking in the windows. Probably waiting for the King and Queen to come out again. Baby supposed that being the King and Queen they'd have to sit through the whole show. Fancy, the three of them getting mistook for actors—funny sort of show it must be. Outside the theatre, behind the little posts with ropes strung between them, the theatre steps still had the red carpet out—it was like new. The street was littered with all the sort of stuff people drop when they're waiting—cigarette butts, sweet wrappers, newspaper and if you looked hard enough...

'There's one!' shouted Fingers.

Peeking out from under a page of the Daily Mirror was a half crown.

'And another one,' said keen-eyed Baby, picking up a sixpence and showing it off.

'Every little 'elps,' said Moll, letting the two girls drop their findings in their own pockets.

A doorman suddenly appeared from behind the glass theatre doors and touched the peak of his cap as he opened the door for a toff. A man with a long white scarf round his neck stepped out onto the red carpet. He tucked his cane under his arm while he lit up a cigar. There it was, that coin stuck on the tip like a little saucer, bigger than a sixpence but not a shilling.

Three times now, this same toff—what did it mean? Were they following him or was he following them? Baby's skin prickled at the sight of him.

Moll said the toff was out of place on the wharf. Was this his proper place? But he should be inside, not out here.

Moll was bent over, picking a penny out of the gap between the cobbles. She hadn't seen him.

'Old woman—it's you, isn't it?'

Moll stood up creakily, her hand pressed into her back. 'Who's calling me old?' She turned round and as soon as she saw him, she said, 'Baby, 'ere—quick.' and scooped Baby into her skirts.

The toff walked down the theatre steps like he owned them. 'I knew it. I knew you had that.' He pointed at Baby. 'Not that many little Indian savages running around the West End with an old woman who collects waifs and strays are there? It had to be you. However, fortunately for you, I have retrieved my sister, and she has come to her senses. She is no longer interested in the... erm item she lost.' He was looking hard at Baby.

Baby did her best to dissolve into Moll's skirts. Fingers hadn't seen what was going on.

The toff strode towards the three of them. 'Scrabbling around in the dirt for pennies. You people are vermin. You deserve to be shot.' He reached inside silk lapels on his tailed jacket.

'Moll, let's go,' said Baby urging her on. They'd already had one lucky escape that evening. She was sure this wasn't going to be as lucky.

But Moll was holding her ground. She put her hands on her hips and stuck her chin out.

The toff pulled out a slim leather wallet. 'What you deserve and what you're getting are so far apart.' From the wallet he took two large white five-pound notes. 'This,' he said, 'is for you to keep that,' he pointed at Baby, 'well away from my sister. If you don't, I can promise you will get what you deserve.'

Moll snatched the two five-pound notes. 'Ta very much.' She rolled up the notes and tucked them down her front.

The theatre door opened, and a woman's voice called, 'Cecil, where were you?'

The toff, Cecil, ran up the steps and shooed the woman back inside. 'Just out for a breath of fresh air. Come, let's not be late for the second half.'

And they were gone.

'Well, me dears,' Moll jangled the coins in her skirts and patted her front. I don't think the pickin's have ever been this good. It's a proper fish supper for us tonight, gels. That eel can go back in the river.'

THE STORY SO FAR
(with hardly any spoilers)

The Wonder Girls are a gang of mostly parentless girls who resist the evil plots of the Blackshirts, British fascists and Nazi sympathisers of the 1930s. So far, they have foiled two such plots.

Wonder Girls—Baby, Fingers, Gin and Brian—mostly hang out in an old railway carriage called 'The Lillie'. But they also spend a lot of time in the local orphanage where the lovely June Lovelock is now matron.

Wonder Girls, Sophie and Ida are at training colleges in Bournemouth. Sophie, Baby's 'guardian angel', is training to be a tailor. Ida is training to be a mechanic. Because of her extraordinary talents, Wonder Girl, Letitia, has joined the Special Operations Executive (British Intelligence). Ida often pops back to Nettlefield to see her little sister Bonnie in the orphanage.

1
THE MUCKRAKER

Brooklyn, New York, New York, late February 1938

VERONICA KNEW THEY WERE COMING. The talk outside Betty Marie's bar blew along the sidewalk to the tiny basement and turned the air sour. Whispers dropped like the marbles the kids were trading on the stoop above. Glances flashed through the railings. *Good riddance*, they said.

Not everyone had had enough of her 'lies'. Jessie and Lorretta upstairs, for instance. They helped out when Archie was ... But she couldn't put that into words yet. How empty the place was without him, the only father she could remember.

Archie's ink-stained work coat still hung on the back of the door that led to the small space they shared. The whole basement, in one way or another, was devoted to publishing their paper, *The Maple Street Reporter*. She unhooked the overall and rolled it into her bag.

She had one last job.

Veronica slid round the printing press; the hulk of iron and ink that dominated the room, now quiet and mourning its master. She stroked the plates, still in place from the edition that had secured her passage to England. 'I don't need you today, old friend.'

Folks said their stories were trash—about *The German American Bund*, for instance, who were playing at Nazis pure and simple. *Just fun and games*, folks said, *what's wrong with good old healthy sporting competition?* But it wasn't just baseball they were playing, that's for sure.

Folks said she and Archie should stop raking stuff up. The kinder ones said they should stop drawing attention to themselves; an old black guy and young white girl was asking for trouble. And the stupid ones said people just didn't want to know.

Tell all that to Mr Schneider. Sewing ten-dollar suits, trying to scratch out a living in South Williamsburg, his window smashed and swastikas daubed on his door. Trouble comes wherever you hide.

Everyone said it was kids, but Mr Schneider had showed Veronica the threat wrapped around the stone. 'They even come for us here,' he said sadly with a shrug of his shoulders, a little Schneider twisting the tassels on her papa's shawl as he spoke. 'When I crossed over, I thought we'd be safe,' he gestured towards the Williamsburg, the huge bridge that joined Brooklyn to the Lower East Side. 'But this is our lot now,' he said, gathering up his little one, still blissfully unaware of her papa's troubles.

Well, Veronica had done the work. She'd found the typewriter with the bent 'J'. It was in the priest's office when she supposedly went to 'confess' one day. And there on the same desk had been the programme of events for the latest 'Friends of Germany' camp on Long Island. Perhaps when they were holding Nazi rallies in Madison Square Garden, folks would start paying attention.

Veronica took a clean sheet from the box of paper under the desk. The truck pulled up on the street above, but wasn't going to hurry. She unscrewed a bottle of ink and picked out a brush from the pot. One copy, that's all she needed.

As Veronica painted in clear brush strokes, boots clumped down the steps. She reminded herself that despite how it looked, she was the one in control here.

Voices, petty and jostling, argued on the other side of the door as Veronica was admiring her work. But then she noticed a dot of blood sunk into an ancient crack in the wood, and her heart ached for Archie.

Her eyes stinging, she blew on the wet ink.

And there it was, the knock on the door, the official rat-tat.

In the last moment before she had to leave the only home she'd really known, Veronica breathed in the scent of the old place and she was filled with certainty that she was doing the right thing.

She pulled her scarf from her pants pocket and tied it around her neck. The scarf was a bright turquoise and reminded her of a vacation she and Archie once took upstate. Veronica patted his old fedora firmly on her head and tucked the scarf under the lapels of her jacket, cravat style. She was ready.

The door handle rattled.

'Alright, alright, I'm here.' She snatched the paper off Archie's desk and opened the door to two officials. One young, lanky and leering over the other, older, grumpy and crumpled. Both squashed together under the stoop.

'Veronica Frances Park, we're here to...'

'I know, I know... give me space,' she said. 'I need to lock up.'

The old grumpy official grunted and backed into the young lanky one, who stumbled backwards up the first few steps.

Veronica slung her bag through the door into the space they'd left. She pulled the door shut behind her, turned the key and reached into her jacket pocket where a little nest of thumbtacks pricked her fingers. She held her freshly painted notice against the door and, as the two men watched over her from the sidewalk above, pressed a tack firmly into each of the notice's four corners:

KEEP OUT

IF YOU DON'T WANT TO CATCH IT!

That should do the trick. Veronica did feel a bit bad about starting a rumour that was clearly (to anyone with half a brain) untrue. But it would stop prying eyes 'til she got back.

She pulled the key from the lock, grabbed her bag and ran up the steps into the early spring sunshine as a trolley car trundled by. 'Well, aren't we going?' she said, putting up the collar on her jacket against the fresh breeze.

Lanky leaned over and whispered into Grumpy's whiskery old ear. 'Catch what?'

'Baloney,' said Grumpy.

But Veronica caught Lanky's look of distaste before he loped through the crowd and slunk into the back of the waiting truck. She couldn't help smiling. Her notice would work, then.

'Take a good look, 'cause you won't be coming back, Missy,' said Grumpy, grabbing her arm.

'We'll see,' said Veronica under her breath.

'What d'you say?' he said, holding the back door of the truck open.

'I said, "You don't say."' She tried the same tone she'd once used for interviewing an old lady who'd lived her entire life in the worst asylum in the state. She shook off the official arm and scanned the little crowd.

She was surrounded by familiar faces, most of them there to gawp. But there was Lorretta, dabbing her eyes. Veronica pushed her way through to her neighbour, hooked her free arm around Lorretta's neck, and kissed her cheek. 'Don't worry. I'll be fine,' she whispered. 'Just look after this for me.' She slipped the basement key into Lorretta's apron pocket.

'I will.' Lorretta sniffed and shook her head. 'I didn't mean you to go, honeychild.'

'I know, but I think Archie did.'

'Take good care of yourself, won't you?' Lorretta did her best to smile.

'I will, dear Lorretta, you know me!'

Lorretta laughed. A tear slid over her cheek. 'I do, and that's the trouble.'

Veronica felt a rough grip on her arm.

'It's time to go,' said the old official, pulling her away.

But there was the little Schneider, squeezing between two old Brooklyn ladies who wore self-righteous pouts. The little girl handed Veronica a small square of cotton, beautifully embroidered with a V. 'From Papa,' she said.

The stitching was so fine. But the child had disappeared before Veronica could say thank you, and she felt her own tears prickle.

Old Grumpy snatched Veronica's bag and threw it inside the truck. It slid across the floor into Lanky's feet. He squished himself further into the corner.

Grumpy thumped the small of Veronica's back with his palm, pushing her inside with Lanky. Was it because she was dressed in pants and a jacket that they thought they could be so rough? Though she'd better get used to calling them *trousers*.

A yellow checker cab with a bent front fender drove up behind. She could just make out a man in a hat on the back seat. How nice to be so untroubled by the world you could doze in a cab.

'Miss Park,' said Grumpy, 'I strongly recommend you don't cause trouble. You have no papers, no record with Immigration. You are an illegal alien. I am sure your family in England will be pleased to see you.' He slammed the little door shut behind her. Veronica grabbed her bag and sat down on the bench, ignoring the young man huddled as far away from her as he could get.

She heard Grumpy scuffle through the crowd. The truck lurched as he got into the cab and the engine gurgled into life.

Family, what family? That was just one of the questions to which she was hoping to find the answer. She slid along the bench and positioned herself in a small of patch of sunlight pouring through a tiny window. She took off her hat and closed her eyes in the warmth.

The engine rumbled as the truck pulled away from the street.

Jerking and joggling in the back, Veronica Frances Park made up her mind. No, she wasn't going to cause trouble. Not that much, not yet anyway, not on this side of the Atlantic. But perhaps for this family in England when she found them, whoever they were. The thought restored her excitement. She was a muckraker, an investigative journalist, and this was going to be her greatest story so far.

2
BABY ON PATROL
Nettlefield, England, Wednesday 23rd March 1938

BABY AND FINGERS HAD GROWN UP together like sisters. Twins even; two halves of the same person, since they were little unwanted street scraps living with old Moll beside the river Thames. They lived together, slept together, thieved together. Nowadays, as they lived attached to Nettlefield Grange Orphanage and wanted for nothing, thieving wasn't as necessary as it used to be. So, together with the other Wonder Girls, resisting the black-shirted fascists had taken its place.

But Fingers had done something amazing.

She had started school.

Baby wondered if it had been the long hot days playing with the Basque kids at the refugee children's camp last summer that persuaded Fingers. Or was it Letitia's bookish influence? After they all uncovered the latest Blackshirt plot to force the refugee Basque kids to 'work' for the Nazi cause, Letitia, the newest Wonder Girl, was now doing something very hush-

hush with the SOE—*'Special Operations Executive.'* Spies and everything. But whatever it was, and to everyone's surprise, when she heard the orphans were back at school last September, Fingers had begged to join them.

There was no doubt that little Florrie Fingers was bright enough. Where Baby struggled, laboriously practising her reading and writing after supper at the table in the orphanage living room, Fingers picked things up as easily as she picked up the Basque kids' football last summer.

Baby was getting used to the wrench of waving her sister off every morning, watching Fingers run to catch up with the other kids, her bird's nest head of red curls bobbing as wild as ever. But the loss of her during the day still felt like a bruise on Baby's heart. She knew it would happen one day, the two of them going their separate ways. It stood to reason. They'd get to America at last, as Moll said they should, find their feet and, well, something would happen. She could feel it. People grew up. They learned to be independent, like she had when Moll died. Her eyes stung at the thought of it all.

To take her mind off the future, Baby turned her attention to the present. If the last year had proven anything, the Blackshirts, like the Nazis over in Germany, were still alive and well in Nettlefield. Mrs Tatler was still running her horrible boarding house, and Mr Winters the grocer was telling anyone who'd listen about the 'good' Mr Hitler was doing for the German people.

So, on her days off from helping Brian out in the kitchen, while Mabel, the regular orphanage cook, was looking after her sister in Bournemouth, Baby took it on herself to patrol the town. To any casual observer, she was just out for her daily walk, but Baby's eyes and ears were open. And as the news from across the English Channel was getting more and more disturbing, Baby had taken to going further and further afield. It wasn't just the Nettlefield Blackshirts she had to look out for. Where were the rest of them hiding?

But it was hard to imagine there was so much wrong with the world on a lovely spring day in late March; the birds singing, blossom budding on the trees, the tide high in the creek.

She left the town centre far behind and headed out of Nettlefield towards Harburton, another town like Nettlefield that sat across the harbour entrance from Portsmouth. Walking into the sun, it felt warm as summer. Baby unbuttoned her jacket, a lovely shade of light blue with many a useful pocket. It was a present from Letitia, just like the one she wore.

'Don't forget,' Letitia had said when she presented it to Baby, 'I've put Sir Hugh's number inside for emergencies. It's in code, but you'll work it out. Just think of me.'

Sir Hugh was their contact at the SOE and now Letitia's boss. He was busy with something very hush-hush up north somewhere. Baby loved still having this connection with Letitia. Since Miss Grenville, she didn't feel the same about her old green silk jacket.

Miss Grenville turned out to be the reason for Baby growing up in London and not in India, her country of birth. Miss Grenville had virtually kidnapped Baby off the street in Bombay, out of her real ma's arms, and smuggled her onto the ship that brought the Grenville family back to England. But little Baby was discovered by Miss Grenville's horrible father and given away in London, wrapped up in Miss Grenville's spare green silk jacket. Moll, the only ma Baby could remember, and a fine ma she was too, took care of Baby, loved her, and taught her everything she knew about how to survive on the street.

When she discovered its history, Baby had stopped wearing the green silk jacket. And now she couldn't find it, anyway. It had most probably slipped off somewhere between the orphanage and The Lillie, their railway carriage home in the woods by Nettlefield Railway Station.

Baby left the road and waded through the long grass in a field that didn't look like it belonged to anyone. It squelched in places, but her shoes kept her feet dry enough. The morning sun sparkled on the high tide, where swans were gliding gracefully across the water.

On the other side of the creek, neatly cut lawns sloped up to one of the big Nettlefield houses. She'd heard this particular big house belonged to the Sparks family, the same family that once owned Nettlefield Grange, the official name for the orphanage. But what use could the last Spark, poor old Abel, have for it, when he was still stuck in Nettlefield Lunatic Asylum?

Baby had to admit that she was pleased with her new shoes, though not so new now. It helped that she'd worn them in. She had to; her old boots had finally fallen apart. The other thing she had to admit was that her old boots were getting a bit tight.

Three of the other Wonder Girls, Ida, Gin, and Sophie, still had a quite a few inches on her, but Baby had grown. She was the same height as Brian now, whose Down's syndrome meant that she'd never be tall. But Letitia, goodness, if she was still growing, she'd probably be a giant by now. Not so good for being a spy!

When Baby told folk she was almost thirteen, they didn't look quite as disbelieving as they did a few months ago. And maybe she was nearly thirteen. That terrible day last May when the orphanage almost burned down was supposed to be her birthday, if Miss Grenville was to be believed. But the woman was gone now. Her family came and got her from the asylum and Baby hadn't heard from her since.

So, it being 23rd March 1938, Baby reckoned she was probably about two months short of her thirteenth birthday.

She passed a large clump of trees and bushes, a small wood really, not far from the water's edge. A bit like their woods by the station. But as she was unlikely to find another railway carriage as beautiful as The Lillie, Baby carried on along the shore, where shingle made walking less squelchy. A boat was moored in the creek. Nearby, birds with long, thin beaks were swooping down to the water. She stopped to watch.

Any other day, she would have turned back. What would the Blackshirts have to do out here? But Baby was enjoying the walk and was imagining what it would be like to be a traveller, an explorer, discovering new places every day. America was a big place. She'd read about cities like New York and Chicago, but there were mountains and deserts too. How exciting would that be? She turned to tell Fingers...

It was like she'd punched that little bruise on her heart. How could she forget that Fingers was at school? She told herself not to be silly.

Baby had reached the point where the creek flowed into Portsmouth Harbour. Portsmouth was a long way round by road, but only a few miles across the water from where she stood. It would be a lot quicker to swim there.

But could she swim? She didn't know. Since she'd been in Nettlefield, the baths June Lovelock had to force her to get in were the nearest she got to swimming. Truth be told, she quite enjoyed a bath nowadays, mostly because that dreadful thing had happened. She'd become a woman. Maybe she was thirteen already?

One thing was for certain: she knew what Nettlefield Creek was like underneath the water when the tide was out, so she certainly didn't want to swim in that.

But something was.

Not far from the boat, the surface of the otherwise calm creek water rippled with bubbles.

A head appeared. Was it a head? It didn't have a face. A mask like something out of *Flash Gordon* covered it. The man, if it was a man, stood up. The water reached his chest. Strapped to it was a tank a bit like a milk churn, with a tube joining it to the mask. He was not just a swimmer. He was a diver. And for the first time, Baby saw something she hadn't noticed before. Behind the diver, in the middle of the creek, a green hill rose out of the water. She wasn't getting it mixed up with the bank on the other side, was she?

No, that was further away.

The green hill was an island.

An island in the creek!

It was just like the book June Lovelock had been reading to the orphans after they'd had their tea. *Swallows and Amazons*. The kids would be proper excited when they found out they had an island too. If they had a boat, it would be exactly like the book. How had Baby never spotted it? Probably because she'd never walked this far.

A sudden breeze brought the familiar, rotten egg smell of creek mud. Maybe the tide *was* on its way out.

Baby trudged up the muddy beach to the field and squatted in the long grass to watch. Could the diver see her? Did it matter?

She ought to go back and report this to the Nettlefield police. Everyone was meant to be on the lookout for suspicious goings-on nowadays. Though most of the time, Baby felt she was the only one taking that instruction seriously. Sergeant Ted Jackson was alright, but she wasn't sure about some of the other coppers. Perhaps she'd just find out a bit more first.

The diver disappeared. Little ripples glinted in the sun where they had sunk beneath the water.

Baby sat on her haunches as seagulls flapped above her, their beady black eyes searching for titbits. A beetle crawled onto her hand. She was watching its armour-like body find its way across her brown skin, when a purposeful squelch of boots disturbed the peace.

Baby skulked lower in the grass and gently nudged the beetle onto a nearby pebble. 'Off you go, little one,' she whispered.

An old man in rubber waders strode past her.

'Marning,' he said in that country accent some of the older Nettlefield folk had. He reminded Baby of the stationmaster, who rarely asked questions. A bucket swung by the old man's side. He carried a shovel propped on his shoulder as he ventured onto the mud.

Baby watched him set down his bucket and start digging. It only took one slice of the spade to find what he was looking for. A cockle, which he dropped in the bucket. He gave Baby a little wave as if to say, *Look, I've found treasure.*

Baby was waving back when she remembered the diver.

But there was no sign of him—or her. The boat had gone too. She shouldn't have got distracted. Perhaps she could even have asked them what they were doing? Perhaps it was nothing suspicious at all. But never mind, she could still thrill the kids with the news about the island.

Baby was really getting hungry now and the smell coming off the mud in the creek was making her feel sick. She'd left soon after breakfast, after she'd waved Fingers off to school, which now felt like a long time ago.

Brian's porridge was getting more and more 'interesting,' as June Lovelock put it. That morning, it had been flavoured with apple and chopped up sausage left over from dinner the day before, with a good dose of pepper. Brian said her dad loved it.

Whatever it tasted like, the porridge had set Baby up for her long walk out, but not quite for the long walk back. Her skirt was heavy with damp around the hem and her belly gurgled as she retraced her steps back through the grass to the little clump of trees.

From this direction, without the sun in her eyes, she could see bricks amongst the greenery; an ivy-covered wall. But her belly was telling her to investigate another day.

The morning was giving her much to think about.

She reached the road and picked up speed. The *'You are now entering Nettlefield'* sign came into view. Baby passed new houses, much bigger than Ida's old house, 'semi-detached' they were called. They looked very modern.

Eventually, she turned onto the main Southampton Road. She waved at Mr Alexander Shaw, Brian's dad, walking through his garden with a small pile of neatly folded cloths. How he got anything to grow under the railway bridge was magic, as far as Baby was concerned.

'Keep going on, Baby!' he called. 'We mustn't be late.'

Late? Late for what? The midday meal was always a mountain of sandwiches, Brian's favourite food. They didn't get cold.

Mr Shaw followed Baby through the orphanage gates that were always open at an attractive and inviting angle. Despite Mr Shaw doing his best to shoo her on, Baby couldn't help pausing to marvel at the beautiful new building.

The orphanage hadn't *completely* burned down last summer. The fire left just the shell of its former self. Though the builders had worked hard, it wasn't until well into the New Year that June and her ma and the kids moved back into their home. They'd enjoyed their time at the Basque Children's Camp, but when the weather turned chillier, they'd all been 'evacuated' to some of the townsfolk who felt the same about the Blackshirts as Baby did.

The renovations had been a cosy mixture of the old Victorian building and up-to-date design features for the modern age. 'Art deco', June called it. The old dormitory was divided into four: two rooms for girls and two for boys. Plus, a row of dormer windows now poked out through the new rainproof tiles, where the builders had even managed to put in an extra floor. The smaller rooms on the new top floor had been given to the older children. Except for two guest rooms where *The Wonders*, as Harry used to call them, could stay on high days and holidays.

So Nettlefield Orphanage was now 'state-of-the-art', according to June Lovelock. And it was just lovely.

Mr Shaw was beckoning from the side of the building

Baby crossed the grounds past the children's playground and the little beds of spring flowers: daffodils, crocuses, irises, and tulips just promising to bloom into their reds and blues and yellows and pinks. Baby had learned all the names from the catalogue she and June had pored over in the autumn.

'You're just in time,' said Brian, shaking out a tea towel at the kitchen door. Baby followed her inside. Wonderful smells were wafting along the corridor.

In the kitchen, *Brian's kitchen* as she liked to think of it, the surfaces gleamed silver. The tiles shone bright white and the checkerboard floor was clean enough to eat your dinner off. It was all heaven to Brian.

'Shall I take the sandwiches in?' asked Baby.

'We're not having them today.' Brian beamed, her cheeks shiny and red with steam.

'Ah Baby, see we're just in time!' said Mr Shaw. 'Brenda is an absolute wonder with flavours!' He could never remember to use Brian's chosen name. Brian said that was because her mum was called Brenda and that was all right.

'So, what is it?' asked Baby.

'Something new,' said Brian. 'It's called curry. It's a stew, sort of.'

'With gravy,' said Mr Shaw. 'An innovation to the traditional recipe. I think your countrymen would be very entertained by it, Baby.'

Baby knew she was supposed to like 'curry', the one word people in Britain had for hundreds of different spicy things to eat. She could remember Moll's friend, Abhi, the Lascar sailor, trying to tempt her with something. But she much preferred a fish supper or, nowadays, a steak and kidney pie. 'Do you want me to do anything?' she asked.

'Dad...' Brian indicated the little pile of folded white cloths Mr Shaw was still holding.

'Oh these, oh yes,' he said. 'They're still warm from the iron. Here you are, Baby, for the table.'

'Serviettes,' said Brian. 'We've got a special guest.'

3
ARCHIE
Brooklyn, October 1929 – February 1938

WITH THE JOGGLING of the old immigration truck, Veronica dozed and let the movie of the life she could remember play out in her head...

***

'Veronica, honey, I'm not going to live forever,' Archie had said not long after Thanksgiving last year. He'd been gently brushing away at a large upper case 'T' at the time.

Veronica remembered pinching her nose against the stink of the lye solution, but it wasn't that which had made her eyes water. *'Don't say that. You're fit and well. You're not going to die, not for ages yet anyway.'*

Why, oh why, had she tempted fate like that? But just saying those words couldn't have made what happened happen. If she believed that, she'd be no better that than the folk who peddled stupid rumours.

'Conspiracy theories,' intelligent folk were calling them.

She could hear Archie scolding her for that now. The notice she'd left on the door crossed her mind again. She shook the thought away and hoped Archie would have laughed. *Playing them at their own game,* he'd have said.

'Well, *that's as may be,*' is what Archie had said. *'The truth is, we don't live forever, and that's a good thing. So as logic goes, you are going to have to live without me one day.'* Gently, he rested his inky, brown hands on her arms and, seeking out her eyes, made her look at him. i He pointed to the top of the bookshelves otherwise packed with files and books and journals.

At the time, Veronica hadn't been able to see anything, but that was because she hadn't wanted to look. She never wanted to think about the day she wouldn't have Archie. Her curiosity took a vacation where he was concerned. Was that because she knew, deep down somewhere in the pit of her belly, that something wasn't right, and knowing it would change her, change everything?

So, Veronica Frances Park grew up in Brooklyn. Her 'school' was Archie's basement, where she learned to write the best copy, the best headlines, how to listen more than talk, how to notice and go unnoticed. *'Keep watch,'* Archie always said. *'Don't be distracted by what's going on in front of you, but look round the edges for what folk don't want you to see.'*

Living with him had certainly made trouble. Archie was a bolshie, a commie, a troublemaker, and judged more harshly for his brown skin. So the fact that somebody with evil in their heart had run down the basement steps, pushed the door to the press room open and shot Archie at his desk, didn't matter to the cops one jot.

Just a few weeks after that awful day in January, Veronica had slumped over Lorretta's kitchen table in front of a cooling cup of coffee. Veronica had refused to celebrate her sixteenth birthday despite Lorretta's best efforts. But as if nature was also doing its best to cajole her into cheerfulness, an unusually warm early spring sun poured through the window. And with the smell of Lorretta's baking, Veronica's resistance was waning.

'Honey, he must have left you something?' Lorretta slid a plate of cookies across the table. 'Chocolate chip. It's a new recipe.'

Veronica wanted to say, *'What do you mean, leave me something? Are the paper and the press and everything not enough?'* But she knew what Lorretta meant. Veronica looked up. 'He did,' she confessed and took a bite of one of Lorretta's cookies. It was warm and delicious.

They passed Jesse on the stoop, returning from his night shift, his work jacket over one shoulder hooked on his finger. 'What's the rush?'

'No rush,' said Lorretta. 'Coffee's on the stove.'

Veronica smiled sadly at Jesse as if to say, *You know Lorretta,* and, with a stone in her heart, followed the woman down to the basement.

The place was still a mess, paper strewn everywhere, Archie's toolbox emptied on the floor and a tin stuck in a puddle of ink under the press. Archie's blood still stained the wall even after a half-hearted attempt to clean up by the cops. Veronica hadn't been able to finish the job, not then, not yet. But she could feel Lorretta bristling to get started.

Veronica pointed to where Archie had shown her, just a couple of months before. 'Up there.'

Lorretta pulled Archie's chair from behind the desk. 'Go on,' she said and gestured for Veronica to climb up.

Her heart as heavy as a tray of lead type, Veronica had stepped up, stretched and felt around in the dust for whatever it was Archie had put there for her.

At first, she could find nothing and was going to climb down. Then she felt the corner of a box.

'What is it?' asked Lorretta, her fists propped impatiently on her hips.

'This.' Veronica climbed down and tried to give the small dusty box to Lorretta.

'No. It's yours. Archie left it for you. I can go if you want to open it in private?'

'No. Stay.' Lightheaded and flushed at the same time, Veronica pulled on the little string bow and eased off the lid.

Lorretta watched intently, wringing her hands in front of her apron.

At the sight of Archie's handwriting and the smell of him coming from inside the little box, a stone rose to Veronica's throat. She swallowed and blinked away tears as she read: *'Don't think badly of me. You should have what's yours. I only wanted to keep you safe. Love Arch.'*

Veronica would never think badly of Archie. He must have known that.

But something in her was stirring. She was losing her balance, her sureness in him.

Underneath the note lay a small black booklet with a hard cover displaying the crest of *The United Kingdom of Britain and Northern Ireland* on the front. Above the crest was the word PASSPORT and below it, a name: *The Right Honourable Mr Howard Campbell.*

Veronica had only been with Archie for a few weeks, when over a bowl of his special corn soup, he said, *'Hmm, Veronica... You'll need something to go along with that—to finish it off.'*

'What, my soup?' seven-year-old Veronica said, enjoying the slurping sound she could make with the

soup brimming on her spoon. Sixteen-year-old Veronica had a feeling that, once upon a time, somebody had scolded her for that.

'*No, your name,*' Archie said, '*if you should ever go to school...*'

Veronica always remembered an icy feeling at the mention of school.

'*Don't make me, Archie,*' said seven-year-old Veronica. And he never did.

A few days after that, as they'd been walking by the park, Archie had mentioned it again. '*This is a good name, like mine. Park... Parker.*'

Veronica remembered looking up through his whiskers, already white in patches but barely hiding a strong, dark brown neck. She wondered what he was talking about. She remembered that icy feeling of school chilling her spine again and his kind but firm grip round her hand that always made her feel so safe.

'*Archie Parker and Veronica Park. How about that? Just for fun, not for school,*' he said, melting her chills. And so she agreed, giving herself the name 'Frances.' It was one of those that could belong to a girl or a boy, and she liked that. She had a sense that 'Veronica' was her own choice, too.

In Archie's basement, on that early spring day in 1938, 'The Right Honourable Mr Howard Campbell' meant nothing to Veronica.

Neither did the photographs of a man, a woman, and a small child. Though Veronica's fingers tingled at the touch of them, she couldn't place them and didn't recognise the names. But there was her date of birth, February 4th 1922.

Underneath the passport was a newspaper clipping, including the same photographs.

The man and the woman had gone missing the day before the crash in October 1929. Most of the story had been torn away, but the header told her that the paper it had been ripped from was called *The Beacon*.

It was about that time in 1929 that Archie had found Veronica wandering around The Navy Yards in a little red coat, her hands tucked into a fur muff, boots buttoned to the ankle, and a little pixie hat tied under her chin. She always remembered her outfit, she remembered feeling uncomfortable in it.

And she knew her name was Veronica. It rang in her ears.

She'd been alone and Archie had taken her in. That was good enough for her.

'Those people mean nothing to me,' said Veronica, replacing each item in the little box and then handing it to Lorretta. 'You take care of it. I don't know what he wanted me to do with it.'

'But Archie wanted you to have it,' said Lorretta.

'I know, and I will. But not right now. Take it for me, please. I gotta tidy up.'

A few days after retrieving the box, as Veronica was oiling the press, the *tap tap tap* of feet hurried down the basement steps. The door flew open and Lorretta burst in. 'You missed something on the back,' she said, waving a scrap of paper.

Veronica wiped her hands down her overall and snatched the paper. It was more hastily scrawled than Archie's neat hand in the other note, but Veronica could still read, *'Go see Betty Marie. She's holding something for you.'*

The words felt urgent. This, at least, was an instruction from Archie. It was something to do rather than trying to ignore the elephant in the room—the two dead people on the passport.

'Well, go on, then,' said Lorretta.

Veronica put the note in her pants pocket. She'd get this over, be done with it, and back to work.

Betty's bar reeked from the previous night's smoke and beer. Somebody was tuning a saxophone on the stage while a janitor leaned on his broom, listening.

Behind the bar, Betty Marie, her hair in rollers and a silk robe falling off one shoulder, polished a glass with a white cloth. 'Ah, Veronica. I was wondering when you'd drop by. I'm busy, big night tonight, Maxine Sullivan, so let's do this thing right now.'

Before Veronica could explain herself, Betty had dipped out of sight.

When she popped up a moment later, she slapped a newspaper on the surface. 'He wanted you to have this.'

Veronica peeled it carefully off the bar, where the paper had already begun to stick. The *Beacon*, a full-size broadsheet, unlike *The Maple Street Reporter*.

Betty leaned over the bar and lowered her voice. 'It was the English guy who left it. That one over there.' She gave a tiny nod towards a shadowy figure in one of the bar's dark corners.

'But why did Archie have it? How did he get it?'

'I don't know nothing 'bout that...' She concentrated her cloth on a stubborn mark on the glass. 'But something tells me it was to do with the Scotsman. Rolled up in a brand-new Cadillac Limousine, he did. Had all the kids crowding round outside. Surprised you didn't see, Veronica. Too busy down in that basement, eh?'

'A Scotsman?' Any wondering about her origins that Veronica couldn't suppress was about England, not Scotland.

'He never got out,' said Betty. 'But his voice boomed out the limo window like a foghorn on the Hudson.' Betty breathed on the glass for one final polish before she placed it on the shelf behind her. 'I recognised the accent. Had a beau once...'

Veronica could kick herself sometimes for being too focused. Wasn't that what Archie always said? *'Don't forget to check the corner of your eye, Veronica. All kinds of underhand things happen there.'*

'What did they want, these men?'

'Oh, the English guy was looking for a child. A girl, lost around the time of the crash. Perhaps he still is. I feel sorry for him. The second guy, the Scot in the limousine, was checking up on him...'

'Did you tell them anything?'

'What do you take me for?'

Why didn't Archie at least mention the man... the men?

But Veronica knew why. She was an investigator. Archie would have been worried that she'd want to check this man out, verify his story, and then what would that mean? What did it mean now? Veronica's stomach churned. She couldn't bury her head in the sand any longer.

The shadowy figure from the corner was getting up—a man in an oversized gaberdine coat, holding a fedora like Archie's. He pinched the crown and put the hat at a careless angle on his head. His coat was undone and the ends of the belt dangled as he walked up to Betty, barely glancing at Veronica. His face was drawn, like he hadn't slept in a week. A lank lock of hair fell across one eye. A white scar cut through his left eyebrow. He slapped his empty glass on the bar, drew the back of his hand across his mouth, and headed for the door without a word.

'Now,' said Betty Marie, 'don't you go blaming Arch. He only wanted the best for you and if he...'

But before Betty Marie could finish what she was saying, the door opened again, and a pretty woman walked in, perfectly coiffured shiny black curls piled on top of her head.

'Ah! Miss Sullivan...' Betty Marie tugged at her robe and, with a look of horror, patted her own hair, still in rollers.

'Don't you worry 'bout that,' said the woman. 'I just wanted to get the feel of the place before tonight.' She looked round the stale-tobacco room, at the guy on the stage packing up his sax, at the little table islands, the bar. Finally, letting her gaze fall on Veronica, she smiled. 'Let me tell you, it feels good.'

'I'll catch you later, Betty Marie,' said Veronica.

'Oh, don't you go on my account,' said the famous jazz singer.

'Pleased to meet you, Miss Sullivan.' Veronica offered her hand.

Maxine Sullivan took it in both of hers.

Veronica felt its warmth course through her whole body.

'Good luck with your adventures,' said the singer, almost as though she knew a plan was already taking shape in Veronica's mind.

Betty hadn't wanted to shop Veronica to Immigration, but Veronica had persuaded her that it was the only way. And it had to be somebody she could trust.

'And I gotta trust you too, girl,' said Betty with a finger that meant business. 'I don't want nobody thinking I'm a snitch.'

'And I don't want anyone thinking I'm that little girl,' whispered Veronica as she leaned across the bar in a jacket and pants suit. Her hair was shaved from her neck to over her ears, with the last few curls parted and slicked flat to one side. She didn't want anyone thinking she was a girl at all.

***

Veronica felt the rumble of the engine as the Immigration truck picked up speed. Veronica Frances Park was just another undesirable now. What would she be in England? She thought about her best clue, the evidence. The paper, the *Beacon*, peeled carefully off Betty's bar, and the one word scribbled on it.

Nettlefield.

4
Sir Malcolm Taggart
Nettlefield, Wednesday 23rd March

BABY CROSSED the orphanage's sunny yellow entrance hall where the stained-glass over the front door made colourful patterns on the parquet. The door was new, the parquet floor was new. Nearly everything was new. The coloured light made Baby think of how Sophie, her guardian angel and Wonder Girl, had led her and Fingers to Nettlefield in the first place.

Baby pushed open the double doors to the orphanage's living-cum-dining room; a large yet cosy, bright, comfortable and happy room. The doors had been salvaged from the fire wreckage and were now as good as new. 'They saved those nippers locked in there,' a fireman had said, so of course they were put back into the new building.

Around the long dining table decorated with spring flowers, instead of benches, there were chairs for comfort. Steam escaped from under the lids of two large dishes set down in the middle of the table.

Around them, Baby counted eight places, each with a white china plate, a polished knife, fork, and spoon. At one of these places, with his back to the window, sat a large, older man. A toff with a full head of steel-grey hair. Though Gin was talking to him, his eyes were scanning the rest of the table. He had the look of a man who believed he was in charge, who talked more than he listened, and expected to be heard.

There was an empty place between the toff and Mrs Lovelock, June's old ma, who sat in her wheelchair, humming to herself. Mr Shaw sat opposite the toff, leaving four more empty places. Baby guessed they were for herself, June, Brian and whoever was giving her a hand in the kitchen.

Baby felt an arm slip through hers. 'Ah, Baby. Did you have a good walk?' said June Lovelock, the orphanage matron. 'Come and meet Sir Malcolm.' She took Baby's little pile of serviettes and handed them to Brian's dad. 'Alexander, would you mind?'

'Oh, yes, we'll definitely need these,' he said, getting up and placing a crisply folded white cloth on each plate. Mr Shaw had had a beard trim for the occasion. It now only reached the second button on his colourful shirt. 'Tie-dye,' he said, 'it'll be all the rage one day.'

June pulled out the empty chair next to the toff. An open briefcase sat on the floor next to him, stuffed with papers. 'Baby, take my place. I'll be back in a moment,' whispered June. Baby sat down between the man and Mrs Lovelock.

The man balanced a fat cigar between long fingers. He wore two heavy gold rings, one on his little finger—not so little. 'Are you abandoning me, June?' his voice boomed across the room.

'I just have to check everything's as it should be in the kitchen,' said June Lovelock, slipping out through the doors.

'Surely your staff can take care of that?'

The doors swung shut.

The man's face was grooved into deep wrinkles. Baby noticed the hint of disappointment—or was it a sneer?—before he returned to his conversation with Gin.

Gin, not quite eighteen years old, always looked more grown up than her age. While she'd been away with her dad in Germany, she'd dyed her hair red like Katharine Hepburn on the movie posters at The Embassy cinema. She'd got thinner, more sporty looking. It worried Baby.

But otherwise, Gin was still her jolly self. 'Darling, we thought you'd emigrated,' she said, peering past the toff. 'You must tell Sir Malcolm your story. He's very interested in everything to do with the orphanage.'

The doors swung open again and June returned, followed by Brian with a steaming pot of the 'curry.'

'Well I never, what a smell! I haven't smelled that since my days with the Raj.' Sir Malcolm turned sharply to Baby. 'Must be jolly familiar to you though, Baby.' They were his first words to her.

And he knew her name.

To be honest, most people in Nettlefield did. But this toff had only just arrived.

'A good, strong, hot curry, what!' The toff then elbowed Baby so hard she nearly fell off her chair.

Robert Perkins, taking each step with special care, was walking behind Brian. He carried a large blue and white stripy jug as if it were the Crown Jewels. A bright white tea towel was draped neatly over one of his arms. 'Gravy,' he announced solemnly.

Baby wondered why he wasn't at school with the others, but was sure June would have a good reason for keeping him back.

Sir Malcolm also appeared very interested in Robert. His gaze was fixed on the boy until he took his place on the other side of the table next to Brian. Blonder than blond, Robert was albino, so quite unusual with his pale skin, scruffy white hair, and grey eyes with a hint of violet. His 'whiteness,' had been of especial interest to Ida's Blackshirt uncle, Arthur Underwood, now in prison for kidnapping blond kids, just so he could get in with the Nazis in Germany.

Brian placed the curry between the two serving dishes already on the table. Her cheeks flushed red with pride, she lifted the lid on a large dish of rice and Robert followed suit with the other dish of boiled potatoes, carrots, and peas.

Mr Shaw took his seat. 'A culinary conglomeration of continents, you might say.'

'Oh dear, in all the excitement, I don't think we've all been properly introduced,' said June. 'Sir Malcolm, you have the pleasure of sitting next to Baby. Baby, this is Sir Malcolm Taggart from London, but Scotland originally.'

The toff nodded approvingly.

June continued round the table, introducing each of them to 'Sir Malcolm,' whose smile dimmed with each introduction.

As they all enjoyed their lunch (the curry was interesting, fruity even), Sir Malcolm talked. He boasted about his houses, the countries he'd been to and the animals he'd shot there. Sometimes, he didn't sound Scottish at all. His eyes mostly fell on June, and anyone who tried to join in the conversation was immediately interrupted.

'I remember once in the Highlands—' started Mr Shaw.

'Yes, the Highlands, my ain country,' Sir Malcom said in a terrible Scottish accent and continued by listing all the 'highlands' he owned. He harrumphed a lot and his shoulders shook every time he said something that amused him.

Across the table, June Lovelock smiled sweetly. Next to Baby, Mrs Lovelock hummed another little tune to herself, only stopping to whisper, 'Let him get on with it, dear. He'll run out of breath, eventually.'

At the end of the meal, June stood up. She tapped her glass to get everyone's attention. Maybe this was when Baby would find out what this all was in aid of?

'First of all,' said June, 'may I say what a delicious luncheon Brian prepared for us. The bananas in the curry were a masterstroke. Let's all give Brian a round of applause.'

'Well, they do say the top chefs are men!' said Sir Malcolm.

'Brian ain't a man,' said Baby.

'And who do you think that is?' he said, pointing at Mr Shaw.

'That's her dad,' said Baby.

It was Sir Malcolm's turn to nearly fall off his chair. 'What? Do you mean to say that... *that*...' he pointed at Brian, his finger shaking as his mouth searched for a word to describe her, '*person* cooked my lunch?'

The room fell silent. Even Sir Malcolm was quiet for a few seconds.

'Hmm, *yes* she did,' said June in a bit of a fluster.

'And a very fine lunch it was too,' he said, recovering himself with a smile that didn't reach his eyes. 'I'm sure her father played a large part?'

'No, I didn't actually,' said Mr Shaw, who was well ruffled at how this bumptious toff, sir or not, regarded his daughter. Baby wondered if he was about to roll up his shirt sleeves, ready to fight Sir Malcolm Taggart.

'Dad, you put the bananas in,' said Brian calmly.

'Oh yes, so I did.'

'Now,' said June, taking a deep breath, 'Sir Malcolm is the proprietor of one of the big London newspapers, the *Beacon*, and he's here because he wants to do a series of articles about the modern orphanage. It will mean that for a short while, we'll have photographers here, newspaper journalists, and maybe even *The World Service* will want to broadcast from here. It's called "human interest." Isn't that right, Sir Malcolm?'

'Absolutely, June. It's selling a lot of papers. People don't want to know what's happening on the Continent. They're much more interested in their home turf.' He took a long drag on his cigar.

'The point is...' said June, stretching herself to her full height.

Baby heard Mrs Lovelock whisper, 'Go Joonie!' under her breath.

'... Is that Sir Malcolm's paper is going to pay us handsomely for the disruption it will cause,' continued June, 'for which we are immensely grateful. So thank you very much, Sir Malcolm.'

'Yes, the *Beacon* wants to cover all aspects of your life here,' said Sir Malcolm through a cloud of cigar smoke.

June glanced at Baby. June's lips were pressed into an upside-down smile.

What did that mean? Would they have to give up The Lillie again? Was this it? Was Baby's and Fingers's time as Wonder Girls coming to an end?

Baby felt something furry round her ankles. Frank, Robert's little white dog, was sniffing under the table for crumbs.

Baby was patting his silky white head when Frank yelped and shot out from under the table, knocking over Sir Malcolm's open briefcase. The papers slipped out.

For a moment, Baby thought she'd hurt the little dog, until a fly buzzed out from under the table and headed for the open window.

Unnoticed by Sir Malcolm, Baby got down and started sliding the papers back into the case.

Above her, Sir Malcom was still in full flow. 'Yes, yes, we'll need accommodation for quite a large team...'

Most of the paperwork looked dull, but among the sheets was a booklet. *Tide Tables, Portsmouth Harbour, North West, 1938*. And on the front cover was a map. Baby recognised it as an outline of Nettlefield Creek because there was the island she had seen on her walk. Inside the booklet were pages of numbers, dates, and times. Before Baby could slip it back inside the case with the rest, a fat hand snatched it.

Baby looked up and was face to face with Sir Malcolm, glowering back at her.

Baby froze.

The expression on his face—the sneer, the disgust—was exactly like looking up into the face of Ida's Uncle Arthur.

5
ELLIS ISLAND
Brooklyn, Late February 1938

AS THE TRUCK BUMPED onto the bridge, leaving Brooklyn behind, the younger immigration official Veronica had nicknamed 'Lanky' slumped on the bench in the corner. He wriggled a bit to get comfortable, crossed his arms over his chest, and closed his eyes.

Veronica stood up to wave goodbye to Brooklyn, her home for the last eleven years.

But all she could see through the tiny window was a web of steel strings and cables criss-crossing above her, separating her from the sky. Was she the fly or the spider? From below, over the noise of the engine, she heard the distant clangs and grinds of construction. The Navy Yard, where Archie had found her, was one of those mysterious places she now only saw from a distance. Archie told her it was dangerous. He said the stories there were for much bigger papers. Where was his ambition? But she remembered how his eyes narrowed, as good as piercing her soul, when he'd said that. So, for once, she curbed her own ambition and left well alone. The place did give her the shivers, after all.

Over the East River, she gazed at the downtown skyscrapers. The city was getting taller and taller. Did they make her feel small? Did they heck! No, it was just a matter of perspective.

The guard had finally fallen asleep, pressed into the corner of the truck, his mouth stretched open. Now or never, here was her best opportunity, in Lower Downtown, by City Hall and Wall Street.

Veronica sat back on the bench and pulled a thick wad of papers from her bag; her parting shot, one last attempt to get these people to pay attention before it was too late. She gave her copy a final read through...

Beware the Bund! Fascism isn't confined to Europe. It is alive and well here in the US! American supporters of Adolf Hitler are spreading their messages of hate right here. Through their happy holiday camps on Long Island, they are recruiting! Beware the Bund!

Perhaps she could have been more direct, but it got the message across.

Veronica slid along the bench and tried the truck door. She was right; Grumpy hadn't bothered to lock it for a 'dumb girl.' She opened it just enough to see where they were. The blare of horns and smell of gas couldn't mask that peculiar sweetness of the city: doughnuts, pancakes, maple syrup... Veronica breathed it in for the last time, for a while at least.

The van trundled past the Woolworth Building, where a cop was directing traffic on Broadway. Yellow checker cabs, cars, trucks, people, all in a hurry. One cab was right behind them, its front fender bent out of shape. No wonder if it drove that close.

Veronica pulled the door shut, holding the handle, as well as her breath, until they'd passed.

She'd been done for littering before, but it was the only way. These people had to know the truth.

She felt a grip on her arm.

'You ain't going nowhere, Missy,' said the guard.

'I'll think you'll find I am,' she said.

'You know what I mean,' said Lanky. 'You ain't escaping.'

'No, but these are.' And right outside City Hall, with her unrestrained arm, she opened the door and flung the last of the flyers to the wind.

Lanky couldn't stop her. She put her fingers to her lips and blew.

Heads turned at the ear-piercing whistle. Veronica's superpower, Archie had called it. A few papers caught the warm blast from the subway below and spun in a whirl, reaching the third and fourth stories of the nearest skyscraper.

A kid with a pile of papers to sell caught one. Veronica waved and blew again, her free arm resisting the guard pulling on the other. 'You oughta know that if these folks aren't careful, there'll be Nazi salutes in Madison Square Garden before long.'

'You shut your mouth with that commie bullshit,' said Lanky, quivering.

'Language. Your momma would have something to say about that.'

'What the hell is going on back there?' shouted Grumpy from the cab.

'You leave my momma well alone,' hissed Lanky, yanking Veronica away from the open door and shoving her back on the bench.

Veronica felt her smile grow from inside her. There was nothing he could do, and he knew it.

She was escaping, though; escaping to England. How much she hoped they were a lot more switched on to the threat there. What was the name of the place again? Yeah, Nettlefield.

The truck stopped. Lanky hustled her out. They were somewhere downtown; warehouses and sheds along an empty street.

Grumpy slammed the driver's door and, in a burst of rage, described exactly how much trouble they were in for letting Veronica litter her trash all over the steps of City Hall. 'And it's all on you!' He poked his fat, stubby finger at Lanky's face, which reddened with the shame of it.

A checker cab drew up on the corner of the block.

Veronica only had time to grab her bag, much lighter now, and slap her hat on her head, before Grumpy shoved her through a shed to a slipway where a boat was waiting. A very small boat, churning out torrents of white smoke.

She felt the mass of the city behind her, spewing her out like the smoke. Grumpy kept close behind, wiser now. She heard him huff, hurrying her along the slipway that bounced with their weight. Lanky watched from the shed.

The sun shone, but the breeze off the river was brisk, so she clamped her hand over Archie's old fedora on her head.

'No more funny business, you hear?' said Grumpy, his fat fingers gripping her shoulder.

She shrugged it off. 'What? D'you think I'm going to jump in the river?' She wanted to tell him he was a fool, that she was escaping, and he was helping her do it. But jumping in the Hudson and swimming to England sure as hell wasn't an option.

The boat's engine churned, impatient to go.

Not having been deported before, at the sight of the little boat, Veronica's chutzpah shrank. 'Is that going all the way to England?' It was hard to keep the tremble out of her voice.

Grumpy laughed. 'No, you fool, girl. That's just the boat to Ellis. As soon as one comes by going your way, they'll throw you on. With any luck, it'll be packed to the gills with dried fish. You'll stink of them by the time you get to Limey land and no one will want you there either.'

He was getting his own back. Veronica didn't mind. He was just another poor misguided fool, his eyes and ears closed to the threat.

A man in a long overcoat, his hat pulled low, with a battered suitcase on his lap, was already sitting on a bench on the deck. A smartly dressed lady sat with him.

'Hello,' said Veronica. She wasn't going to ask anything awkward, like what they were done for. Just a couple of questions about their dashed hopes perhaps, for *The Maple Street Reporter*, when she got back.

But the woman shuffled closer to the man, slipping her arm through his. They were scared. Where were they going? What were they going back to face?

Veronica just smiled at them, trying to let them know she understood their fear, before she turned away and stared across the river to New Jersey and Communipaw, where the Dutch first settled in America. Archie always said the whole nation was a nation of immigrants, except for the rightful folks, who were here first, who had no say in the matter at all. So what right had anyone to tell anyone *you're not welcome here?*

The pitch of the engine went up a notch. This was it, the first leg of her journey.

But footsteps were thumping down the slipway. The planks swung from side to side, but it didn't bother the man carrying a small case, a thick coat over his arm and, like Veronica, gripping his hat low over his face against the wind.

'Wait!' he called from just a few feet away. 'Got room for anymore?'

Veronica looked up into a face with a lank lock of hair escaping from under a fedora, and a white scar cutting through his left eyebrow.

The man from Betty Marie's was climbing onto the boat.

6
June Under Pressure
Wednesday 23rd March

BABY LINGERED in the hall while June and Mr Shaw waved goodbye to Sir Malcolm. She glimpsed his car, big, black, and posh. Ida would know what model it was, but she was back in Bournemouth with Sophie. The person driving the car was hidden under a peaked cap. It reminded Baby of that time she saw the King and Queen in their car on the way to the theatre. You could see why all the fuss was made about Sir Malcolm Taggart.

Brian held the double doors open for Robert, who was carrying a pile of plates so clean that the top one looked as if it hadn't been used at all. At Robert's heels, Frank's tail wagged nineteen to the dozen.

'You have to wash them too,' said Brian. 'Properly,' she added with her best frown.

'Don't you worry 'bout that. Come on, Frank.'

Frank trotted behind, his claws clicking on the parquet.

Baby helped in the kitchen with the rest of the clearing up, until June had settled her ma back in her new sitting room. June and her old ma now had their own little 'flat' on the ground floor, the sick bay having moved to its own well-equipped extension at the back of the building.

When the kitchen was gleaming, Baby dried her hands on the fresh roller towel on the back of the kitchen door and stepped across the corridor.

June's office door was shut. Baby heard voices inside; June's and Gin's.

'They are so alike, June. There's no doubt this time.'

'Don't say anything, will you?' said June.

'No, *I* won't, but the school...'

Baby knocked.

'Come in!' said June, a bit too quickly.

June was sitting in her big brown leather swivel chair that she often let the little kids have 'a go' on. She twirled a pencil between her fingers. Already, the office walls were covered with a fresh stock of children's art. Bright smiley paintings, mostly of June herself.

Across the desk, Gin lounged in one of the comfy visitor chairs. The whole room smelled of her perfume. 'Baby, darling,' she said, getting up, 'I'm at The Blue Bonnet, just for a few days' work. You won't believe how much the landlord has spruced the place up!' With her manicured finger, she pointed between Baby and herself. 'We'll catch up later. Now I must dash. Much to organise!' She picked up the clutch bag on June's desk, stabbed her hat with a pin and swooshed out with her cardigan over her shoulders.

Gin had been able to look grown up for as long as Baby had known her. She was very convincing as 'Aunt Constance', for instance. 'Aunt Constance' was a very posh old lady who came out when they were in a certain kind of pickle. But now that Gin was practically grown up, good and proper, it made Baby feel sad. Over and over, Baby learned that nothing stayed the same. It was a hard lesson. Their lives would never stop changing.

'Baby,' said June, getting up herself, 'Is everything alright? I must open a window.' She slid up the sash. One or two of the children's paintings and drawings fluttered with the breeze that wafted through the office. 'Gin does love her perfume, doesn't she? I gather her father has sorted out his money problems.' June sat down and began shuffling the papers strewn all over the desk. 'I'm just trying to make sense of the accounts after all the building work.'

'This Sir Malcolm,' said Baby, taking Gin's chair, 'I don't like him. There's something about him that doesn't feel good.'

'But Baby, he's the owner of a big London newspaper. He's very well connected.' June tapped the desk with the end of her pencil.

'That's as may be, but...' Baby wanted to say that he reminded her of Ida's Uncle Arthur. But that was just a feeling, not evidence. Though there was the book about the creek and the diver she had seen on her walk. What were they about? More coincidence?

Baby continued, 'Are you sure you want him and his people all over the place here? Do you know what he's going to say about us? Don't forget what Letitia's doing. I don't think that's something that should be in the papers, do you? And Harry, can we trust the kids not to talk about Harry too?'

June's frown deepened. 'I do see what you mean. But look at all these.' She waved her hand across the papers, the accounts. 'These are debts. The council funds us so far, and we've had some generous donations, but there's still a shortfall from all the repairs and renovations. I'm not begrudging all the little extras. The children deserve it.' June clenched her fist. 'But we need the money that Sir Malcolm is going to pay us. And, like Gin says, this kind of publicity could be good for us and the children, especially. They'll be known as a *Nettlefield* boy or girl. It could really help them get on...'

'But haven't they already been in the paper, what with the fire and everything?'

'But that was just the *Courier*. I can't imagine many people outside of Nettlefield read our local paper.' June put her finger to her lip. 'Though I was sending it to Gin when she was in Germany...'

'Alright, but I'm going to keep an eye on 'im,' said Baby. She was going to more than keep an eye on him;

she was going to investigate him. But best not to worry June with that yet.

'You do that, Baby,' said June, shuffling the papers into a neater pile.

Baby forgave the shortness in June's voice. She was under pressure.

'I'm sorry, I mean thank you,' June added and put the paper in the in-tray on her desk. 'And yes, I think we all picked up on his old-fashioned attitude. Thank goodness dear Brian is so accepting. But the money, Baby. It would really make a difference.'

Through the open window came the sound of the children returning from school, the creaks of the swings and the see-saw, and the squeals of delight from the roundabout.

'I oughta be getting back to The Lillie,' said Baby.

'Yes.' June turned her gaze to the accounts in her in-tray. 'Feelings... Should we trust them more?'

Baby wanted to say yes, we should. She'd learned a word for it, 'intuition'. Feelings were always worth checking out.

Her hand was on the door handle when she remembered about Robert. 'Is Robert alright? He didn't go to school today.'

'No, Sir Malcolm specially requested to meet him. He said he'd seen his picture in the *Courier* report about the fire. His teacher was happy for him to have the opportunity. More "human interest," I suppose.'

The goose bumps on Baby's arms popped up. If she didn't have to run back to The Lillie for Fingers, she'd be going for it right now. But the very first thing she'd do in the morning was buy a copy of the *Beacon*.

7
VERONICA ARRIVES IN NETTLEFIELD
The Week Before, Wednesday 15th March

THE SHIP THAT VERONICA found herself on carried grain, not fish, thank goodness. It finally docked in Southampton nearly two weeks after setting sail from New York.

At the railroad station in Southampton, when she asked for the right platform for Nettlefield, Veronica heard garbled stories about orphanage fires, Spaniards and spies. But it all sounded as fantastic as Nazi rallies in Madison Square Garden.

Barely an hour later, her train was slowing into the station.

'Next stop, Nettlefield!'

Veronica stirred, tilted her hat up off her face and peered through the window at long thin backyards, vegetable plots, and chicken runs.

'Nettlefield, next stop,' repeated the guard and continued along the corridor.

Veronica pulled her bag off the luggage rack and plonked it onto the seat. As she tucked her shirt into her pants and straightened her jacket, she felt the cold stare of an older lady pressed into the opposite corner of the compartment. All these masculine traits were becoming second nature to Veronica. And she was getting to like her new male persona. So far, it had only been to her advantage. How long could it last?

Nettlefield Station was tiny. Half a dozen steps and she was across the platform, past the ticket booth and out into a broad space where a few cars were parked. Beyond them, she saw a laundry, a small mountain of coal, some sheds and, just beyond the cars, a dense clump of trees. With her carpet bag firmly in her grip, Archie's hat tilted at a jaunty angle and her scarf cravat style, she headed away from these random things down a slope towards the main street.

She spotted a big house where brightly coloured playground equipment decorated the grounds. An expensive hotel that entertained children? Did they have that sort of thing in England? She walked past a row of townhouses that reminded her a little of Brooklyn, though they had no basements as far as she could tell.

Why had Archie wanted her here? What was with the man in Betty Marie's bar? Or the paper? What connection had this little place to do with the *Beacon* or her family? And where had the man from Betty

Marie's disappeared to? He'd stepped onto the ferry, tipped his hat politely, settled himself at the other end of the boat to Ellis Island and not bothered her the whole trip. Did he even get on the same ship?

Veronica hit the main street and was heading towards a church. The church clock showed a few minutes after three. Past the church, she was becoming aware of an unpleasant smell. A little further and boy oh boy, it got bad! So bad; rotten egg bad. She tapped the shoulder of a kid staring at some movie listings, a slingshot sticking out of his back pocket. 'Hi there, I'm new in town. Can you tell me what that terrible smell is?'

'What smell?' His faced screwed into a frown. 'Oh, *that*. You gets used to it. It's the creek. Whole place stinks when the tide's out.'

How could a little creek stink out a whole town?

The smell aside, her plan was to find the nearest bar. In her experience, if you wanted to know anything, convince folk you're old enough and hang around the nearest bar.

She left the kid drooling over a new film. According to the poster, it would be 'Coming soon.' The first full-length cartoon, *Snow White and the Seven Dwarfs*.

She came to a store selling newspapers. But with curled corners and yellowing with age, the papers were piled unattractively in the windows. One broken pane was itself covered in newspaper. Above, in flaking paint, the store declared itself to be The Nettlefield Courier. The sign, hung wonkily inside the door, said 'Closed,' but Veronica banged on the glass with her fist, anyway. Nobody came.

She eventually found the bar, The Blue Bonnet (How did it get a crazy name like that?) tucked away up a side alley. The sign creaked on a hinge above the door. Two men with violin cases brushed past her. Gosh, this place didn't look that different to the States after all. Gangsters in broad daylight! It was broad daylight on the main street, at least. The church clock she'd passed a few blocks back now showed only fifteen minutes after three, but the alley sucked the light from the day.

She pulled her hat low again and opened the bar door.

Tables were pushed back against the wall. A large man in a long, brown apron was lining up chairs in front of a makeshift stage. 'Ere, what you doing? We ain't open yet.'

'The door was open,' said Veronica.

'Not for you, it wasn't. Come back at opening time!'

Two men carrying a harp of all things barged past her on the step.

'Over in the corner's the best place for that,' said the large man in the brown apron, who seemed to be in charge.

He pushed Veronica out of the door. 'What you doing, gawping like that? Off with you.'

'Where's the nearest boarding house? I'm looking for a bed for the night. Somewhere to stay?'

'Doris Tatler'd be your best bet. Now, do I have to tell you again?'

'You're not sending him there are you, landlord?' said a kinder looking man, who'd snuck in behind the harp carriers.

The man in the brown apron, the landlord, grumbled and shut the door, leaving Veronica on the step.

'Well, it's a clue, at least,' said Veronica to herself. "Dorcas Rattler," was that what he'd said?'

The door opened again with the smell of old beer, and the kinder man popped his head out. 'Doris Tatler, just down there on the right, er... son.' He pointed back down the alley, the way she'd come from the street. 'Though as soon as you can, find somewhere else.'

Veronica was about to ask why, but the landlord called him in and the door shut with the clunk of the key in the lock.

Veronica picked up her bag and headed to where the kinder man had been pointing.

The door was unmistakable. It was the only door. She'd noticed a shop just inside the alley, but it was closed, the windows obscured with dirty white paint and the door boarded up with no means to get inside.

In contrast, the boarding house doorknob shone like a mirror. Veronica could see herself distorted in it. She was all nose.

Veronica straightened her jacket and brushed herself down. She was conscious of her unwashed state but hoped the lady would accept her excuses. She raised her fist to knock, then hesitated. What reason could there be to find somewhere else as soon as she could? There was one way to find out. Veronica knocked, took off her hat and held it respectfully against her chest.

As the sound echoed in the dark alley, Veronica noticed an unfriendly sign fixed to the wall: 'Working Gentlemen Only. No Ladies.'

She replaced her hat on her head and stepped away from the door with a sigh.

But with the slide of a bolt and the creak of a hinge, the door opened. A little old lady with fierce eyebrows squinted up at her from the doorstep.

'Good afternoon, ma'am. I was told at the bar just up the way there that you have a room for rent. I'm new in town and need a place to stay, but...'

As soon as Veronica spoke, the little woman's face twisted into a weird smile and her eyes widened with a kind of wonder. 'Ooh, I say.' She patted her hair and pulled off her apron. 'Might you, by any chance, be an American? You have the look of Mr Gary Cooper.' The lady smiled awkwardly, as if she didn't really know how.

'I've just come from the States, yes ma'am,' said

Veronica truthfully. She was aware the passport left to her by Archie told a different tale.

'As a matter of fact, I do have a room for a nice young man like yourself. Come in, why don't you?' The lady reached out, grabbed Veronica's jacket sleeve and pulled her into a dark hallway smelling of overcooked vegetables. 'This way, my dear.'

The way the lady said 'my dear' made Veronica feel like one of the children in *Hansel and Gretel*.

Veronica passed a hallstand, where a long list of house rules was displayed in writing too small to read. The jug beside it was old and had a face on one side. It wore a horrible leering expression that looked up at Veronica from the stand, as if to say, *'You mind these rules or there'll be consequences.'*

'Keep up, dear,' said the lady, Mrs Tatler, from the stairs. 'Then we'll have time for a nice cup of tea.'

Veronica followed the lady up three flights of stairs, past a dynasty of somber family photographs in dull wood frames, to a room in the attic. It was bare except for a bed covered with the thinnest of blankets, a white ceramic sink, a wardrobe whose doors were tied together with string, and a chest of drawers. Out of a small gable window, all Veronica could see was sky. That was the nicest thing about the room.

Mrs Tatler bustled around, trying to hide the fact that, had it not been tied with string, the wardrobe door would be falling off. 'The handyman will be here any day now to repair that,' she said, smiling awkwardly again. 'Come down when you've got yourself settled and we'll have that cup of tea. What should I call you, dear?'

'V...Ron,' said Veronica. 'My name is Ron. She quite liked this shortened version of her name and now felt like a very good time to use it.

Veronica put her carpet bag on the bed and took off her hat and jacket. She checked the inside pocket for Archie's letter and tip-tapped down the stairs. Only on the final flight were her steps deadened by carpet. A kettle whistled, rattling on a stove somewhere. She followed the sound to the back of the house.

In the middle of the kitchen, she found Mrs Tatler carefully setting two ornate china cups with matching saucers on the table covered with an oilcloth. Veronica smelled a cheap perfume, which didn't quite mask the smell of old boiled cabbage. The lady had her back to Veronica, humming a little tune and bobbing in time to it.

Veronica coughed to alert the lady to her presence.

Mrs Tatler turned round. She had exchanged her apron for something much frillier and her lips were inexpertly smeared red. The effect of the bright lipstick on a face that rarely wore it was a bit alarming. 'Oh hello, dear. Do sit down. I'm nearly ready for you.'

Veronica sat on the chair that Mrs Tatler offered and looked about the kitchen while Mrs Tatler poured the hot water into a fancy china teapot and positioned it with the cups and saucers on the table.

Beside the kettle, a large pot sat on the stove, the source of the cabbage smell. On the dresser, plain white plates and bowls were displayed, with an unfriendly little reminder to clean up after yourself and not to take any more than your fair share. A grumpy brass owl weighted a pile of assorted papers: letters, handbills, newspaper clippings. Above the owl, in the middle of the dresser shelves where you might expect a small collection of family photos, there was just the one photo, quite a large one, cut from a magazine but framed in a fancy silver gilt frame. It was the most extravagant thing in the room. The photo was of the actor Gary Cooper, in a Stetson hat for his first talking picture, *The Virginian*.

Mrs Tatler filled the teapot and placed it on the table with a jug of milk and a silver bowl of sugar, which she took from the dresser's topmost shelf. 'Oh, it's so interesting to have an American person in my house,' she said, pouring a drop of milk into each cup. 'To have that wonderful accent...' She poured the tea. 'Tell me all about your marvellous country. And have you seen Mr Gary Cooper's latest moving picture? *Souls at Sea*, I believe it's called. Sugar? Do tell me all about it. Though I actually prefer him as a cowboy.'

Mrs Tatler sat there, rapt with attention, her teacup poised at her lips and her eyes fixed on

Veronica, as Veronica made up some baloney about Gary Cooper. How he was a natural horseman, how everyone loved him on set, and how, so she'd heard, he was looking forward to returning to England someday. Veronica remembered something she'd read about him having to go to school here when he was a kid. Any time Veronica paused to ask Mrs Tatler a question—a good open question like Archie taught her—Mrs Tatler shooed it away with another question for Veronica.

'So, Mr Cooper actually was a real cowboy! Oh, how wonderful! I had heard, but to hear it from a real live American... It's so wonderful to have another gentleman lodger and such a fine young man, may I say too. I thought my last was an honourable, right-thinking gentleman, but it turned out not to be the case.' She sighed and laid her hands demurely in her lap. 'I am quite particular as to who I take in. This was my family home, you know. Now, where were we? Ah, yes, you were telling me how Mr Cooper was a real-life cowboy, too. Tell me more about his ranch...'

Although Veronica was a lover of the truth, stories served their purpose too, and telling a few about a Hollywood actor wasn't going to hurt anyone. When she felt she was getting a little fantastical—'Oh yes, he rode bareback from Dodge City to Tombstone in eight hours, beating the railroad by five minutes and thirty-three seconds!'—she attempted a polite withdrawal from Mrs Tatler's company. 'Well, thank you kindly, ma'am.' *Thank you kindly*. Where did that come from? 'I'll not take up any more of your time.'

'Nonsense, dear,' said Mrs Tatler. 'You stay here and watch the kettle, while I get a counterpane for your bed and a nice eiderdown that I reserve for my more *special* guests.' She relit the burner under the kettle and bustled past Veronica out of the kitchen. 'I'll just be two ticks!'

'Wouldn't it be easier if I came too?' called Veronica, doing her best to keep her voice in its lower register. But Mrs Tatler was already out of earshot, padding up the stairs.

Veronica gazed around the sparse kitchen. For a room often called the heart of the home, Mrs Tatler's kitchen was a heart of stone. She could see why the kind man from the bar didn't recommend the place. Her gaze fell on the grumpy brass owl paperweight. It was cold and unpolished, unlike the front door knocker. She picked it up. The pile of paper it held seemed to breathe a sigh of relief. The top torn piece of newspaper, a coupon for Doswells' Department Store, wafted to the floor, revealing a small folded card. It was a programme of events for 'Hamwell and District, British Union of Fascists.' Inside, the main event in larger type, was the visit of a *'Sir Malcolm Taggart, owner and editor-in chief of the Beacon,'* whose topic would be: *'The Anchsluss, what it will do for Germany and its benefits for Britain.'*

The card trembled in her hand. Was the *British German Bund* why she was here? Was this why Archie had left her a copy of the *Beacon*, whose owner and editor-in-chief was Sir Malcolm Taggart? She'd scoured the copy from Betty Marie's. If she had read his name, it hadn't left an impression. Apart from trying to persuade the British people to lock their doors against the German refugees, the whole paper was full of nonsense about the movies, the latest fashions, and soccer. She'd tried to match her clipping to one of its pages, but the yellowing clipping was much older. Even the typeface was different.

She heard the creak of Mrs Tatler's feet on the stairs. She refolded the piece of paper and tucked it with the shop flyer back under the grumpy owl. Darn, she hadn't made a note of the date of the talk. She could have snuck in.

'I've put them ready on your bed, dear,' said Mrs Tatler, sporting a fresh coating of lipstick.

Veronica's stomach churned at the sight.

'Now let's have another cup of tea and you can tell me some more about Mr Cooper's ranch...'

Veronica picked up her hat off the table and stood up. 'I mustn't keep you from your chores.' She no longer felt the need to be courteous.

Mrs Tatler's face fell in a clown-like grimace before attempting another smile. 'Well, never mind, dear. Perhaps we'll sit down over another cuppa after dinner.'

Veronica could feel the Bund's claws reaching out for her. Seething at all that Mrs Doris Tatler represented, Veronica did her best to shake off the notion.

Was she going to have to take these people on by herself?

Her family, whoever they were, would have to wait.

8
The Nettlefield Courier
Wednesday 16th March

SITTING ON THE HARD BED piled high with a princess quantity of eiderdowns (cold, slippery things that Mrs Tatler had delivered at intervals the previous evening), Veronica counted the few coins she had left after paying her first week's rent. In her hand she had eight large brown pennies and a few tiny silver sixpences. After some simple math, she worked out she had two shillings and two pennies, which didn't sound much at all. She slid the money into the coin purse and snapped it shut. She had to find some paid work and find it fast.

That newspaper store could definitely use some help, if it did actually open for business. She was sure going to find out and find out who was responsible for it. Veronica dressed in a fresh shirt, forced a smile through the breakfast of lumpy, cold porridge provided by Mrs Tatler, and left her new lodgings.

From the dark little alley, Veronica emerged into the town's main street, West Street, according to the sign fixed to a wall in front of her. To her left, the sun was just peeping over the old building at the far end. Columns framed a heavy-looking door and steps led down to the sidewalk. The place reminded Veronica of the stories of ancient Greece. The building must be ancient too, because it was propped up on one side by scaffolding. West Street skirted past it, where a road sign said, 'Portsmouth 12 miles.'

But above, the sky was a bright, hope-filled blue. A store owner in a brown work coat was unwinding his awning. Over the street, a woman in a headscarf tied as a turban and wearing a frilly apron, not dissimilar to Mrs Tatler's, was sweeping outside a store where boards covered the windows. A large British policeman, a bobby, a copper—she'd heard them called all three names—wobbled past on his bike.

The Nettlefield Courier did not have an awning or anybody to unwind one. Litter had gathered in the doorway and some of the upstairs windows were broken. Apart from the wonkily hung sign, now saying 'Open,' there was little to show much selling of news went on at all. The store reminded her of Mr Schneider's place in South Williamsburg. It looked attacked.

She pushed the door open anyway.

Veronica heard the familiar clunk, click, and flap of a printer working hard somewhere out the back. 'Helllooo!' she called. 'Shop! Anyone at home?' But whoever was in charge out there didn't hear her over the noise of the press.

She sighed, but with her next breath told her herself she could turn this place around.

She tripped over a stack of old newspapers. They slid across the floor. Veronica picked up a copy. *The Nettlefield Courier*, dated July 1937. Nearly a whole year ago. It fell apart where the front-page article had been slashed through. It was a piece about the British fascist, Oswald Mosley, having to hide in a tram to get away from protesters on Southampton Common. She remembered Archie telling her about the incident at the time. It certainly didn't occur to her then that she'd end up in practically the same place.

Apart from the front page, the rest of *The Nettlefield Courier* was nearly all advertisements: 'A miracle grow fertiliser! Feed those marrows now for winners in September!' One whole page was devoted to a department store that seemed to sell everything. Whoever owned that had to be a big cheese in this town.

A rack for magazines and comics stretching along one wall was almost empty. Opposite, on shelves behind the counter, jars that contained only sugar dust and a few pieces of hard candy stuck to the sides. On the counter, a tray for chocolate bars was empty, too. But next to the tray sat a very clean, very new stack of today's paper. Thick, expensive to print, busy copies of the *Beacon*.

On the front page, above a picture of Adolf Hitler heading up a motorcade driving through an excited crowd waving swastikas, the *Beacon's* headline read: *'AUSTRIANS SALUTE THEIR NEW LEADER! The two countries are now one, as they were meant to be.'* That didn't sound at all right to Veronica.

A beefy young man barged into the shop behind Veronica and grabbed a couple of Beacons from the top of the pile. He threw one of those large brown pennies on the counter and ran out. When Veronica noticed the price of the paper, she realised he hadn't even paid for one.

'Stop!' she shouted. 'Wait, that's not enough!' She ran after him down the street, kicking over a pile of brooms propped against a display. 'Sorry,' she called to the old store owner, who huffed out to pick them up.

The short-change thief dodged a trolleybus over the street. Veronica suspected he had more muscles than brains.

She shouted after him, 'Hey there, you didn't leave enough money!'

'What's it to you! No one cares about old man Coombes!' shouted the young man.

She put her finger and thumb to her lips to whistle, but he'd already disappeared down a side street.

'This is one screwed up place,' said Veronica.

She trudged back to the shop, passing the broom seller standing in his doorway, his hands on his hips.

'I'm sorry, sir,' she said.

'Never mind, young... err, lady? You were trying to help old Arnold out. He hasn't been the same since... Anyway, you'll get 'em next time, I'm sure.'

'Thank you, erm... Mr Clarence?' She guessed the old guy's name from the sign above the shop. 'I'm Veronica.'

'Yes, that's me,' he said, offering his hand. 'How do you do, Veronica?'

'Very well, thank you, sir,' she said, taking his firm, warm handshake.

'Now, I must be getting on,' said Mr Clarence, and he disappeared inside his store.

Back at The Nettlefield Courier, Veronica tried the door at the back. It led to a dark hallway, where, at the end, the press was still cranking away.

A sign, a little pointing finger, directed her up to the 'Office.'

She stepped over a loose section of disintegrating carpet on the bottom stair and made her way up. At the top, she faced just the one door. 'The Nettlefield Courier' was etched in an ornate font on the window, underneath 'Alfred Coombes, Editor-in-chief, 1898 to1925.' And underneath that, 'Arnold Coombes, Editor-in-chief, 1925.' Through the clearest section of glass, Veronica peered into the office. It appeared deserted, but she knocked and listened just in case. When no one replied, she turned the doorknob and let herself in.

It was like walking into Archie's place all over again, though on a slightly larger scale. But there was no busy clack of a typewriter keys, or a cheery 'Good day.' The one typewriter she saw was silent and unattended. Three other desks marked where other typewriters might have once sat. On one, a trilby hat with a band for a press card was slung carelessly with dead flashbulbs; on the other, a messy stack of papers and a few teetering piles of books.

More stacks of old *Nettlefield Couriers*, yellow with age, were piled up by the door. A grey knitted jacket, darned in odd colours, threads trailing, hung on the back of a chair. And on the one desk in use, judging by the abandoned cup of tea—she *was* in England, after all—a half-written piece was in progress on the typewriter.

There was a stale smokiness about the place, though she couldn't see any overflowing ashtrays. It smelled a bit like Betty Marie's bar and Archie's basement combined. The saving grace was a large window or wall of windows which looked out onto West Street. She counted four of its panes covered with newspaper, and lined up along the windowsill, four lumps of red brick.

Behind the desk, fixed to the wall, was a pinboard of photos, faded and curled in the sunlight, of community gatherings, children's tea parties and patriotic celebrations. It was all small-town news, nothing hard hitting. But like the rest of the office, the board was very disorganised. Veronica pushed aside the chair for a closer look. Most of the pictures were from years ago, just after the Great War, before she was born. There were significant gaps. She traced her finger over the thumbtack holes. Under a picture of a proud farmer and his prize-winning cow, she found the corner of a photo with its tack. There was no way she could tell what the photo was of, but it had sure been ripped off the board in a hurry.

She imagined herself sitting at the desk. She could really sort this place out. On the desk, a tall spike on which you might collect bills and receipts, was heavy with large sheets of paper. Letters, headed 'Beacon Newspapers, Publishing Happiness and Pride in our nation since 1922.' The *Beacon* again. What did the *Beacon* have to do with this place?

She was sliding the top letter up off the spike for a closer look, when a rustling, creaking sound stopped her. It was coming from underneath a tasselled silk shawl. Veronica pulled on the silk and the birdcage rattled into life.

The green parrot inside practically leapt for joy on its perch. 'READ ALL ABOUT IT READ ALL ABOUT IT READ ALL ABOUT IT,' it screeched.

Veronica dropped the shawl and crashed back into the pinboard as the sound of tumbling boxes and the heavy pad of footsteps came from the stairs. 'I'm coming, I'm coming, Houdini!' said a voice getting louder with its approach.

A dishevelled man with a thin covering of greying hair and braces holding up baggy brown corduroys stumbled in. His shirtsleeves were rolled up to his elbows, cuffs flapping.

'Oh hello, miss.' He pushed his unruly strands of hair back over his head. 'It is "miss," isn't it?' He pulled out a pair of wire spectacles and, with his ink-stained fingers, hooked them round his ears to squint at Veronica. 'Would you like to place an advertisement?'

Behind the desk, Veronica knew she was somewhere she shouldn't be, but there was nowhere to run, so she just had to brazen it out. 'I just came to say hi there,' she said. 'Fellow reporter to fellow reporter.' She showed off her own ink -stained fingers. 'Newsprint, you just can't get rid of it! I'm in the newspaper business too.'

'Oh,' said the man, presumably Mr Arnold Coombes. He nodded slowly, thoughtfully, almost as if a movie was playing out in his mind. He gazed at Veronica for a few seconds.

Veronica felt a warmth under her collar.

'Well, hello there,' said Mr Coombes at last. He turned away from Veronica and started shuffling the messy pile of paper on one of the unused desks.

'I was hoping that you could give me a job,' said Veronica. 'I can write good copy, fast, and set type; we have a Unitype back home...'

Mr Coombes nodded his approval, his back still towards her. He'd taken off his glasses and appeared to be wiping his eyes.

'And I can operate a press safely, look.'

Mr Coombes turned around, replacing his glasses, and examined her full complement of fingers, proving she could switch printed copy for fresh paper without getting them caught.

'And I can even make tea, but I'm better at coffee...'

'Yes, I can certainly give you a job.' He picked up the shawl and threw it back over the birdcage. 'Doing all those jobs would be really handy and more besides. But if you were looking to be paid, I'm afraid you're out of luck.' He glanced at the spike of letters and the lumps of brick on the windowsill. 'I won't be in the newspaper business much longer.'

'What happened to your other reporters?'

Mr Coombes stifled a laugh. 'Other reporters! That was years ago, in the paper's heyday. Dad and I had a tip-top team—alliteration.' He sighed. 'Where are you staying?' He leaned against the windowsill, undoubtedly trying to hide the lumps of brick.

'Just around the corner.'

He tutted and shook his head. 'Doris Tatler's...'

'Perhaps I could help, stop you going under?' Veronica didn't have a clue how she would do that, but this place, thousands of miles away from Maple Street, Brooklyn, felt a lot more like home than Mrs Tatler's. 'I could stop people stealing your newspapers, for instance. You need somebody downstairs to mind the store.'

'Yes, I do,' said Mr Coombes, rubbing the bristles on his chin. 'Perhaps I could give you a few coppers if you sell that pile of papers downstairs for the cover price. And if you sell some *Couriers* too, I'll double it!'

Veronica wasn't sure what he meant by a few coppers. Weren't they policemen here?

Seeing her confusion, Mr Coombes reached into his pocket. 'These,' he said, holding a large brown coin between his thumb and forefinger. It was a penny, like those the thief had chucked across the counter earlier. 'But listen, you'll need some proper money. To pay the Tatler woman off, at least, so when something else comes up, you take it. You can start with me now if you like?'

'Sure!' said Veronica, itching to attack the mess downstairs.

'Now, I need to be getting on,' said Arnold Coombes. 'The next edition's due tomorrow. We're weekly now.' He opened the door to the stairs, shooing her out. 'Make yourself at home, Veronica, and call me Arnold.'

The door closed smartly behind her. Through the clear bit of glass, she watched Arnold Coombes pull the cardigan off the back of the chair, put it on, and sit down at the typewriter.

He dragged the back of his hand under one eye, then straightened his glasses. But instead of typing, he tugged the half-written story off the carriage, scrunched it up and threw it in the trash.

9
Arnold Coombes
Wednesday 23rd March (half-day closing)

VERONICA IMMEDIATELY FELT at home with Arnold; so different to Archie in so many ways, not least of all the colour of his skin. But so alike in others. Though she still had to sleep at Mrs Tatler's, Arnold made sure Veronica was well fed and needed to spend as little time as possible in the horrible woman's horrible boarding house. Veronica's cover as a young American man was still intact for her landlady, at least.

The Nettlefield Courier had the same concerns as *The Maple Street Reporter*. The British *Bund*, nicknamed the 'Blackshirts,' had the sympathies of a lot of the town. Though just as many people were speaking out against them, that didn't stop them from reading the *Beacon* newspaper. Veronica was coming to the conclusion that this was why she was here. Nothing to do with finding her family at all. But then she returned to the passport and the clipping from the *Beacon*. Her parents, really?

And what could Archie have had to do with this little place?

But these questions had to wait, because Arnold had kept Veronica so busy tidying, sorting, and learning how to use his Typograph so she could compose the front page, that she'd barely had time to do anything else at all.

She hadn't even been able to find out when or exactly where this 'Sir Malcolm Taggart' was speaking, let alone sneak in to hear what he had to say. When she raised the subject with Arnold, he either set off on a rant about the 'Tory press,' or changed the subject entirely. Veronica now supposed Sir Malcolm Taggart was back in London and out of reach.

'My, Veronica, you've picked that up quickly,' said Arnold when she showed him her first line of hot metal type. 'Fancy you still having an old Unitype when you were practically on Mergenthaler's doorstep?'

'Archie sure was proud of that. He said Mergenthaler was just going to send the Unitypes to the trash, so where was the crime?'

'The crime,' said Arnold, 'was Mergenthaler's. Destroying perfectly good machines to monopolise the market with their overpriced Linotype. The waste and the greed made my blood boil. If I'd had the money, I'd have been over there with a truck collecting them all up and giving them to the folks who'd write the truth.'

Arnold was certainly very well informed.

Two small stacks of the latest edition of the *Courier*, due out the next day, sat on the counter hiding the day's one remaining *Beacon*. Veronica gazed at her typesetting and felt a little glow of pride bloom on her cheeks. The story was about the Town Hall and how the current council had allowed the building to fall into disrepair. Veronica had read it a hundred times on the Typograph. She agreed with Archie; their attitude to one of the town's oldest and once-upon-a-time fanciest buildings didn't make sense for the traditionally conservative council.

She was pleased that she'd persuaded lots of *Beacon* readers to take a discounted copy of the *Courier*. 'For the local news,' she told them. 'And I believe Mr Coombes is considering some kind of loyalty reward for regular readers...' *Keep it vague,* Veronica muttered to herself. She'd help Arnold to get them thinking for themselves one way or another.

'Ooh, I say,' said an older lady in a headscarf when she heard Veronica's offer. She tucked both papers into her shopping bag on her way out of the store. It was the same woman who, every day, swept the doorway of what Veronica now knew to be the old undertakers' place. Veronica had heard the story about Underwood, the Blackshirt undertaker, now in prison for kidnapping.

Veronica dashed out from behind the counter and opened the door for the woman. 'Why do you do that?'

'Do what, dear?'

Veronica pointed at the boarded windows of Underwood & Son across the street. 'Clean for a business that's obviously gone under.'

'I'm not sure what you mean, dear. I just do as I'm told. The council like to keep the town looking spick and span. They pay my wages, after all. Now I must be getting on. Mr Allemby will be wanting his dinner.' She bustled off past Mr Clarence's brooms, and some pots of red and yellow tulips brightening his display of hardware.

The door to the print room nudged open. Veronica left Mrs Allemby and grabbed the door for Arnold as he wheeled his bike through the shop. The sturdiest bike she'd ever seen, with a large tray fixed to the front. He propped it against the counter and plonked one stack of *Couriers* in the tray. The piece on the Town Hall was part of his series on local institutions. 'Everyone wants to know what goes on behind closed doors. Pity I couldn't pay the orphanage...'

'What do you mean?' asked Veronica, catching his bike as the pile of papers unbalanced the front wheel.

'Oh, nothing,' said Arnold. 'Perhaps we'll try to get you into the asylum for an interview with old Mr Spark, for your first report.' He picked up the last *Beacon*. 'I'll get rid of this at the same time.' He rolled it and wedged it between the tray and the stack of *Couriers*.

Veronica was pleased she was going to be reporting again, muckraking, truth-telling... 'Who's Mr Spark?'

Arnold was struggling to remove something a bit too big for his pocket. 'Abel Spark? He's somebody who had the misfortune to be different.' He pulled out one of the lumps of brick that had decorated the windowsill upstairs and put it on top of the papers in the tray. 'Useful paperweights, I suppose,' he said, reaching again in his pocket. 'And this is for you.' He put a large silver coin in Veronica's hand and wrapped her fingers around it. His fingers were warm, if a little dusty.

'You're worth double this, Veronica, and I hope that one day, half a crown's what I'll be able to pay you every day. But for now, my girl, take the afternoon off and remember, if something else comes along, something that'll pay you properly...'

'Yes, yes, I will, and thank you. When I do, you won't need to pay me at all. But are you sure about this? I didn't sell all last week's *Couriers*.'

'You sold a sight more papers than I would have. Now there's some sandwiches for you out back. Why don't you take them down to the park? The tide's in,' he said, and wheeled his bike out the door.

Veronica had easily sold all the *Beacons*. They sold out every day. Though it was the last thing she wanted to read, it would give her some insight into the man behind the paper, the Nazi sympathising Sir Malcolm

Taggart. But she could never find any old copies lying around anywhere in the shop.

'Whoops, nearly forgot.' Arnold unhooked a key on a shoelace round his neck and gave it to Veronica. 'This is yours, Veronica. You'd better lock up, now the old place is looking so inviting.' He gazed round at the colourful display of magazines and comics on the racks; the tray of fresh candy on the counter; and, on the shelves behind, the four new jars of hard candy—'boiled sweets,' they were called here—with a set of scales and some little paper bags on a string. Arnold refused to sell tobacco. 'Think about it, Veronica, all that tar going into your lungs. How can that be good for you?'

'If you come back later, I was going to have a go at making some hamburgers. I hear they're quite the thing in America and maybe...' Arnold pushed his bike off the sidewalk.

Maybe what? Arnold often drifted off into his 'brown study' mid-sentence. Sometimes, he'd forget she was there. Whatever was going on for him on the inside would rise to the surface. As if all the troubles of the world were pressing on his brow, his head would droop, and he would slope off upstairs. She'd seen the odd liquor bottle in the trash. They were in the business of telling the truth, but could you have too much?

Whatever the rest of Arnold's sentence was, he shook it away with a smile and swung his leg over the crossbar. 'I'll be off then, Veronica. Don't forget to lock up.'

She was getting to know his habits and eccentricities. She liked it, especially when he used her name. It made her feel valued, like Archie used to. Though something also troubled her about that, but she couldn't quite put her finger on it. Come to think of it, she couldn't remember telling him her name. But she must have, mustn't she?

Veronica watched Arnold pedal off on his bike, over the trolleybus rails and up the street until he took a right turn opposite the church and was out of sight.

She didn't really want to go to the park, in spite of the tide covering the stink of the town's creek, so she ate Arnold's deli-sized brisket sandwich while leaning against the large white sink in the tiny kitchen beyond the print room. He still called it 'corned beef,' though it came out of a can. When she'd finished, she unbuttoned Archie's old ink-stained overall and hung it on the back of the kitchen door, swapping it for her jacket. She grabbed Archie's fedora, tapped it on the back of her head and felt ready for a bit of exploring, a hunt for her first story. Where was the asylum, anyway?

The telephone was in full view in the darkroom. Veronica understood why Arnold kept it in there. He told her the last one had gone through the upstairs window.

Also in full view, though locked in a glass-fronted cabinet fixed to the darkroom wall, was a gun. It looked quite old, possibly a war relic. Didn't the British also fight in Africa at the end of the last century? Anyway, Veronica was well aware of the second amendment, though Archie was always against it, and she assumed the right to bear arms was the same here. She closed the darkroom door.

Also in full view to anyone peering through the shop window were the press and the Typograph, cleaned and oiled, ready for next week's edition. But they were too heavy and awkward to steal, let alone throw.

She was locking up with her new key when Mr Clarence clattered through his shop door with a couple of galvanised buckets and an armful of brooms. 'Half-day closing can't come too soon for me this week, young lady. I've had that much trouble from the Teasdale lad...'

Other shops in West Street were winding away their awnings for a half-day vacation, too. 'Does everyone take a break on Wednesday afternoons, Mr Clarence?'

'You might get a cuppa and a rock bun at that smart new Lyons' tea shop.' He pointed towards the station end of the town. 'Or you might be interested in the library? She doesn't get that many visitors nowadays.'

Veronica couldn't help feeling frustrated that everything was closed on her first free afternoon in this place. But 'rock buns' sounded intriguing, and she loved listening in on other folk's conversations; you could learn a lot that way. So that was here she headed.

Through the 'tea shop' window, on the corner of the road that Arnold had disappeared into, Veronica saw waitresses in black dresses with frilly white aprons and similarly frilly white bands tied round their heads. They bustled about, balancing fancy china on silver trays, mostly serving older ladies of the town, teacups in hand, leaning in for gossip. It looked just the sort of establishment to get the lowdown on this place. She was just about to push the door open when she saw one of those older ladies was Mrs Tatler talking to another woman in an ominous black blouse.

What a darned nuisance! Mrs Tatler still mistook her for a guy, but Veronica wasn't so sure her Blackshirt companion would be so easily fooled. She pulled the fedora lower over her forehead and backed away. She wasn't hungry, anyway.

A policeman wobbled past on a bike similar to Arnold's but without the useful front tray. It was the same 'bobby' she'd seen before. He bore down on the pedals as the road steepened, then dismounted by a short terrace of houses with tiny patches of front garden. The policeman leaned against the handlebars and caught his breath. He was a sergeant, by the looks of the three stripes on his sleeve.

She could ask him for directions to this orphanage Arnold mentioned, but then remembered Archie's clipping still in her pocket. She didn't want the orphanage at all.

Mr Clarence had told her where to go, but all she'd heard was 'rock buns,' whatever they were.

10
Miss Oswald & Mister
Later Wednesday Afternoon, 23rd March

VERONICA CAUGHT UP with the old policeman as he was lifting his leg over the crossbar on his bike.

'Hello... er, miss. And what can I do for you today?' he said, lowering his leg again and straightening up with a small groan.

'Good day to you, officer. I'm new to these parts. I was wondering where I might find the nearest library?'

The New York City Library and even the Brooklyn Library seemed to keep a copy of everything ever printed, so perhaps it was the same for this small town? But she had the feeling her hope might be misplaced.

The policeman took off his helmet and scratched his round head, almost hairless except for the walrus moustache under his nose. 'Hmm... library, you say? We haven't had much call for a library these past few years. People in this town think they know it all.' He laughed. Presumably he thought he'd made a joke.

Veronica wished she'd risked the tea shop.

'Last time I looked, it was that way.' The policeman pointed towards a tree-lined avenue on the other side of the street up from town. 'But the easiest way for you, a stranger in these parts, is turn right at the end of this road, turn left all the way along West Street and at the Town Hall, left again.' He replaced his helmet. 'I'd best be getting on.' With some effort, he mounted his bike and pedalled off along the road.

Sitting under the cow-eyed gaze of Mrs Tatler and her friend wasn't really that appealing, so Veronica followed the policeman's directions.

At the crumbling Town Hall she turned into a street that was even older, where the buildings were large and important looking, historical even.

And a little way up it, sandwiched between two of these important-looking buildings, was the Nettlefield Public Library.

Like the Town Hall, the library needed some repair or a lick of paint at least, but there was no scaffolding to hold the building up. The more imposing buildings on either side were doing that, as if the library were under arrest. A paint-chipped board outside advertised opening times: '11am to 4pm, Monday to Friday. Librarian O. Oswald.' Veronica wasn't wearing a watch, but surely was well in time.

However, at that moment, the library door opened, and an older lady in a battered straw hat with a large daisy hatpin stepped out. She carried a carpet bag similar to Veronica's, hooked over one arm, and a set of keys in her hand. She put her bag down on the top step and pushed a key in the lock.

Veronica hailed the lady from the street. 'Excuse me, ma'am, is it closing time already?'

'I'm afraid it is, young lady. As we were quiet, I've decided to close early. Mind you, we're always quiet.'

'But I'd love to come in.'

'You're not one of those...' She very cautiously pointed to her shirt and tentatively mimed a shrunk Nazi salute. 'We've had some trouble with some of the more enthusiastic young men and women coming in and checking for unsuitable books. It was very worrying, but as our collection is quite ancient, they didn't find a lot to burn. Money from the council hasn't been forthcoming for quite some years now.'

Veronica reassured her and was wondering who the other person in the 'We' might be when she saw a tortoiseshell cat poke its nose out of the lady's bag.

'Oh, don't mind him, he's rather old. Mister Mephistopheles or just "Mister" for short. He keeps me company all day.'

Was this the O. Oswald on the noticeboard? The lady unlocked the front door and held it open. 'How exciting, a visitor from overseas as well. You are from America, aren't you?'

'Yes, ma'am, I am.' Veronica stepped inside a small vestibule. 'I was wondering, do you keep back copies of the *Beacon?*'

'Oh. You mean the newspaper?' She dropped the keys into her bag with the cat and raised her hand to the large daisy pin stuck in her hat. 'Yes, yes, we do. We have plenty of those. One thing the council was keen on. Now, are you sure you're not one of those over enthusiastic young people?'

'No, Miss Oswald. I can assure you I'm not.'

Patting the hatpin in place, the lady frowned and said, 'Have we met?'

'No, your name is on the board.'

'The board?'

'Outside.'

'Oh that. That was Father.'

'So, you are...'

'Miss Oswald, Olivia Oswald.' She turned the lock on the inner door with a clunk. 'Now, do come in.' The lines on the lady's face faded, and she didn't look as old as Veronica first thought. 'It's actually nice to have someone in here. And what is your name, dear?'

'Veronica,' said Veronica, smiling her friendliest smile.

Miss Olivia Oswald pushed open the library door. Its hinges squeaked. She unpinned her hat and left it next to a small date stamp on a lectern by the door.

As Veronica followed Miss Oswald inside, she couldn't help noticing what an exceptionally long hatpin it was.

The smell of ancient manuscripts, dust, mustiness, and damp mixed with kerosene hit Veronica. Miss Oswald's shoes tap-tapped on the floor. With the hiss of gas, she lit a lamp over a large table. Its greenish glow brightened the room, if you could call it that. 'There, that will help. This is not the best lamp to read by, but new lighting is expensive, they tell me. I'll open the curtains.'

The flood of natural daylight from a high window took away some of the feel of the Ghost Train on Coney Island. Bookcases surrounded them. There were lots of gaps and some of the remaining books had tumbled over to fill the spaces. Veronica felt the shelves tower over her.

'Now, sit down here.' Miss Oswald pulled out a chair.

It wobbled as Veronica sat down.

'Just how far back would you like to go?' asked Miss Oswald. She positioned the carpet bag containing Mister the cat on the table under the lamp. 'It's his favourite spot,' she said and tickled him under his chin.

Veronica knew the year she went to live with Archie. It was 1929, the year of the Wall Street Crash, when the value of shares on the stock market plummeted: a lot of money was lost; businesses went bankrupt; and there were so many people out of work and unable to feed their children. It was awful. So 1929 *might* be a good year to start.

'How far do they go back?' asked Veronica.

'That would be from when from when Sir Malcolm Taggart took over in 1922.'

That would be even better. Get some insight on this man. Then perhaps she could persuade Arnold a profile of the man behind the *Beacon* could be her first article. 'Perfect,' said Veronica.

'Can I ask what you are looking for? Perhaps I could help. I do love a treasure hunt!'

Veronica didn't know what to say. With no idea of what she was going to find out, she wasn't sure what she was looking for. 'No, that's fine, thank you.'

'Oh, that's alright, dear. I'll bring them out in batches,' said Miss Oswald. 'Mister and I will be quite happy with our book. It's by Mr Orwell about his time living with the down and outs in Paris and London. Though I don't think the council would approve of it on the library shelves.' Her forehead creased, and she looked like she was going to ask if Veronica really was sure she wasn't one of those young people again before she shook her head and thought better of it.

'I'll be back in a jiffy.' Miss Oswald disappeared through a door between the bookcases.

Mister's fur was the most orange Veronica had ever seen on a cat. She wondered how silky it would feel. But before she'd even lifted a finger, the cat meowed a warning hiss before settling inside his bag.

Miss Oswald returned with a huge pile of newspapers. She plonked them in front of Veronica. 'Mister reminds me not to put paper too close to the gas.' She reached inside the bag and gave him another affectionate tickle. 'Now, I've brought one of our earliest sets—1922 to 1925. The cellar's full of them. If we should ever catch fire... Somehow I don't think the present council will be building a new library!' She laughed nervously.

Veronica opened the first paper. January 1st 1922, the year she was born. The front page was a headline wishing the country a happy and prosperous new year. She turned to the editorial written by Malcolm Taggart himself. In it, he wrote about the loss of his twin sons in the last weeks of the war but also hope for the future in that his late brother's son, the banker, was expecting their first baby. He went on to talk about the need to rebuild and not punish. He seemed angrier about the British government and their slaughter of a generation than the Germans for starting the whole war in the first place.

She scanned some more editorials and ploughed through more papers where a new editor had taken over. They became more like stories rather than news. So much so that Veronica often doubted their truthfulness. She read a story about the Royal Family—

how perfect all the children were. But she remembered Archie telling her about another prince who they kept hidden away. Sometimes in the hunt for truth, it was very difficult to recognise it when you found it.

Miss Oswald suddenly appeared at Veronica's shoulder, making her jump. 'Would you like another lot yet, dear?'

Veronica didn't really want to read any more of this stuff, but she did want to find the rest of her cutting. It was what she came for. 'Could I jump ahead a few years, to 1929, perhaps?'

'Oh dear, yes. That was the start of our troubles. The year of the Financial Crash, wasn't it? And the start of the Great Depression, you poor Americans.'

The later papers were no better. Much worse, in fact. Barely taking in any headlines at all, Veronica scanned editorial after editorial. Each more ridiculous, salacious or libellous than the last, expressing terrible opinions about different groups of people. Jewish people, the lame and crippled, the poor... She was getting very tired of this rumour-mongering designed to manipulate readers' opinions. Was no one interested in the truth these days?

She closed the last paper she could bear reading. It was for a date in November 1929 and full of commentary about Wall Street, accompanied by various ridiculous theories on its cause—from outer space monsters to an underground group of Bolsheviks.

But nothing of any value. If the stories were in a storybook, they'd be very entertaining.

Miss Oswald was napping in her chair with Mister on her lap. Her book had fallen to the floor. The light outside had faded and the clock on the library wall made it seven o'clock. Had Veronica really been here that long? She'd probably missed both Mrs Tatler's meagre rations and Arnold's hamburgers by now.

She was tidying the pile of papers when she noticed that one had slipped to the floor. Thursday October 31st, 1929, three days after 'Black Monday.' The frontpage headline was like a slap round the face. How had she missed it?

But The *Beacon* had not run with a headline about the fallout from the biggest stock market losses in recorded history.

Instead, it ran with:

'MISSING IN AMERICA: HOWARD AND SYLVIA CAMPBELL.'

It was dedicated to the disappearances of the Campbell family, nephew and niece-in-law of the newspaper's owner Malcolm Taggart, and their only daughter, seven-year-old Euphemia Grace, affectionately known as Veronica.

11
It's a Market Economy!
The Next Day, Thursday 24th March

BABY ARRANGED the washed and dried breakfast bowls on the shelves of the extra-large dresser. Baby gave the dresser a quick 'flippy doo' with the tea towel, as June's old ma, Mrs Lovelock, liked to say, before hanging the towel on the range to dry out. 'When's the new help coming, Bri?'

'June said the advert would be in the paper soon,' said Brian, dishing out a bowl of porridge from a fresh pot she had made for her dad according to his special recipe.

'Oh, that's good,' said Baby. It wasn't as if she didn't want to help. It was only right, but in the kitchen she was not much more use than that waster, William Teasdale, brother of jailbird Bill—their ma had very little imagination—Arthur Underwood's henchman.

'I think someone will come and help very soon.' Brian rubbed Baby's arm kindly before she covered the steaming bowl of porridge with a cloth and put it on a tray with the latest copy of the *Courier*. 'I am just going to take Dad his breakfast.' Baby held the door open for Brian and helped her navigate the washing lines at the back of the orphanage.

Baby nipped back inside and hung her own apron on its special hook in the kitchen. She checked that her purse was where it should be, in one of her many skirt pockets, then headed out through the gates and up West Street to poor old Arnold Coombes's paper shop. He delivered the *Couriers* himself, but today Baby needed the *Beacon*.

Baby was sure Malcolm Taggart, *Sir*, was a Blackshirt. She could smell them now and she'd tried to tell June, but all June could say was, 'But the money, Baby. We need the money.' What Baby couldn't work out was *why* this man was so interested in them and a small town like Nettlefield. Malcolm Taggart was a proper toff who knew folks like the Prime Minister. He'd told them so himself. Baby wouldn't be surprised if he was in with the old King too, the one that got himself abdicated.

Reading newspapers, the *Courier* mostly, was an education for Baby. It was how she knew about what was happening in Germany and the other countries in Europe and across the world. Though from the headlines on the copies of the *Beacon* she'd seen around town, she didn't like the shine the paper was putting on Adolf Hitler and his like. And she was getting more and more concerned about what was going on in India. If that Miss Grenville was to be believed, Baby had family there.

She didn't have long before she had to be back to give Brian a hand with the lunch. They'd all taken to using the posher word for the midday meal now. So, Baby hurried past the big houses that Fingers had promised she'd finally given up burgling. Goodness knows how Fingers never got caught. But then she was Florrie Fingers, quiet as a mouse and sneaky as a rat. She could get in or out of anywhere. She picked a pocket with those long fingers of hers without the pocket owner feeling a thing, but next they knew, they couldn't pay for their tea in the new Lyons' tea shop opposite old man Winters's greengrocer's shop.

At that moment, the very same old man Winters, one of the town's Blackshirts, was rocking on his heels in his shop doorway, his arms folded across his brown apron. Even though it was nearly two years ago when Baby had last painted on his shop window, Mr Winters still hadn't given up watching her under his bushy eyebrows.

'I've got my eye on you,' he said with a throaty growl.

'I know,' said Baby. 'Same 'ere.' She pointed from her own two eyes to his.

His latest assistant was shouting from inside the shop. 'Mr Winters, I need some more coppers for the till!' They wouldn't last long in the job.

So, just for fun, and because Winters was an old Blackshirt, Baby tipped an orange teetering on the edge of his fruit and veg display into one of her many skirt pockets. Moll's old skirt was getting a bit short, but was still as useful as ever.

Distracted by the pinched orange bouncing against her legs, Baby collided with a man in a large gaberdine coat outside The Embassy cinema. 'Oops, beg your pardon,' she said to the man, who had a strange expression caused by the white scar that cut one of his eyebrows in two. He grunted as Baby extricated herself from the flaps of his coat. He pulled his hat over his face as if to hide the scar and hurried across West Street.

Baby strode on but she couldn't help noticing the scarred man was heading for the corner by Underwood's old place, opposite Arnold Coombes's shop.

Arnold Coombes was not a Blackshirt, but had to sell the Beacon. 'I've tried putting them out of the way,' he'd told her when he stopped by for a cuppa in the orphanage kitchen one day. 'But it doesn't stop them from buying it.'

'But some of 'em don't actually *buy* it. They pinch it, don't they?' Baby had said.

'Yes, you're right, Baby.' Arnold Coombes had sighed and shaken his head. 'June, don't get me wrong, I'm really grateful to you for taking a few copies of the

Courier, but it's a drop in the ocean. Even the folk who shouted down the march in '36 get the *Beacon*. They like the football and stories about the Royal Family. There's a crossword too. They told me the bits that there *were* to read in the *Courier* were too serious and the rest of it was just adverts. But that's the only way I can keep the thing running. My old dad would be turning in his grave. I tried a crossword, but it's not my forte.' He looked hopefully at June Lovelock, taking a sip of tea on the other side of the table.

'Perhaps it's something Mother might be interested in; just a simple general knowledge one maybe, just a few clues?'

Baby seriously doubted that. It was not that Mrs Lovelock didn't have the brains to do it; it was that she liked to keep that fact well hidden. 'People let out all kinds of secrets when they think you're a silly old lady in a wheelchair!' she once told Baby.

Baby wasn't a regular visitor to Arnold's shop, but after waving to Mr Clarence between the buckets and brooms in his shop window next door, she could see The Nettlefield Courier had undergone a makeover. Nowhere near the scale of the orphanage rebuild, but it did look like an actual shop now. The chocolate bar tray was full, jars of sweets sat on the shelf behind the counter, and she could even see a copy of that new comic, *The Dandy*, on display.

But there was something even stranger about Arnold Coombes's paper shop today.

Someone else was in it.

They were standing behind the counter, where Arnold should be, or his parrot at least.

Baby hesitated on the doorstep. The someone was busy counting papers. The latest edition of *The Nettlefield Courier* was on prominent display next to the tray of chocolate. Baby picked up a *Detective Weekly*. It was well out of date, unlike *The Dandy*, which was brand new. Perhaps she'd come back for both when she had the money.

She couldn't see the *Beacon*. The paper she'd come to buy. Oh, darn it. She was too late. They'd sold out. Well, she'd have to try again tomorrow.

The person behind the counter looked up, their thumb marking their place in the stack of *Couriers*. At first glance, Baby thought it was a young man, quite a dashing one at that, in a billowy white shirt, sleeves rolled to the elbow and a jaunty little turquoise scarf around their neck. For one icy moment, they made her think of the wicked Nazi, Easton Fitzgerald. But being used to Brian's taste in men's clothes—her dad's—Baby realised that it wasn't a young man at all but a young woman looking back at her with fashionably cropped hair, shorter than Baby's, flopping over her face.

'Hello there! What can I do for you, er... miss?'

She was a fine one to talk. But she had an accent, an American one. Baby could feel the goosebumps popping up on her arms. She was actually meeting a full-blown American.

'I want today's *Beacon*,' said Baby. 'Please,' she added, trying to make a good impression.

'Really?'

Baby heard disapproval in the girl's tone. Baby's goosebumps faded. Her politeness had gone uncredited.

The girl leaned across the counter and flapped the latest *Courier* in Baby's face. 'Are you sure you wouldn't like the *Courier* better? It's local, national, and global news about the real world and how it really is.'

'Yeah, I know,' said Baby, feeling strangely threatened by the girl's insistence. 'But I want the *Beacon* and you've sold out.'

The girl was much taller than Baby, perhaps as tall as Letitia. She towered over Baby, even from the other side of the counter.

'We haven't,' she said with a frown. From under the counter, she produced a crisp, clean new paper with today's date and today's Blackshirt headline, something complimentary about Adolf Hitler. 'That'll be four cents sorry, pennies, four pennies.'

'But the price on the cover is tuppence. *Two* pennies.' Baby translated for the benefit of the American.

'Too bad, we're selling them for four and for that you get a copy of *The Nettlefield Courier* as well. It's a market economy. Didn't you know that?'

'No, I didn't,' said Baby, not knowing what the American girl was talking about and wondering what was it with *we*? As far as she knew, Arnold worked on his own. This was not how she expected her first meeting with a real, live American girl to go. Usually so sure of herself, Baby felt unbalanced. 'Where's Arnold?'

'Upstairs, working on a story,' said the girl, picking up half the stack of *Couriers* and stashing it under the counter.

Baby was trying to work out the best thing to say. She didn't want the girl to think that she liked the *Beacon,* but she also didn't want to go into a long, rambling explanation about why she was buying it. This girl should be able to see that Baby wasn't a typical *Beacon* reader. If the girl wasn't so dim, Baby would have asked her about where she'd come from in America, for some tips for getting by, if Baby did actually get there one day.

'Did you want anything else?' asked the girl, her tone getting frostier by the second. She was trying to give Baby the two papers, the palm of her other hand waiting for payment.

'No thanks,' said Baby. 'I don't need the Courier.'

The girl harrumphed and snatched back both papers. *"Being ignorant is not so much a shame, as being unwilling to learn."* Ben Franklin,' she said haughtily.

'What?' said Baby.

'It's a quote,' said the girl. 'About you,' she muttered under her breath.

'So how long will you be here for?' asked Baby. Maybe if she was only there for the day, Baby could come back tomorrow and get a *Beacon* for tuppence. She could easily pinch one as Arnold was hardly ever in the shop, but she wouldn't do that to him. She suddenly became very aware of the stolen orange warming her pocket.

'For as long as I need to be,' was the girl's drawling reply. 'And what's it to you?' She looked down her nose at Baby, her frown deepening as she replaced *The Nettlefield Courier* back on its pile while holding the *Beacon* between an ink-stained finger and thumb like it was a dirty rag.

Through the open door, Baby could hear Mr Clarence with one of Nettlefield's older ladies. The woman, one of the cabbage-throwing women at the Blackshirt March in '36, walked past the Courier's open door and waved to this rude American girl.

'Just curious,' said Baby. She really didn't like the way the girl was making her feel. The girl's attitude looked and sounded like the Blackshirts who shouted abuse at Baby about her height or her brown skin. It was one thing to be called nasty names about what you chose to be—a one-time thief and a dauber of slogans on Blackshirt shops—but the rude words for those things you had no choice about were horrible. Not that she'd want to change those things, but the names made her feel worthless. So when she felt like that, she'd think about all the people who loved and, yes, admired her. Then Baby could pick herself up again and, in a manner of speaking, walk tall.

Baby did have a sixpence. It was a new little silver sixpence that she had been saving for a trip to the Lyons' tea shop. She didn't want to spend it on the nasty old paper. But if she had to... Reluctantly, she reached into a pocket in her skirt and placed the sixpence on the counter. 'I need the change,' she said, taking the paper.

Baby was sure this girl thought she *liked* the *Beacon*; that she was one of *them*, that she was actually a Blackshirt. To be so completely misjudged, to be thought the opposite of what you were. That. Was. Terrible.

Why should Baby have to explain that she didn't need the *Courier*? Why didn't the girl know that, to help Arnold, June got a few copies for the orphanage on account, and sometimes comics too for a special treat? The stories in *The Nettlefield Courier* could be a bit too real, so June always told the orphans what was going on in the world, but in a way that still made them feel safe. Sometimes Arnold wasn't so good at that. Baby wondered if Taggart had spotted the *Courier* around the orphanage when he came for his lunch the previous day? Or had June replaced it with a *Beacon*, just for show?

That was a thought! Baby had a memory of seeing one on June's desk, well out of the way of the orphans but well in view for Sir Malcolm Taggart, when he called.

'Just remembered,' she said, 'don't need the *Beacon* either.' Baby snatched the sixpence off the counter and replaced it with the paper before dashing out of the shop.

Relieved that she still had her sixpence for the Lyons' tea shop, Baby's feelings about America were changing. If that was what Americans were like—knowing what was best for everyone and assuming what a person was like without finding out—she wasn't too sure she wanted to go there.

'You can't do that, you've bought it!' called the girl from the shop door.

'And now I've sold it back!' shouted Baby. 'Market economy!' She threw the words back, guessing what they meant. Buying and selling, that must be it.

Over the road, she glanced at the boards covering Arthur Underwood's old undertakers' shop window. The place still gave her the shivers. But through the dark cracks between the slats, she caught a flash. Like someone had briefly switched on the electric light in his office. At first, she thought it could be Fingers. Fingers had been in there before, but there was no way she'd turn the light on.

Baby wanted to investigate, but the church clock was striking twelve. She had to be back for lunch. It was only for a few of them, Gin and the adults, but she'd promised to be there.

She'd have to leave Underwood's until tomorrow. How she hated that place. Why couldn't someone buy it and turn it into a sweet shop or something?

Taggart's fancy car drove past her. Was that him in it? Wasn't he supposed to be back in London? Though Baby was focused on getting back to the orphanage, behind her, she was sure the smart car turned off West Street towards Underwood's yard.

12
Muckraking in Nettlefield
Thursday 24th March

IN THE LIBRARY, the day before, Veronica had stared and stared at the picture on the front page of the old Beacon, trying to make herself feel something, remember something about these people. She refused to believe she could be a Taggart. That wasn't the name in the passport. That was a 'Campbell,' not a Taggart, though to her mind, 'Veronica Park' worked a lot better even than 'Veronica Campbell' and she certainly did not feel like 'Euphemia Grace' at all.

But an itch like a bug crawling inside her shirt niggled her. How was she going to get rid of it? She could feel a connection there and didn't like it.

She knew Archie found her wandering in the Navy Yards and that he took her home to Maple Street. She'd always simply accepted that. He was kind; he was nice; he *listened* to her. But, thinking about it, wasn't that strange? Should he have been allowed to do that?

Why did nobody come looking for her? Where were 'Howard and Sylvia?'

But then somebody did come. The man in the limousine Betty described had to have been Taggart himself. And the other man, in Betty Marie's, the one in the oversized gaberdine coat, with the scar, and the newspaper had to have been an employee of some sort. Was he the man who killed Archie? Why? And where was he now?

She was glad Archie had taken her in. He smelled right. He smelled of ink and paper and words. He had so many words. And his wisdom was deep: *'Everything you write is as much about what you don't say as you do. Don't underestimate your reader. Many of them can read as much between the lines as on them.'* She remembered writing her first report about a drugstore owner who was paying kids half as much as adults for the same errand job. Was that right? She left the reader to decide. *'Tell them the facts, Veronica, not what to think,'* he always said.

Were those really the facts about the man and the woman on the front page, Howard and Sylvia? They had looked familiar, but was that Veronica trying to make them look familiar? Because according to this report, they were her parents:

> *The Beacon community today is anxious for the safety of banker Howard Campbell and his wife Sylvia, beloved nephew and niece of our proprietor and editor-in-chief, Sir Malcolm Taggart. Their seven-year-old*

daughter Euphemia Grace, affectionately known as 'Veronica', is also missing. The British couple were last seen at their holiday home in the Hamptons, Long Island, New York. They were awaiting the arrival, on the Queen Mary, of their daughter on an autumn break from her English school. The child's chaperone is being questioned by the New York Police. No ransom notes have been received, but reports of strange lights in the sky over Long Island have led the Taggart Campbell family to believe that something otherworldly may have occurred. They are consulting renowned expert in anomalous phenomena, Charles Fort, for some clues as to the family's whereabouts. The Beacon community hopes and prays that this sad story soon finds some resolution.

'Sad story? No. It's a crazy story,' Veronica had said in the musty darkness of Miss Oswald's library.

'But it's what the readers of the paper like to read... and believe,' Miss Oswald had said, with Mister the cat purring in his shopping bag. Miss Oswald had then ushered Veronica out for the evening. 'I'll keep that out for you for tomorrow. It's lovely to have library visitors, you know. Perhaps you'd even like to take a look at some of our books?'

At least that girl coming in for a *Beacon* and not accepting Veronica's 'buy one get one half price' offer gave her something else to think about. How had a girl like that been persuaded fascism was on her side? Yes, Veronica might have made one or two assumptions, but it was totally clear the girl despised everything the *Courier* and, therefore, Veronica stood for.

Arnold's footsteps thudded down the stairs. In a crumpled jacket that Veronica hadn't seen before, he hooked the camera round his neck. 'Did I miss a customer?'

'Yeah, you sure did. But they changed their mind,' said Veronica.

'Oh, rightio. But well done on getting that stack of papers down.' He nodded towards the smaller pile of *Couriers* by the candy tray.

Veronica didn't want to burst his bubble by letting on about the rest of the pile under the counter, so she just smiled and straightened the top copy, the unwanted *Beacon* having already rejoined its diminishing stack under the counter.

'I was thinking of a series of profiles on our ARP volunteers,' he said, indicating the camera. 'Nice to have a few shots of them in their day jobs... By the way, a few new ads have come in. Just text, if you wouldn't mind a bit more practice on the Typograph? And I completely forgot to show you this one from a couple of weeks ago. It doesn't have to go in again. They're interviewing next Wednesday, I think.' He handed her a folded piece of paper, then patted his trilby hat onto his head. The curled press card was stuck in the band.

And with a spring in his step, he sauntered out into West Street.

In just a week, Veronica had seen a change in the man. Perhaps she could do something to consolidate that? Really give him something to be happy about and even perhaps help secure the *Courier's* future. Her brain buzzed with possibilities.

She put the piece of paper Arnold had just given her, still folded, into her pocket with Archie's cutting. She'd attend to that later. Because right then, Veronica wanted to shake that small brown girl; make her see sense. How could she, the sort of person the Bund wanted to persecute, not see that? That she was actually choosing to read the *Beacon* proved the power of newspapers. Why couldn't people see the hate bubbling below the surface on every page?

Veronica would have to get busy. Arnold alone obviously couldn't write enough to make the folks in this town realise what was going on right under their noses. The report on the asylum, wherever it was, would have to wait. It seemed it was down to Veronica to take the lid off the simmering cauldron of hate. And she was going to start with someone who should know better. That would be the *Beacon* reader who waltzed out of the shop not five minutes ago.

Veronica's encounter had put her library discovery into some perspective.

Before the small brown girl, that crazy story about 'Howard and Sylvia' had filled her head. Now the girl had even displaced Veronica's curiosity about the rest of Archie's cutting, which was still burning a hole in her jacket pocket. Yes, she would go back to the library, but the curious girl who wanted to read the *Beacon* had prompted a new obsession.

Veronica needed to write.

As soon as the last *Beacon* flew out the door and the pile of accompanying *Couriers* was sufficiently reduced for the day, Veronica closed the store. She locked the front door, flipped the 'Open' sign to 'Closed' and ran upstairs while Archie was still out with his camera.

She sat down at his desk. From her pocket, she took the neatly written ad Arnold gave her before he went out. Interesting. Yesterday, he'd been trying to keep her away from the place. Perhaps she'd deal with that tomorrow. Right now, she had next week's front page to write.

She wound a clean sheet of paper onto the carriage of the typewriter and started typing...

13

HEWETT ISLAND
Almost a Week Later, Wednesday 30th March

IT WAS ALREADY DAYLIGHT when Baby leaned against the doorframe of the 'room-bed,' the compartment of The Lillie covered in mattresses where Baby, Fingers, Brian, and Gin slept with whoever else was at home. The Lillie was not so much a hideout anymore, but it was still very much 'home' to Baby. She hadn't seen any more of the American girl in Arnold's shop. All week, she'd avoided that end of West Street purposely.

Gin sprawled across the middle of the mattresses, asleep amongst the piles of quilts and blankets and pillows, still dressed from the night before. She'd been out again at The Blue Bonnet. 'It was absolutely ethereal, darling,' she'd whispered to Baby when she got home. 'Like the angels.' She'd then sighed, kicked off her shoes, collapsed, and fallen asleep.

The pub? Like the angels? Baby struggled to imagine that.

In one corner, in her own little nest, Fingers was pretending she was still asleep, her ginger curls exploding on the pillow. Her school tunic was screwed up in the opposite corner of the room-bed and her many-pocketed skirt lay where Baby's had half an hour before.

'Psst, we'll be late,' said Baby, not fooled by the little fake snores.

Fingers tugged her patchwork quilt over her head and curled into a smaller, harder, and even more determined little ball. 'I ain't going today,' came her muffled voice.

'You can't pick and choose which days you go,' said Baby.

'Oh yeah, I can.'

'Why don't you want to go? You were liking it. Has your teacher changed? What's happened?' asked Baby.

'Nuffin'.'

'Is it the gas masks?' All the schoolchildren had been given the horrible face masks to wear in case Adolf Hitler tried to gas everyone. They had to practise wearing them for an hour a day.

'No.'

'Well then, let's go.'

Fingers didn't move. It was clearly not 'nuffin', but as Fingers was still there and not doing one of her disappearing acts, Baby decided to let her sister explain in her own good time. Besides, Baby had bigger fish to worry about: the island in the creek; Sir Malcom Taggart; his interest in the orphanage; and in the very white, albino orphan, Robert Perkins.

'Come on, I'm hungry. Breakfast'll be done soon.'

'I'm not stopping you.'

Baby considered bouncing across the mattresses and dragging her sister out, but that would mean undoing the laces on her shoes and doing them up again. So instead, she threw the orange she had pinched from old man Winters the day before.

It bounced off Fingers's back and sank into a soft white pillow.

'Ow! You can't make me go.'

'I'm making you get out of bed.'

'Alright, alright.' Fingers threw off the quilt and sat up, her red curls now even more of a tangle than usual.

'Well, what are you going to do all day? You can't... you know. You promised.' The promise was to stop burgling. No longer a necessity, nowadays it was more of an illegal hobby.

'I'll come with you,' said Fingers. 'It's your day off, innit?' Fingers pulled on her clothes, including a skirt like Baby's, though Fingers's skirt still covered her knees. She shook her short red curls and crawled out.

Fingers was right, it was Baby's day off. Plus, Brian, Mr Shaw, and June were interviewing prospective new kitchen assistants.

Sitting on the edge of a mattress in the room-bed doorway, Fingers tied her bootlaces. Though June had offered her new shoes like Baby's, Fingers insisted on another pair of boots.

Her laces tied—at last Fingers had got the hang of it—she ran out of The Lillie and across the little clearing. 'Come on! What are you waiting for?' she called from the bushes.

Baby took her new blue jacket off the hook where her old green silk one used to hang. Leaving Gin asleep, she ran after Fingers who was already halfway through The Lillie's bushy tunnel leading out to the station.

They skipped round the only car parked outside, scurried down the bank and over the road to grab whatever was left over from the orphanage breakfast.

If she was honest, Baby loved having her sister along. So, with one of Brian's bacon sandwiches each, they walked under the railway bridge, waving to Mr Shaw in his miraculous garden and taking the same route Baby took just over a week ago, the day Sir Malcolm Taggart came into their lives.

Very soon, they had left the town behind and were walking past fields that stretched out towards the creek. The creek, as creeks go, was very big and smelly. It was here the Nettlefield River flowed out into the furthest corner of Portsmouth Harbour. The darkest corner, some might say.

Fingers trudged along, head down, under her own little rain cloud. Baby had to run to keep up, occasionally shouting directions. 'No, not down there, this way!'

They'd been walking for about half an hour when Baby recognised the little clump of trees from her previous walk this way. Today, the creek was just one narrow channel of water flowing through the middle of a lake of mud. 'Follow me!' she said, and turned off the road into the field, following the stink.

'What do we want to go this way for?' said Fingers, her hands on her hips. 'It smells 'orrible.'

'I saw something here last week,' said Baby, pressing on past her through the long grass. 'Look at that!' she pointed. 'It's just like in your book.'

Fingers's brow furrowed.

'*Swallows and Amazons!*' said Baby. Fingers had told Baby about the book the teacher was reading at school, about kids having adventures on a boat. Though from experience they knew real life could be a lot more adventurous, having picnics on an island you'd got to in your own boat sounded marvellous. Wading across the mud, less so. 'And I saw somethin' else too...'

'What?'

'A diver,' announced Baby, 'Like *Flash Gordon* at the pictures.'

'In this?' said Fingers, swirling her foot in the sticky mud. 'Are you daft?'

'No, the tide was in then. It was all water. Come on.' She beckoned Fingers along what was the shoreline a week ago.

The old cockle digger was out with his tin bucket and garden spade again, trudging across the mud in his boots. It looked almost as if he was going to walk to the island. The green hill rising out of the creek water that Baby had spotted on her last patrol now rested on the drab brown sludge. It reminded her of the colour the orphans made when June got the painting easels out.

But on top of the green hill, there was now a shed; not as big as the hangars where they keep the planes at Hamwell airfield, but bigger than the garden shed Brian's dad wanted for his garden. Were the two people outside both divers? Maybe it was where they wanted to keep their helmets and breathing tubes. It was a bit far away for Baby to see exactly what was going on. But surely the pipe the two of them were carrying into the shed was nothing to do with diving?

But then she remembered the tide tables in Sir Malcom Taggart's briefcase, and a tingle of suspicion rippled across her shoulders.

The old cockle digger was trudging back towards them.

'Are you alright walking on that?' asked Baby.

'As alright as I can be,' said the cockle digger. 'You got to know where to go... Sometimes a few old bits of board help.' He pushed his spade into the mud and started digging again.

Before Baby could ask how the boards could help, Fingers was tugging on Baby's sleeve. 'Can we get a boat, for when the water's up?' Fingers pointed to a line of little boats stuck on the mud that would have been floating the week before.

'You better ask up at the clubhouse,' said the cockle digger.

'What is that place?' Baby pointed. 'Over there?'

The old man straightened up, his hand pressing into the small of his back as he creaked upright. 'Nothing of any use to anyone.' He picked up his bucket. Only a few cockle shells rattled around inside. 'Perhaps a few birds' nests. But don't you go out too far, looking for eggs and getting stuck in the mud, will you?'

'So, if that's all there is, what would a diver be interested in?'

'A diver, you say?' He shook his head. 'I don't know about that. Though at one time there was talk of putting a fortification on it to protect the harbour. Portsmouth's just over there.' He waved his hand in the general direction of the water. 'Old Adolf's getting busy, isn't he? Who knows when he'll be having a go at us, eh?' He creaked over again and continued jabbing at the mud with his garden spade.

'Is that what that hut is, d'you think?'

The old man squinted at the island. 'That?' He laughed. 'I reckon that's something to do with the big house. They say all sorts go and visit. Royalty, if you believe some of the old gossips. Now, you let me get on, or I'll have nothing for the missus's tea. You're better off following that path.' He pointed towards the hedge. 'That field has a bit of an adder problem this time of year.'

'Adders?' asked Fingers.

'Snakes,' he said.

Fingers grabbed Baby and pulled her onto the well-worn track. 'Let's get out of here.'

But Baby wanted to investigate. There was that little clump of trees. But she wasn't too keen on the idea of a snake wrapping itself round her ankles, so she called, 'Bye,' to the old man and followed Fingers back to the lane.

They were stamping their feet to get rid of the mud when they heard the purr of a well-tuned engine. Baby had learned how to recognise a well-maintained engine from Ida. The sound always gave her goosebumps.

Coming up the lane behind them was a very smart car. The very same sort of car Sir Malcolm Taggart was being driven about in.

But it wasn't just the very same sort of car. It was the very same car.

Baby felt Fingers cling to her back as the car drove slowly past.

A chauffeur with the flattened profile of a boxer's broken nose under a large, peaked cap was at the wheel. Baby's skin tingled. Was that Blackshirt Bill Teasdale out of jail? When did he get out... *again*? She'd heard rumours.

On the back seat, two people were in conversation.

One had the unmistakably imposing outline of Sir Malcolm Taggart.

And the other was a woman in a close-fitting hat pulled over the side of her face. Red hair curled out round the brim.

Baby tried to pull Fingers out from behind her back. 'Look who's driving.'

But Fingers just clung tighter. Bill Teasdale was a thug, but Fingers had never been afraid of him.

As the car motored smoothly on towards Nettlefield, the woman's face appeared in the back window.

Baby had seen a face like that before and she couldn't help but be reminded of Wonder Girl, Sophie, when she was being stolen away by Arthur Underwood before Baby and Fingers had ever heard of Nettlefield.

14
IN UNDERWOOD'S YARD
The Same Day, Wednesday 30th March

THE FACE IN THE BACK of Taggart's car still haunting her, Baby reluctantly left Fingers at the orphanage and went to investigate Underwood's old place.

June said she'd write Fingers's teacher a note. Instead of going to school, Fingers could help with the interviews for a new kitchen person. 'You could be like a tour guide for the orphanage, show anyone who's responded to the advert around. And then, you could give your opinion on whether or not that person would be a good fit.'

At that, Fingers's smile had widened, and her frown lifted. She turned to Baby. 'You go and have a look round 'is old yard, I'm gonna 'elp out 'ere.'

'Oh, all right,' was all Baby could say.

It seemed one prospective kitchen assistant had already arrived. From the other side of June's office door, Baby heard June telling them about the orphanage, so she left them to it. She tried to skip along

West Street, but her heart was a bit too heavy to skip very far. At the church, she slowed to a walk.

Since seeing the light on in Underwood's the previous week, she'd been wanting to check out the place. Waiting for half-day closing when the town was quieter also seemed like a good idea, and with Fingers off school, it was the perfect day. Or would have been the perfect day if her sister hadn't been lured away.

Last time they were there together, the place was as dead as the folk Underwood used to bury. But today, something about the old undertakers' shop made her shoulders tingle with foreboding.

But Baby was here now. She told herself to stop being silly and get on with it. She peeped through a gap in the boards that covered the shop's front windows on West Street. It was all dark inside today. For a moment, she persuaded herself she'd imagined the light *and* Taggart's car heading towards the yard, almost a week ago now.

But she hadn't imagined Taggart's car today.

'Hello Baby, how's things?' said a voice from across the street.

Baby turned away from the boards and saw Ida's special friend, Mr Rogers, from the garage, coming out of Arnold Coombes's paper shop with a copy of the *Beacon* tucked under his arm. 'Have you heard about the toy vouchers they're giving away?' he said, pointing to the newspaper. 'Could be handy for the orphanage. Me and the missus have started saving them for next Christmas.'

Baby had heard about the vouchers. She'd seen them, carefully cut out and sitting in a little neat pile under a paperweight on June's desk.

'Good idea,' was all Baby could think of to say to Mr Rogers.

'I'd best be getting on. Give my best to everyone.' Mr Rogers collected his bike, propped against Arnold's shop window, and scooted across the road to the church.

Baby turned the corner to Underwood's yard. Folk generally gave the place a wide berth. They'd got superstitious about it; said it was an unlucky place. So she was surprised to find the tall wooden gates padlocked with a shiny new lock and chain.

This was where she could have used Fingers's help to climb over them. But Fingers was busy giving 'her opinion' on kitchen assistants, wasn't she?

So, having first checked for traffic from the middle of the road, Baby ran at the gates. With a leap that would impress Letitia, she grabbed the top of one gate and scrambled over. Perhaps it was something about Letitia's jacket that helped. The leap and the scramble scuffed Baby's shoes a bit, but a dab of polish would sort that out.

Inside the gates, Baby brushed herself down.

In the centre of the yard sat a big pile of broken fence slats, old furniture, and assorted rubbish, all piled in a heap, as if for a bonfire. The workshop window had been broken when they were there the previous May. It was now covered in boards, like the windows onto West Street. The back doors were also padlocked. Baby peered through the gaps in the slats over the window, but it was all dark inside there too.

Queenie's old stable stood empty in the corner. She wondered what had happened to Underwood's old horse. Baby hoped she was happy in a lush green field somewhere.

Around the heap of rubbish, the rest of the yard looked very tidy, swept even. Except for the bit of fence in the corner that led to the overgrown alley at the back of the church hall. Nobody had bothered to fix that yet. Last year, that was where Easton Fitzgerald and his gang of Blackshirts did the awful indoctrination of the Spanish children. Baby shivered when she remembered those poor kids and the fears they had for their families.

Baby pulled a loose slat away and squeezed through to the weedy path. She looked around for something to stand on. This was where Fingers would have been useful, too. Not just useful; all this would have been so much more fun with her. What was happening to them both?

Fresh spring shoots were poking through the earth, but at the far end of the path, a wooden crate lay abandoned. She didn't really need the crate because she could hear what was going on through the open window. But she fetched the crate and climbed up, anyway.

The newly formed Nettlefield ARP—which stood for Air Raid Precautions—were inside. And as it was half-day closing, all the town's shopkeepers were there too, for drill practice and what to do in the event of an air raid should the country go to war with Germany again. This was looking more and more likely, despite the assurances Mr Chamberlain gave on the newsreel.

Baby spotted Mr Rogers putting his *Beacon* on a chair and joining the rest of them on parade. She spotted a few more copies of the *Beacon* on chairs, too. Her heart sank at the sight of them. Most of these were good people, not Blackshirts. They didn't believe everything they read in that paper, did they?

Still, it made Baby feel safe that it was the ARP in the church hall instead of the Blackshirts, but she was certain those devils were hiding out somewhere. What a turnabout! Two years ago, it was Arthur Underwood obsessing about where *they*, Baby and the other Wonder Girls, were hiding out!

As there was nothing to see in the church hall, Baby returned the crate to where she'd found it. Careful not to squash the new green shoots (more daffodils perhaps?), she slipped back through the fence to the yard.

There may have been nothing to see in the church hall, but she couldn't help wondering who had tidied up Underwood's yard, and why?

Just as she was a pondering over a neat stack of new red bricks from the brickworks, she heard the padlock rattle on the other side of the gates.

Baby dashed back to the loose fence slat and squeezed through. In her hurry, her skirt caught on some splinters.

The chain rattled through the rungs on the gates.

There was a time when she wouldn't have worried about ripping her clothes. But her many-pocketed skirt was almost all she had left of Moll, the only real mother she and Fingers had known.

Somebody was pushing the gates open. They juddered, and the chain rattled.

Her fingers trembling, Baby carefully unhooked her skirt. As soon as it was free and with her heart beating a little harder than usual, she slipped behind the bit of fence that was still standing.

The gates scraped over the freshly swept cobbles.

Baby looked for a knothole as she heard a pair of smart shoes tap inside.

Sir Malcolm Taggart, tall and rigid, carrying a cane—why did toffs love a stick?—made his entrance with the air of someone who owned the ground they walked on. Did he own it? Had he bought the old place?

Taggart looked about him, inspecting, judging. Had it been tidied up enough for him? Bill *jailbird* Teasdale, minus chauffeur's cap, showing off his broken nose and a sharp haircut, swaggered in behind. Baby wanted to punch both of them. Bill Teasdale flaunted a large ring of keys.

Baby noticed Queenie's old stable had a new shiny bolt on the outside. Why would you put a new bolt on the outside of an old stable door? Especially when the horse was gone?

Sir Malcolm was tapping his cane on the boards covering the window by the back door to Underwood's old workshop. 'Come on boy, I haven't got all day.'

Bill lost his swagger and fumbled with the ring of keys until he found the one to open the door. Baby wondered if the woman was still waiting in the car.

When Baby was sure that Sir Malcolm Taggart was safely inside Underwood's old place, she squeezed back through the gap between the slats.

What had to be kept inside in Queenie's old stable with a new bolt? Just a quick look.

She ducked under the boarded windows; she wouldn't put it past Bill to be on the lookout.

Baby slid the bolt, and the door swung open. Aha! The bolt was just to keep it shut.

Inside, the stable floor was swept and clean like the yard, but there was no pile of rubbish inside. Baby had the impression the stable had recently contained much more than the one metal box that remained.

Ooh, Baby loved a mysterious box. She unclipped the lid and carefully lifted it to reveal something like an Enigma machine. She felt something of an expert about Enigma, codes, and code-breaking nowadays, having discovered one in the orphanage last summer. It wasn't an Enigma, but the panel of dials and knobs and switches did remind her of one of Brian's dad's contraptions, 'Inventions', according to Brian, that he liked to tinker with. She wished she could show Mr Shaw. He'd know what it was.

A hand grabbed the back of her jacket.

The fabric tightened, the hand twisting. Her top button cut into her throat. The hand pulled her out of the stable, away from the mysterious machine into the middle of the yard. She grabbed at her throat to undo the button. 'Get off me, Bill Teasdale,' she wheezed.

But the hot breath in her ear did not belong to jailbird Bill. 'What are you doing here, you little rat?' said Sir Malcolm Taggart. 'I know who you are and what you've done. Your little schemes have no chance this time.'

With some effort, Baby undid the button and twisted to face him. She held on to her steel, her resistance giving her strength and confidence. 'Course you know who I am! I sat next to you, didn't I? Or are you too old to remember what happened last week?' The lines on his face were deep. He could have been a hundred years old. 'What are you up to, eh? You're not really interested in the orphanage, are you?'

Sir Malcolm Taggart almost exploded with laughter. 'You think I'm not interested in your orphanage? How little you know!'

She felt his hand grab more of her jacket, winding it in his fist.

'But I know all about you, you nasty little piece of vermin.' He spat the words in Baby's face before dragging her through the gates, out of Underwood's yard, and dropping her like a bit of rubbish on the pavement.

Her knees grazed, pavement grit pressed into her palms, and her shoes all scuffed, Baby watched Taggart stride to the waiting car. Not even from Underwood had she felt that much hate. It soaked her like mud.

The back seat of the car was empty.

Bill Teasdale closed the passenger door after Taggart, his grin as wide and shiny as the ridiculous peak on his cap.

Baby knew that she did look a bit different to when she and Bill had last met. A smart blue jacket instead of the missing old green silk one, shoes instead of boots, and she even brushed her hair now. But she was sure he still recognised her. He flicked a rude finger in her direction as he swaggered round to the driver's seat. Whenever it was that Bill got out of jail, Baby had a fair idea how he'd got out. Taggart must have a firm grip on power.

But what did Sir Malcolm Taggart have against her? It was a lot more than the colour of her skin or him being a Blackshirt. She sensed something else.

She sensed revenge.

15
BRIAN'S NEW ASSISTANT
Wednesday 30th March, Afternoon

BABY WAS PICKING HERSELF UP off the pavement as Constable Spencer rattled past on his bike, concentrating on the road ahead. If it had been Sergeant Ted Jackson, she might have run after him, but she wasn't sure where Spencer stood regarding the Blackshirts nowadays. So she brushed herself down, straightened her new jacket, and watched the huge black car glide away. You could barely hear its engine as it manoeuvred onto West Street.

Perhaps Taggart was going back to the orphanage? Baby ran round the corner after it.

The shop awnings were wound up for half-day closing and the door signs were flipped to 'Closed.' Just past the church, she lost sight of Taggart's car disappearing under the railway bridge. If he wasn't going to the orphanage, where was he going? Back to the creek?

Baby suddenly remembered how, at his special lunch, he'd especially asked to see Robert. For a while, Arthur Underwood had been very interested in the albino Robert. But hadn't they already dealt with Blackshirt kidnappers?

Baby was hungry now; her belly was rumbling. The church clock said it was well past lunchtime, but she was sure Brian would have saved some sandwiches for her. So, with her belly rumbling like Leonard Cook's old laundry van, she trudged the rest of the way to the orphanage, her mind going over and over why Taggart hating her felt so *personal*. Was his connection to Arthur Underwood more than them just being Blackshirts?

Baby pushed open the orphanage's big front door, now painted a cheerful primrose yellow which went with the jug of daffodils from the railway embankment sitting on the telephone table.

A delivery van was parked outside, and a man in a flat cap and brown work coat excused himself past Baby. He was pushing a triangular package resting on a trolley. 'If you could, miss?' He indicated the double doors to the orphanage's living room.

Baby held one of the double doors open and watched him push his load through, setting it down in front of the large fireplace decorated with a jar of bluebells from Brian's dad's garden. The sight of the package, its size and shape, produced a small flutter in her chest. She took a deep breath and tried to swallow it away, but it wasn't going anywhere.

Laughter was coming from the kitchen. Baby crossed the hall in its rainbow light. That, and the friendly familiar voices, helped. She felt a calming warmth as she reached out to open the kitchen door.

Then she heard another voice. Not exactly new, because she'd heard it almost a week before. A loud voice, sounding like its owner was permanently chewing. An American voice.

Through the little window in the kitchen door, she saw them all. Gin, Brian, June, Mr Shaw, and Fingers. Fingers, who should really be in school. They were all sitting at the kitchen table, gazing up at the same American girl from Arnold Coombes's paper shop.

In a man's suit, hair shorter than Baby's, and with that flashy turquoise scarf tied round her neck, she was sitting on the table with one foot on a chair and the other long leg stretched to the floor. She was in full flow, telling them some story she'd probably just made up.

Baby felt like someone had stabbed her through the heart. What was she doing here? And then it occurred to her. She was the new kitchen helper! But she already had a job at the paper shop. Baby was all set to put June Lovelock straight when June saw her peering through the bottom corner of the window in the smart new kitchen door.

'Oh Baby, you're back. Come in and meet Veronica.' June opened the door for her.

Veronica tried to smile as she looked at Baby, but all it did was turn into a sneer.

'Hi,' said Veronica. 'Pleased to meet you.' She offered her hand as if they hadn't met before.

Baby couldn't even manage a 'hello.'

She looked for her plate of sandwiches on the table, the dresser, the draining board. Brian usually put some under a damp tea cloth for anyone who wasn't there when they sat down to eat.

Baby couldn't see a cloth covered plate anywhere, but she did finally notice what was in the American's hand. A half-eaten corned beef sandwich. And beside her on the table, a damp tea cloth... and a plate of crumbs.

Baby wanted to turn right round, pinch some buns from the Lyons' tea shop and eat them sitting on the church hall roof. Letitia always said roofs were the best place to think. Or in Baby's case, fume.

Why was Fingers clinging onto the American's arm like that?

Baby knew why. They'd all been taken in by her and her silly accent. Talking about 'In the States this, in Brooklyn that,' and 'You've gotta see The Big Apple at least once before you die.'

'What big apple?' asked Fingers. 'From a giant tree, you mean?'

'No,' said June. 'I think Veronica is referring to New York City. I've read it's what jazz musicians are calling it nowadays.'

'Maxine Sullivan, anyone?' said Veronica. 'I met her, you know, just before I left.'

The faces round the table looked puzzled.

'Oh, you must meet...' But June stopped before she finished her sentence. What was she going to say? Harry? Ida? Letitia? Sophie?

'I'm not really American. Nobody is except the Indians,' said the girl.

'Like Baby?' asked Brian.

'No, my dear,' said Mr Shaw. 'Our friend means the people to whom the land truly belongs, mistakenly referred to as "Indian" by Christopher Columbus.'

'So, you all could be American too!' said Veronica.

At which Fingers clung even closer to the girl's arm.

Baby had had enough. 'I've got things to do.' With her belly rumbling from a lack of corned beef sandwiches, she huffed out of the kitchen.

She didn't hear anybody say goodbye. They were all still fawning over the American show-off.

When she first met them, Baby had thought Ida was 'uppity', and Letitia far too 'goody-two-shoes', but this one... There was something about her that made Baby dislike her a lot more than the others. Though she was reluctant to put it into words, she recognised the feeling.

Jealousy.

It was true that Baby had made Fingers a bit jealous over Sophie; but that was different. Sophie desperately needed their help. It was life or death. But this one didn't look like she needed anybody's help. Not ever.

Baby was too fed up even to climb the bank to the station. Plus, she was in her nice jacket and shoes that she didn't want to scuff any more. That thought was a surprise.

Since they were all cosied together in the new orphanage kitchen, Baby thought she'd go back to The Lillie. There had to be something to eat there.

She trudged up the slope, past the laundry. Was that Leonard's van parked outside? She could do with a friendly face. But there was no cheery 'Hello Baby!' to lift her mood.

Outside the stationmaster's office, she heard a lot of kerfuffle coming out of the ticket hall.

The station porter was pushing a trolley piled high with luggage, followed by a group of fashionable young people. Two very elegant women and four dapper young men with briefcases, cameras, and loud voices that didn't care who might be listening.

'Dear old Malcolm had better be paying us a ton of cash for this job,' said one of the elegant young women, balancing a cigarette holder in her gloved hand.

'How long are we committed to staying in his little hole?' said one of the young men, his hands in his pockets as he watched the porter struggle with their cases.

'He sold it to me by saying we could get back to town in about an hour,' said a young man linking arms with the other young woman.

'Oh, that would be about just less than two hours, darling. We left Waterloo at two minutes past twelve,' said the first woman through a cloud of cigarette smoke.

A car drove up; not Taggart's Daimler, but it was one Baby knew. The open-top cream-coloured car she'd last seen at the Basque Children's Camp, belonging to Moles, the disgraced council official. It passed Baby and stopped at the far end of the station buildings. A laundry van was parked nearby. For a moment, she thought it was Leonard Cook in the front seat, but when she looked again, the front seat was empty.

But a young Blackshirt that Baby didn't recognise was driving another black van; Underwood's old van. It passed the parked laundry van, then parked beside the open-top cream-coloured car. Had Taggart bought Underwood's place lock, stock, and barrel? There was no doubt now that he was up to no good and the Blackshirts were with him at the heart of it. Well, this would take her mind off stupid American girls.

With a lot of effort, the station porter steered the trolley piled with luggage to where the open-top car and Underwood's old van had parked. He dumped his load and hurried back to the ticket office—before he was asked to unload it as well, Baby guessed.

Another porter with a trolley of typewriters excused himself through the group. Baby was sure they really were typewriters, rather than Enigma machines; an easy mistake to make. He was heading towards the open-top car, too. Baby grabbed one of the handles. 'Need a hand?'

'Thanks a lot, Baby.'

'Mr Coombes!' said Baby.

'Shhh,' said Arnold Coombes, putting his finger to his lips. 'Just watch,' he whispered.

Together they pushed their trolley, leaving it alongside the cream open-top car. Baby pretended to be heading back to the ticket office, but instead she nipped behind the waiting trolley.

Arnold Coombes crouched with her. From under his jacket, he pulled out an old box camera on a strap round his neck and started taking pictures. 'I've got a few from Underwood's Yard,' he whispered between snaps. 'I saw you in there. Be careful, Baby. Taggart's a dangerous man. We just need the evidence to prove it.'

Baby knew all about evidence. How good it had to be; how watertight. 'You be careful too, Mr Coombes.'

The boot of the car was open, and the driver was leaning on the bonnet reading a newspaper. The *Beacon*, of course, while the young Blackshirt driver of

Underwood's van loaded bags and cases and hat boxes into the back. He didn't look very happy about it.

Click, click, click went Arnold Coombes's camera.

'Don't forget that lot,' ordered the *Beacon*-reading older driver, flapping the paper in the direction of Baby and Arnold's trolley of typewriters.

The young Blackshirt grunted. He looked like he was about to say something very rude to the older man, when Arnold winked at Baby, tapped his nose, tucked his camera inside his jacket and stood up. He picked up a typewriter. 'Need a hand, young man?' he said to the Blackshirt.

The young Blackshirt looked surprised but didn't refuse the help and loped off to pick up his own copy of the *Beacon*.

As he helped, Arnold took the opportunity to snap a few more photos of inside the van.

The group of fashionable young people were making their way grumpily to the waiting vehicles.

'Why couldn't they have stopped outside?'

'Who are these country bumpkins that Malcolm has taken on?'

'Oh, I say, careful with that!'

One of the elegant young women let herself into the front seat of the cream-coloured car. 'Where are we going?'

'Hamwell, miss. This side of the river,' said the older driver, folding his paper, too late to open the door for her. 'Sir Malcolm has organised a tea for you all with the group there.'

'Oh, tea's nice, but I'd die for a glass of champagne,' said the other young woman, sliding into the car's back seat while the driver held the door for her.

Hamwell? That place kept cropping up. It was where Underwood tried to fly away with Bonnie. And José had said something about Hamwell airfield last summer.

In the muddle, Arnold Coombes rejoined Baby. 'Shouldn't you be getting back to the orphanage?'

'I'm on my way to The Lillie.' Baby had no intention of going to The Lillie now, but he didn't need to know that.

'I'd better get back and start developing this film,' said Mr Coombes, showing her his camera. 'You take care, Baby,' he added earnestly before sloping away towards West Street.

Two of the young men let themselves into the back seat of the open-top car, sandwiching the young woman already there.

'Giles and Bertie,' she said, waving like a toff at the remaining two young men, standing pathetically by the emptying trollies. 'You'll have to go in the van.'

'What? I don't want to go in that,' said Giles, waving his finger at Underwood's van as 'Bertie' was already climbing into the front passenger seat.

'Oh, don't be such a wet blanket,' said the smart young woman in the front seat of the car, shooing Giles towards the van's back doors. 'There's plenty of room.'

'But Bertie's got the best seat!' he whined.

As crammed as the seats of the open-top cream car were, the boot, apart from a tartan blanket, was empty... and open.

There was only one way to find out exactly what was going on at Hamwell, and it wasn't by 'taking care.' The way to do it was right in front of Baby. So, while the drivers and their passengers were arguing over who was going where, and while the boot lid hid Baby, she climbed inside the boot of the open-top cream-coloured car. She covered herself with the blanket, crossing every finger and toe that whoever shut the boot wouldn't notice the Baby-sized tartan lump inside.

The engine coughed, spluttered, then purred into an even hum. The car reversed and turned.

'Oh, I say!' said a young woman's voice. 'The boot lid is still open!'

'I've got it, miss,' said a passing porter.

After a slam and a judder, the car gathered speed and Baby was on her way. She'd get this thing sorted out, find out what Taggart was up to, and send them all packing.

She was beginning to sound like Ida Barnes.

Baby had only been locked in the boot for a minute or two when the flutter in her chest turned into a pain, an ache far worse than the one in her hungry belly. She desperately missed her sister. Baby and Fingers usually got into these sorts of scrapes together.

But then she remembered her last sight of her sister, hanging on to the American's every word.

Moll, dear old Moll, was wrong.

America was not the place for them.

16
Veronica's Guilt
Wednesday 30th March, The Same Afternoon

VERONICA COULDN'T BELIEVE her luck getting a job with such a fine bunch of folks.

The work was going to be easy. Washing dishes, putting them away, and doing anything Brian the cook asked of her from midday until the kids had eaten in the evening.

It wasn't her favourite sort of work, but it would pay enough. Everyone was really swell and the matron, who said to call her 'June,' said there was a room for her in the orphanage if her present lodgings didn't work out. 'I know Mrs Tatler quite well,' said June Lovelock with a wink.

Sometimes she really did think there was a huge divine hand guiding her. Being found by Archie in the Navy Yards, when she could have been found by any manner of lowlife. Finding Arnold, like another Archie, and now finding this lot. Funny little Fingers with that amazing head of red curly hair, who was so interested in the States that it hurt. She reminded Veronica of someone from the movies. Ginger Rogers? No, that wasn't it. Someone else.

But the minute Fingers found out that Veronica was intending to go back to the US someday, it was like the girl was handcuffed to her wrist. And then there was Brian, so peculiarly intelligent in a very unusual way, looking after her pa and everyone. How did the small *Beacon* reader fit in with them?

Veronica's 'story,' the one of which she was so proud, her first for the *Courier* and a surprise for Arnold, was going to be printed today. She was proud of it when she tugged it off Arnold's typewriter. But as she was sitting at the Typograph, while each line of type cooled, she could hear Archie: *'Have you checked your facts, Veronica? Remember our responsibility as journalists; we're not in the business of spreading rumour.'*

At first, she'd intended her story for the front page. She had been going to swap it for Arnold's investigation into the dilapidated Town Hall, but as her first flush of enthusiasm—and her conviction—waned a little, she decided to edit it down and tuck it in amongst a page of ads.

But after a very pleasant afternoon learning her duties as Brian's kitchen assistant, listening to the others talking about the girl, the same girl who inspired her story, curiously named 'Baby,' the feeling grew in Veronica that she may have been a little hasty in her judgement. She didn't name the girl, but from her observation of the town so far, Baby was possibly the only small brown girl in it. So, her shock report about some of Fascism's biggest supporters in Nettlefield being brown-skinned could only be about Baby.

June very helpfully allowed Veronica to telephone Arnold to let him know that she'd got the job and was staying at the orphanage for the afternoon.

It took Arnold a while to pick up the receiver. 'Hello, Veronica, is that you?' he shouted over the noise of the press in the background.

'Yes! I got it!' Veronica shouted back.

'Of course you did!' He didn't seem in the least surprised.

'I'm staying at the orphanage for dinner and June says I can move in here too!'

'Good-oh! I'm a bit late today so I'd better get on!' The line went dead before she could ask him to hold back the ads pages.

Veronica felt her cheeks flush warm. It was too late to do anything about it now. Nobody would read it, would they?

Fingers wanted to take Veronica to see 'Lillie.' Fingers said it was where they slept. Veronica imagined another matron like June in some annexe or something. It was all very progressive here, rather like herself. The sort of thing that went on in Greenwich Village on the Lower West Side, a part of town she aspired to.

'Come on, it's this way,' said Fingers. 'You coming too, Bri?' Fingers was pulling on Veronica's jacket sleeve.

'Alright,' said Brian. 'Dad, will you watch over the curry?'

'Of course, my dear... Does it need tasting at all?' said Alexander, which was how Veronica had been introduced to Mr Shaw, who seemed to be a frequent visitor to the orphanage.

'No Dad, not today,' said Brian, surprisingly firmly. 'It's just how the children like it.'

'Oh, very well.' He pulled out a chair, sat down at the kitchen table and took a rolled-up newspaper from a briefcase propped against the chair legs.

Veronica wondered which newspaper it was, but Fingers was already dragging Veronica out of the kitchen and along the corridor. She grabbed her hat.

At the desk in her office, June Lovelock was poring over a mass of paper. She looked up. 'If you're going to The Lillie, bring Baby back for some food, won't you?'

'Will do,' shouted Fingers, leaping across the threshold of the big bright yellow door. She skipped past the orphans' playground, over the main road, and up the slope to the station.

Veronica ran to keep up. Where were they taking her? Wherever it was, it looked like they were getting on a train.

Brian dawdled behind. Every few feet or so, she was looking over her shoulder.

'Aren't we buying tickets?' said Veronica outside the ticket hall.

'Don't be daft,' said Fingers, striding past the station buildings, her many-layered skirt swinging as she walked.

Near a coal heap, they took a sharp right and the next thing she knew, Veronica was being pulled through a dense clump of greenery.

They emerged into a little glade where the setting sun gave everything a golden glow, where the birdsong suddenly increased in volume, and the ground felt like foam rubber. In the middle of this little piece of heaven sat an old railway car.

The door opened and a young woman, draped in a silk gown, stood there. 'Oh darlings, have you got Baby?'

'Isn't she with you?' said Brian, padding across the glade.

'I thought she'd be back 'ere by now,' said Fingers. 'Oh well, she's just gone on another one of her walks. She'll be back before it's dark.'

Veronica estimated that would be within the next hour.

'Alone? I thought you were blood sisters, never to be parted...' The elegantly dressed young woman turned to Veronica. 'Oh, hello.'

The girl-woman wouldn't look out of place on Fifth Avenue.

'Gin, Ronica. Ronica, Gin,' said Fingers, pointing to each young woman. 'Ronica just started helping in the kitchen.'

'Well done,' said Gin to Fingers. 'Names aren't usually our Fingers's forte.'

'It's Veronica,' said Veronica.

'Ooh, and you're an American! Well I never,' said Gin, offering Veronica her hand. 'Enchanted.'

'Yep, more or less...' replied Veronica, shaking Gin's elegantly offered hand. It was warm and soft. Being 'more or less' American did not seem to bother her. Should Veronica bow or curtesy or something as well? 'Gin' seemed like a lady.

'You certainly have a cosy little place here,' said Veronica, trying to get away from the formal British niceties.

'There's room for you too,' said Fingers, wide-eyed and hopeful, tugging again on Veronica's sleeve.

'We love it in here, I'm sure you will too,' said Gin. 'I don't think I shall ever grow out of this place. Come and sit down and we can chat.'

Veronica took off her hat and followed Gin, who swept up the railway car in her fluid silk gown to a table under an electric light with a large, enamelled lampshade. She wouldn't have been surprised if Gin produced a pack of cards and started dealing. Veronica noted a kettle on a little stove, a line of books on some low cupboards that lined the wall, a sink, and a door. She assumed—hoped—the door led to a bathroom.

As soon as they'd all sat down, Gin leaned across the table. 'So, where's Baby gone, and why?'

'I dunno,' said Fingers, turning her attention to the tabletop. 'I think she was hungry.' Then, lowering her voice, she said, 'Cause I gave her dinner away.'

'What is it with you two? One moment you're joined at the hip and the next... Oh Bri, darling, why are you looking so worried?'

'It feels bad,' Brian said, slumped in her chair. 'I think something's happened to her.'

'You know Baby can look after herself better than any of us, and she's only been gone for the afternoon. I really don't think there's anything to worry about. I'm sure she'll be back for her dinner.' Gin turned to Veronica. 'Now darling, tell me all about yourself.'

'Er... I met Baby last week,' said Veronica. 'Maybe she wasn't too pleased to see me again. We didn't exactly hit it off. I can tell a lot about a person by the paper they read. That's my other job, newspapers, you see.' She told them about 'muckraking,' *The Maple Street Reporter*, and how she was helping Arnold out at the *Courier*, how he couldn't pay her much, which is why she needed the job at the orphanage. She also said that her 'pa'—Archie—'died' and that she arrived in Nettlefield 'by chance.' She didn't tell them about *how*

Archie died, the passports he left her, nor the man with the white scar over his eye. She didn't know how much these girls could handle.

'Arnold told me about the job. But it was an excellent ad; I read a lot of them.' From memory, she recited the neatly written ad that Arnold had given her the week before: *'Assistant needed for Brian, the orphanage cook. Only kind and nice people need to apply. You don't have to be good at cooking.'*

A smile replaced the frown on Brian's face.

'Oh, yes, of course,' said Gin. 'June only takes the Courier. Well, she always used to. Of course, now she has to get the Beacon, now that the orphanage is going to be featured in it as a major "human interest" story.'

'What? Featured?' said Veronica. A coldness shot through her like the murderous icicle favoured by mystery writers.

'Oh yes, we've been waiting for the team of reporters and photographers to arrive. It's such an opportunity for the orphans to be in a national newspaper. Daddy and I met him in Berlin, you know.'

'Him?' Veronica disguised a gulp as a cough. She knew what Gin was going to say.

'Sir Malcom Taggart, of course,' said Gin.

The guilt about her report, along with the cold dread of her possible family connections to Taggart, the Beacon and all it stood for, were all turning Veronica's insides into a cauldron of lumpy oatmeal. But before she could work out how to express her concern, Fingers had launched into an explanation about Gin being a proper 'Lady,' Lady Virginia something or other. 'She was on holiday with 'er dad for a long while last year to celebrate him getting out.'

'Out?'

'*Out*... You know, out of the clink... Jail.'

'He'd had some financial issues,' said Gin.

Fingers rolled her eyes.

Who were these girls? And what had Veronica gotten herself into? What was she already into? This man, Taggart, her family—really? Whatever all this meant, she couldn't believe it was going to be good, but it was going to be a great story for *The Maple Street Reporter* when she got home.

If she got home.

'But about this man, Taggart,' said Veronica, trying to sound casual and not as if he might be her great uncle. 'I think he and his paper are somewhat inclined to the right?' She was trying to find a word that wasn't too threatening... but she couldn't find one. 'Just a little bit... fascist?'

'Tell us about it! Half the town is,' said Fingers. 'But at least he ain't trying to kidnap the kids.'

'Are you sure?' said Veronica.

'Now, you're sounding like Baby,' said Gin.

The guilt about her report was beginning to suffocate Veronica.

'Anyway, 'es probably back in London by now. We saw 'im go off in that car of 'is earlier,' said Fingers.

Veronica's face burned with the news that Sir Malcolm Taggart had been in town the whole week without her realising. Why? The talk he was supposed to give to the local Bund was over a week ago.

'What could a newspaper baron like Sir Malcolm Taggart possibly want with our children?' continued Gin. 'He's no Arthur Underwood, or Easton Fitzgerald. But yes, that little bit of tension at lunch a couple of weeks ago didn't go unnoticed. Baby is very hot on purging Nettlefield of the fascist menace, as are we all. But what harm can a little newspaper report do? And after the fire last year, the orphanage desperately needs to raise some extra funds of its own. It's a condition of the council continuing to support us.' Gin tucked her chair under the little round conference table, like a period to the conversation, and strode, silk rippling, to the other end of the railway car. 'Come on, let's go for dinner. Did I hear 'curry' again, darling Bri?'

'Yes,' said Brian, her face brightening into a smile. 'Not too hot.'

Gin threw off her gown to reveal a smart day dress. 'It catches on the bushes,' she explained as she pulled a colourful quilt from a room that seemed to be carpeted entirely with mattresses, and draped that around her shoulders instead.

With a newfound lightness, Brian joined Gin, wrapped in the quilt, at the open door.

'I expect Baby will already be there, famished and tapping her wrist. Are you coming too, Veronica?'

'Sure,' she said, tucking her chair under the table.

The more Veronica learned about Baby, the more discomfort she felt about what she'd written; it was like hugging a porcupine. She couldn't believe that she'd even suggested that some Indians were in league with the Nazis because of their threat to the rest of Europe, and especially their British oppressors. *'Wasn't the swastika a Hindu symbol?'* Her words in the article stabbed at her now. Whoever said *'the pen is mightier than the sword'* was so right. But Veronica was sure its mightiness wasn't intended for the writer.

Fingers barged between the two girls at the door. 'Race ya!' she said and bolted for the tunnel.

'You're on!' said Veronica, hoping to leave her guilt behind. She excused herself between Gin and Brian and ran after Fingers. She'd just caught sight of Fingers's scampering feet before the bushes surrounding the little glade became an impenetrable black.

By the station, Veronica could see the first lights of the town twinkling in the gloaming.

Fingers scampered down the bank. Veronica's longer legs took the path and met Fingers at the orphanage gates.

At the open front door, June was clapping her hands, summoning the kids on the swings to wash their hands for dinner. Was it just the yellow front door or the women's kindness that gave her an angelic glow? 'Come in and wash your hands, it's teatime!'

The British had far too many confusing words for meals.

'Oh, what good timing!' said June, catching sight of Veronica. 'Is Baby with you?'

'No, she's not,' said Veronica.

'Oh. Well, I'm sure she'll be back soon. She is rather an independent spirit.'

The excitement of the race faded from Fingers's features, with the news of her friend's continued absence. She plodded round the side of the building to the kitchen entrance, followed by Brian and Gin, who remained cheery. Veronica guessed Gin's cheeriness was for Brian's sake.

The only good thing about Baby's absence was that she wouldn't be there to read the *Courier* if Arnold had delivered it. And of course, as Veronica kept reminding herself, people don't *read* the ad pages, not properly.

In the orphanage kitchen, a lovely smell wafted from the large pot on the range. Plates ready for serving were piled on the kitchen table with a large dish of rice surrounded by a sunburst of meat and vegetables in a bright orange sauce.

'Ah, Brenda, my dear, you're back,' said her father, looking up from his paper, open on the table at the ads that formed most of the *Courier's* middle-page spread. 'We're all ready for another of your delicious meals.'

Veronica cleared her throat but could only manage half her usual volume as she enquired, 'Is that this week's paper?'

'No, no, not out yet. Funny, Arnold usually brings them over on a Wednesday, stops for a cup of tea and a chinwag...'

June appeared, holding one end of a towel on which a small girl with grazed knees and a tear-stained face was drying her hands.

'I'm sure that's good enough now, Betsy. You've been a brave girl.'

The girl ran off to join the happy chatter in the big room across the hall.

'Alexander, Arnold telephoned to say he'll be over with the papers after dinner,' said June, folding the towel.

With a look of glee, Brian's pa stroked the open *Courier* from the previous week. 'I do like to read everything, you know. I find some of the advertisements especially amusing! Such an insight into human psychology...'

Who was Veronica kidding? Of course folk would read her story! Goosebumps popping, neck tingling, and—she was sure—cheeks flushing bright red,

Veronica gripped the frame of the open kitchen door. 'Give my apologies to June. There's something I have to do.'

She turned and bolted out of the kitchen, through the door, and across the playground. At top speed, she hared out of the wrought-iron gates and up West Street.

Maybe, just maybe, she'd be in time to stop her first disaster…

17
VERONICA CONFESSES
Wednesday 30th March, Evening

VERONICA RAN TOWARDS the green glow of the streetlights.

The lamplighter passed her with his ladder. 'Evening... er, miss,' he said, and touched his cap. 'Roll on daylight saving, eh? Just a couple more weeks.'

She nodded and went to touch the brim of her hat in return, but it wasn't there, and she remembered she'd left it on the table in the railway car. Would they have her back? If they didn't, it would only be what she deserved.

Arnold's bike was outside, propped against the Courier's shop window. In the distance somewhere, she heard raucous foot-stomping piano jazz and the beer-soaked shouts and cheers that went along with it. It sure sounded like some party at the bar, or 'The Bonnet,' as Arnold called it.

The shop door was locked. She reached for the key on the string round her neck.

But before she could push it in the lock, Arnold was already there, on the other side. Through the glass, she could see he was carrying a pile of new *Couriers*. As he opened the door, Veronica looked at them miserably.

'I thought you were having your dinner at the orphanage,' said Arnold, dumping the stack of papers in the front tray on the bike. He rummaged in his pocket and produced another paper-weighting rock.

'Yes, yes, I was, but I have to tell you something.' She gulped a bellyful of courage. 'Arnold, I have to confess.'

'Come on in,' he said, pushing his loaded bike through the door into the store.

Veronica felt well and truly reprimanded. Arnold had been halfway through printing the edition when he noticed Veronica's report. A bit later than usual because he'd been out and about with his camera. 'I hope I caught them all, but I was that tired after a long day...'

Arnold said everything Archie would have said. Everything she should have known. 'Do your research! Don't make sweeping judgements! Check your facts... We are not the *Beacon* and you are not a gossip columnist!' He pushed his hair off his face and sighed. His softness returned. '*Did* you get something to eat? Because I can fry you some sausage and egg before you have to go back to Mrs Tatler's?'

'Yes,' Veronica lied. She didn't feel worthy of one of Arnold's dinners. She couldn't let him cook for her when he'd done a double shift, resetting and reprinting this week's *Courier*. 'I'd better go back to Mrs T's. She locks the door after nine. But the girls said I could stay with them in future, in their railway car, if I like.'

'Good,' said Arnold, beaming. 'You'll do well with them. And well done for getting the job. Shall I see you home?'

'No, I'm a Brooklyn girl. It's only round the block.'

'Alright then. I'm bushed. And don't dawdle.' He wagged his finger and added, 'I heard a group of Mosley's lads heading for the Bonnet half an hour ago.'

'What about the papers?' Veronica pointed to the bike propped against the counter. She was sure she could ride it. 'I could do the deliveries?'

'No, it's too dark now. We'll begin again tomorrow.' Arnold unhooked his glasses and rubbed his eyes. 'I know you meant well, Veronica,' he said with a weary smile.

The relief that filled her belly was as good as one of his steak and kidney pies. After returning Veronica's hug, Arnold trudged upstairs towards the tiny room next to the office where he slept.

Veronica wondered what she could do to make it up to him, to impress him again. But then she realised trying to impress Arnold was what got her into trouble in the first place.

'I'll leave you to lock up on your way out?' called Arnold from the top of the stairs.

'Sure,' said Veronica, feeling for the key on the string around her neck.

But she heard his feet tap down again. 'No, on second thoughts. I will see you round the corner.'

At the other end of the alley, The Blue Bonnet was pounding with a singalong to the music bashed out on the bar's piano. The door flew open and a young man tumbled out. With an unintelligible cry, he pulled himself up and barged head first back into the packed bar.

Arnold saw her all the way into Mrs Tatler's. 'Nighty night, Veronica. We'll start again tomorrow.' After a little wave and a smile that so reminded her of Archie, Arnold stepped briskly away.

The familiar smell of overcooked vegetables was wafting around the hall, which made Veronica realise she was hungry. Brian's interesting sandwiches, corned beef with cucumber, lettuce and peas, had been hours ago. The ugly jug on the hallstand leered up at her. She would have loved to smash its horrible face.

Why did she say no to Arnold's offer of food? But that was all her own fault, so she would just have to lump it. What made Archie and Arnold so alike, despite their physical differences? It must have been the newspaper business—the honourable newspaper business. The goodness of the muckrakers shone through, whatever they looked like on the outside.

18
BURGERS & CHIPS
Thursday 31st March – Friday 1st April

THE NEXT MORNING, Veronica helped herself to a second helping of Mrs Tatler's cold, lumpy porridge. It would plug her empty belly, at least. Her job for the day was helping Arnold with the deliveries of the new edition of the Courier. The new, *new* edition, free from any rumour-mongering, poorly researched reports by V. Park. Keeping her away from the print room for a few days was Arnold's idea of a punishment.

But on their rounds, she loved seeing a bit more of the town and meeting the good people who supported the *Courier*. She also loved having a go on his bike, which, for such a big, heavy, and unwieldy thing, was really good at hills. She'd already written her notice for Mrs Tatler and packed her few things into Archie's old carpet bag. She wasn't leaving a forwarding address. The plan was to move into the orphanage on Saturday. 'I'll have a lovely room ready for you, then,' June had said.

The following day, she did her first shift with Brian 'sandwich' making. Brian's dad helped, in a manner of speaking.

Mr Shaw sat at the large kitchen table with a notebook, chewing a pencil, jotting ideas, and suggesting bizarre fillings. 'Raspberry jam, sliced tomatoes, and a dash of ketchup? What do you think, Brenda?'

'It would be very red.'

'Hmmm... yes.' He tapped the end of his pencil on the notebook before turning to Veronica. 'How about you, my dear? Do you have an opinion?'

This threw Veronica because, obviously, it would be disgusting, but she didn't want to be discourteous to Mr Shaw, not on her first day. 'I think,' she said after a moment's thought, 'it may be a little wet?'

'Oh well, back to the drawing board, as they say!' he declared and gleefully added, 'Happy April Fools, my dears!'

'Oh, Dad!' said Brian.

That evening, to celebrate Veronica getting the job, Arnold made his hamburgers, which they ate together in the little kitchen behind the *Courier's* print room. You could fit six of Arnold's kitchens into the one at the orphanage. But despite his reduced amenities, Arnold's hamburger fillings were spot on. He even added pickles and a slice of cheese to the minced 'scrag end of beef' patties he made himself. They were delicious and had certainly been well worth the wait. It was like being home in Brooklyn. She told him so as the juices dripped over her chin.

'I learned from the best,' said Arnold, wiping his own bristly chin on the threadbare towel hanging on the back of the door to the yard. 'Now it's getting dark. Let's get you back to Mrs T's for a good night's sleep before you get hooked up with the girls and their adventures.'

Veronica persuaded Arnold that she'd be fine by herself. It was just around the block and the Bonnet crowd hadn't really got started yet. Plus, it wasn't nearly as late as the other night.

In the alley, she could hear music, but no raucous singalong to go with it. The music, in fact, was heavenly. Strings accompanied by barely a whisper from the drinkers. Was there even anyone in the bar? The door swung open. No tumbling youth fell out, though the place was packed again. The Bonnet crowd had been silenced by the mesmerising music. She felt a pang of sadness that she'd put Arnold off, that he wasn't with her to hear it. Surely a sound like that would help soothe whatever Arnold's worries were about the *Courier*?

So, for the last time, she hoped, Veronica crept up Mrs Tatler's stairs, keeping to the edges where they were less likely to creak. Mrs T was still mad keen on talking about Gary Cooper movies and drinking weak tea with 'Ron,' at any time of the day.

Her note telling Mrs T that she'd found alternative accommodation—she didn't say where—was ready on the sink drainer in her attic, and her bag was packed.

She tried to take Arnold's advice and get some sleep, but her new job and those swell girls could not suppress the dread that she was related to a Nazi-sympathising newspaper man.

Under the only eiderdown with enough friction to stay on the bed, Veronica felt the judder of the front door slamming shut. Was that someone coming in or out?

She pulled on her pants and crept down to the second-floor landing.

Veronica heard Mrs Tatler's voice, and a man's; one she hadn't heard before. She crept down the next flight of stairs, crouched behind the banister on the landing, and listened to the voices coming through the open kitchen door.

'Your current houseguest, Mrs Tatler, h'is of great h'interest to Sir Malcolm.'

'Oh, really?' said Mrs Tatler.

Veronica recognised the tone in her landlady's voice. It was the same eager tone she used when she mistook Veronica for a film-star like Gary Cooper.

'Yes, he has been trying to h'ascertain her whereabouts for some time.'

'Did I hear you correctly, sir?' said Mrs Tatler. 'You seem to be talking about a young lady?'

'Yes, that h'is correct.'

The man had an overfondness for the letter 'H.'

'Oh, what a pity. I have a young man staying with me,' replied the jittery voice belonging to Mrs Tatler.

'H'I'm afraid you don't. They h'are a male impersonator; a young woman in disguise.'

'What? No...'

'H'yes.'

Mrs Tatler made a noise like a cat being strangled.

Veronica heard a chair scrape across the kitchen tiles. She dashed upstairs, slipped her feet into her sneakers. Archie always used to say sneakers were better for a quick getaway. She took her one pullover from her bag and put it on—the spring air was quite fresh in the evening—and grabbed her jacket. She fastened the bag strap and hurtled with it down the last flight of stairs. She pulled the front door open and leapt over the step into the alley. On West Street she peeped round the corner to see who the mystery voice belonged to, but she only got a back view of a man in a fedora like hers, and a cape-like oversized gaberdine coat, striding up the alley and pushing his way through the door into the crowded pub.

There was something very familiar about that view. Of course! He was the man from Ellis Island and Betty Marie's bar. Not just a man; a PI—a private investigator—who was looking for her. Then he wasn't looking for her; and now he was again—all under the orders of Sir Malcolm Taggart.

Had Sir Malcolm always been looking for her? Ever since the *'Tragedy on the Brooklyn Bridge'* that she had no recollection of whatsoever? Why hadn't he just come and taken her? She was mightily glad that he hadn't, but someone with that much influence and money could do whatever he wanted.

Of course, there was always a chance the little girl left behind after the tragedy was another Veronica. It was not an uncommon name. Maybe that was why she chose it? It was much better than 'Euphemia Grace.' But whatever the truth, this man and, therefore, Sir Malcolm, believed they had found the 'Veronica' they were looking for. And whatever the truth, Veronica was certain she did not want to be found.

So why, oh why, did Archie send her here? Was it just some horrible coincidence? How could *she* be part of a family like *that*?

So, her cover was blown with Mrs T. Oh well, at least it had lasted long enough for her to find a much nicer place to stay. For a moment she thought of following the man, undercover. That wasn't a bad idea, but such an operation would need planning; an alternative disguise, at least.

The revelations of the previous week, displaced for a while by her ill-fated report, returned and flashed in her mind like the cameras outside Carnegie Hall. Her belly rumbled. It couldn't be from hunger, though. Butterflies flitted about her insides like moths round a lamp at the returning thoughts.

Retracing her steps, she hurried along the street, swinging the satisfyingly heavy carpet bag to take her mind off the butterflies.

She was passing the greengrocer on the opposite corner to the Lyons' tea shop when she saw the beefy young man who had stolen copies of the *Beacon* from Arnold's shop on her first day. He was running across the street, dodging a trolleybus. She was wrong about Baby. She was convinced of that now. But this young man was in his black shirt; there was no doubt about him. And he was a thief.

When the trolleybus had passed, she noticed the beefy young Blackshirt had joined the queue outside a glowing vision, the source of a tantalising smell of 'Fish and Chips.' She could tell why the Brits loved them so much!

Everyone in the queue seemed to know the young Blackshirt. Either stepping away or, in the case of one or two, patting him on the back like some kind of returning hero.

Veronica crossed the street and reached inside her pants pocket for some coins. Arnold's hamburgers could have been weeks ago, rather than hours. After those, she hadn't been hungry at all, but she was now and not just for French fries, or 'chips' as the Brits called them. She was a muckraker, wasn't she? She was just as hungry for information.

'You alright there, er... missy?' said a man in oily overalls on his way out of the chip shop.

'Yes, I'm fine, thank you,' said Veronica. She wasn't sure of the man's intentions, but there was no harm in being courteous.

When she'd found the coins, two small silver sixpences and a handful of those big brown pennies, she joined the queue.

The beefy young Blackshirt was enjoying being the centre of attention. 'Yeah, I know, I've been down Hamwell way and I'm in with 'em. They're letting me into their secret meetings an' all.'

'You're only making the tea, Bill,' said a man clutching an empty string bag.

'And driving them about, driving *him* about sometimes. They gave me a cap, didn't they?'

'You won't be doing that for long, son,' said a man near the front of the queue. 'Not if you go around blabbing about all their doings.'

'Does your William know you're out?' said another man, taking a newspaper parcel of fish and chips from a girl in a white cap with shiny red cheeks on the other side of the counter.

'No, but when 'e does 'e won't know what's hit 'im. Well 'e will—it'll be me! 'im and that orphanage are going to be sorry when they get what's coming for 'em.' Bill tapped his finger against his nose.

Luckily, the queue moved quickly. Blackshirt Bill snatched his parcel of chips and barged his way out, past the queue that submissively moved aside.

Veronica was surprised to find she just needed one of the big brown pennies for a 'pennyworth' of chips wrapped in the *Nettlefield Courier*. 'Salt and Vinegar? Sir... or would that be miss?'

'It's "miss,"' said Veronica. 'And go ahead!' Veronica got the impression this was a good man. It seemed to her that the good people in this town didn't judge by appearances. They looked past how a person appeared on the surface and then they either guessed—correctly—or asked. Which was better; guessing or asking? She wasn't sure, but both involved looking past how a person appeared on the outside. And that had to be a good thing.

The chips were hot and golden and delicious. She had to blow on each one, but when they were cool enough to eat, she enjoyed every bite as she ambled along the street towards the orphanage.

She heard a train whistle. Now that she knew she didn't have to feel guilty about her article, she decided to go straight to The Lillie. That was if she could find her way through the bushes. She hoped the girls were true to their word about her staying.

In the near-dark, the streetlamps were glowing a gassy green. Veronica finished her last chip outside the orphanage gates. She was about to screw up the greasy paper when she noticed the photograph on the newsprint.

She now understood Arnold's logic that the people of Nettlefield got the truth one way or another. Under a streetlamp, Veronica closely studied the photo on the crumpled page. It was of a group of people in black shirts, surrounding a tall, proud looking man with a cigar between his fingers. She had seen enough pictures of Sir Malcolm Taggart with important people, royalty even, in the old copies of the *Beacon*, to recognise him.

The paper, an old *Courier*, was a little greasy, but she could pick out the faces of several of the townsfolk. The greengrocer was there, as was Mrs Tatler, beaming away in a very large hat at the front. The faces weren't looking directly at the camera, as you might expect, which suggested Arnold had tried to make himself inconspicuous to get the shot. The caption underneath read, *'British Union of Fascists Hamwell and District Branch executive committee welcome Sir Malcolm Taggart.'* The short report underneath listed the members' names, so no *Courier* reader could be in doubt as to who these people were.

Veronica folded the newspaper and put it in her jacket pocket. She crossed over the road and made her way up the slope to the station. The coal heap loomed dark before her. She made out the distant outlines of empty trucks, the engine shed, and the dense bushes opposite, but it was impossible to see The Lillie's entrance in the near dark.

Outside the ticket office, she heard footsteps, steps on a mission, getting louder. Steps that knew where they were heading, not into town, but towards Veronica. Had Sir Malcolm Taggart's private investigator found her? What had Mrs Tatler told him? Had any of the Nettlefield store owners, Miss Oswald even, talked about an American in town? What was the gossip in The Lyons' Corner House? She really shouldn't have dawdled with the chips.

Under the station light, Veronica took the quickest of glances behind her. It was a man; it had to be. Great Britain was a traditional sort of place, after all. The man wore a peaked cap and oily overalls

.

19
WHERE IS BABY?
Friday 1st April, Evening

VERONICA STOPPED, and the footsteps behind her stopped. She walked, and the footsteps walked. She passed the coal heap and the engine sheds. In a cap and overalls like that, they were probably just a railroad worker heading in to work for a late shift.

But she wasn't buying it.

Her heart beating that little bit faster, she peered hard at the bushes for the tunnel entrance to that railroad car.

The bushes all looked dark, dense, and the same. Veronica guessed at the entrance and made a dash for it, anyway. If she could just lose her tail, whoever it was.

But the footsteps dashed too.

'Wait!' said a girl's voice. 'Are you lost? It's this way. Follow me.'

The voice belonged to the overalls. It was not a man's voice, and it was beckoning Veronica.

'You went too far,' said the girl. One strand of hair had escaped from the cap. 'It's Veronica, isn't it?'

'Yes, how did you know?'

The girl was already half hidden by the bushes.

She knew Veronica's name, and she knew where to find the entrance. It could be a trap. But Veronica decided to take her chances. She lowered her head and followed the girl.

'Oh, you're big news at the orphanage,' said the girl in front of her.

'What?'

'Don't sound so worried. Bonnie, that's my sister, says Brian is thrilled to have an American assistant.'

Veronica followed the girl to that warm homely glow made by the railroad car they called The Lillie.

'Ida! You're back!' Brian burst from The Lillie's door and wrapped her arms around the girl in overalls. 'And so are you, Veronica!' Brian wrapped her arms just as warmly around Veronica. At that moment, Brian's smile was bigger than her face.

The girl, Ida, said, 'It's just for a little while, but I'll be back properly for the Easter holidays.'

'Darling, why such a short visit?' said Gin from The Lillie's doorstep.

'Mr Rogers needed me at the garage. My car's nearly ready!'

'Wow-wee!' said Gin. 'You've actually finished it?'

'Practically, with Mr Rogers's help,' said Ida. 'It just needs a test run. We might do it tomorrow.'

'Can we all come?' asked Brian.

'Of course!' said Ida.

Fingers burst past Gin and grabbed Veronica's arm ''urray! You're 'ere!' Fingers's grip was heavier than Archie's old carpet bag as she pulled Veronica inside.

Cute little wall lamps, lit for the evening, made The Lillie look especially cosy.

Veronica dropped her carpet bag by the door to the room-bed, hoping she really could stay, for the night at least, as Fingers hauled her over to the table, where Brian and Gin had already sat down. 'I was helping Arnold today,' Veronica explained, with a brief pang of leftover guilt about her report.

Ida took off her cap, shook out her hair and joined Gin and Brian at the table. She invited Veronica to take the chair next to her. 'Where's Baby? Why isn't she here?'

Fingers's hand loosened and slipped from Veronica's arm. 'Gone,' said Fingers, her mood darkening on this dime of information. She avoided Ida's gaze.

'Gone?' said Ida. 'Gone where?'

Fingers leaned against the cupboards, where Veronica spotted her hat in pride of place perched on top of the row of books. One chair at the table remained empty.

'We don't actually know,' said Gin, giving Fingers a hard stare. 'If you ask me, I think she might have felt a little bit jealous. So, we were just giving her a bit of time to herself.'

'Really. How much time?'

'Two days, seven hours and twenty-six minutes, so far,' said Brian.

'Then why aren't we looking for her?' said Ida, leaning forward, apparently ready to leap out of her chair and start the search immediately. 'Do we have any idea where she might be?'

'She showed me the island, the other day,' said Fingers, still perched against the cupboards.

'What island?' asked Ida.

'The one in the creek. The one like *Swallows and Amazons*. It's a book we're reading at school,' said Fingers.

'Sounds a lovely place for a picnic,' said Gin.

'We saw him there the other day.' With a sad smile, Fingers gestured towards Veronica. 'It was the day 'Ronica came.'

'Who's "him?" Names, Fingers! We need names,' said Ida, sounding exasperated.

Brian explained. 'I think Fingers means Sir Malcolm, who was in his car with a lady who...'

Fingers shot Brian a fiery look.

'What? How can you possibly know that, Brian?' said Ida.

'I've seen her,' said Brian. 'I mean him…'

Fingers picked up her story again before Brian could explain any more. 'Anyway, 'e was being driven about in that car of his and she was in the back.' Fingers made a strange stroking sign with her fingers. 'It was where they go digging for cockles sometimes. They said that once upon a time there was a castle or summat on the island. He called it a forty-cayshun.'

'I still don't know who "him" is,' said Ida. 'Gin, can you help?'

'Ida, I'm sorry, you weren't there.' Gin explained about the lunch to introduce Sir Malcolm, who wanted to publish a big story about the orphanage in his newspaper. 'And he's going to pay us handsomely for it,' she finished.

'Oh, Sir Malcolm Taggart,' said Ida, 'I've heard of him, of course. Doesn't most of the town read his paper? I'm sorry to say Mr Rogers does too, but he says he gets it for Mrs Rogers, for the crossword, and the coupons. But why would an influential London newspaper baron be interested in Nettlefield, islands in the creek, or our orphanage?' Ida leaned back in her chair and folded her arms. 'Do you know what?' Ida continued, 'I'm pretty sure Baby would have asked that question too. Fingers, who was the woman with him?'

But Fingers had sloped off to the room of mattresses they called the room-bed. Just her feet, booted, but laces trailing, poking out.

'Does this help?' Veronica unfolded the chip paper from her pocket and flattened it as best she could on the table. 'Have you seen these guys before?'

Brian pulled a cord and light from the lamp above flooded the table.

Ida swallowed and nodded slowly. 'Yes, I know who one of them is—very well!' She pointed to the tall, dark, attractive man standing next to Sir Malcolm. 'That's my Uncle Arthur. This must be an old photo. My uncle has been in prison for over a year now.'

'Ah, so that's him,' said Veronica. 'I had heard.'

'This isn't looking good, is it?' said Gin. 'June told me that Baby wasn't that thrilled about Sir Malcolm. She said Baby wondered if the newspaper articles were all he wanted to do. I should have listened. But I just got too excited about us all being in a national newspaper. Do we really have Blackshirts at our doors again?'

'I think we always have,' said Brian.

'Underwood's? That's the place opposite the Courier, isn't it?' said Veronica.

'Yes,' said Ida, 'but that's not where they are in this photo. Look, that's a pub sign above them. It's at the wrong angle to read it, but my guess is that that would be Hamwell. Last summer, José said something about having to wait at Hamwell until the Spanish kids' ship came in.'

'Ah, I know about that,' said Veronica. 'Arnold showed me his double-page spread about the refugees and the camp. He said there'd been some infiltration. I'll ask him if he has other pictures, ones he didn't publish.'

'I'm sorry,' said Gin, 'I think this all is my fault. Dad and I met Malcolm in Berlin and I told him all about the orphanage.'

'I think he had Nettlefield in his sights well before that,' said Veronica, wondering what Gin, her father, *and* Taggart were doing in Berlin. 'That picture proves it.' She carefully peeled away a greasy corner to reveal the date: *'9th November 1935.'*

'Can I see, please?' Ida took the paper and held it closer to the light. 'Uncle Arthur certainly looks younger, and pleased as punch with himself. Who do you think that is?' She pointed to the person on the other side of Sir Malcolm Taggart.

Gin leaned over the table and peered closely at where Ida's finger was pointing at a smart man, wearing a hat at a very dapper angle, beside a lady similarly half-obscured under an elegant hat. 'No!' Gin looked up, her face round with wonder. 'It could be. It really could be them, you know. Edward and Mrs Simpson. They have leanings...'

'Well, whoever they are, they're not helping us find Baby. But this place,' said Ida, tapping the blurred pub sign, 'may help.'

Veronica wasn't sure what else to tell these girls yet. They had enough on their plates already. But it was only fair to let them know one thing. 'I think,' she said, 'somebody is looking for me too, and I don't want them to find me. Not yet, anyway.'

But a loud banging on The Lillie's door and a frightened voice on the other side crying, 'Help! 'e's out and 'e's after me!' saved Veronica from an onslaught of questions.

20

Ida Doesn't Steal a Car
Friday 1st April, Late

VERONICA SAW FINGERS heave herself off the mattress floor and out of the room-bed to open the door.

In tumbled a lanky young man. For a moment, Veronica mistook him for one of her guards from Brooklyn. Had he followed her across the Atlantic too? This young man had the same loping, hangdog walk.

'What's the matter with you, William Teasdale?' said Ida impatiently, not bothering to get up from the table.

'It's me bruvver. He's out, and he's after me.' The young man barged past Fingers, shuffled over to the table, and sat himself down on the empty chair.

'What do you think you're doing?' said Fingers.

'Can't I join you lot?'

Though she was half the size of this William, Fingers strode over and hauled him off the chair. 'Go and wait by the door, but first tell us 'ow he got out.'

She made herself comfortable in the spare chair next to the window.

'I dunno,' said William Teasdale, loping off to the door.

'I expect it was the same way Mrs Bullar did,' said Brian. 'Dad says it's called corruption.'

Gin quickly explained that Mrs Bullar, in league with Ida's Uncle Arthur Underwood, was the bad Blackshirt orphanage matron before June.

William obediently slumped under a rack of coat hooks.

'And don't think you're stopping,' said Fingers. 'We're full. You're going to have to find somewhere else to hide. What's wrong with Leonard's place?'

'Won't have me. 'e says Auntie Alma don't trust me.'

'Well, that's a surprise. *Not*,' said Gin.

'Who's Leonard?' asked Veronica.

'Darling Leonard is a good friend to us all. He's got us out of a few scrapes with his van. He drives for the laundry, you see. William and Bill—their poor late mother had no imagination—are his cousins. William, unlike Bill, is "trainable," shall we say.'

'That's being generous,' said Ida.

'Yes, but compared to Blackshirt Bill...' said Gin with a tilt of her head and a finger that meant business.

Ida nodded. 'True.'

'I think I might have met him, the brother,' said Veronica, 'or seen him at least. He was in the same queue as me for chips. He certainly has a big mouth. He was boasting about working for the Hamwell group.'

Giving Veronica a queer look, up and as far down as the table would allow, William said, 'Yeah, 'e's right and I think Baby hooked up with 'em too.'

Gin stood up, letting her chair crash into the sink unit behind her. She marched over to William, hauling him up by the collar. 'What? With Hamwell? What are you saying?'

On his knees, William flinched under Gin's gaze. 'Sh... sh... she jumped in the car with 'em, she did, at the station. A new lot came down from London. I saw 'em.'

'*How* did you see them?'

'I was hiding from Bill in Leonard's van, or one of them laundry vans, at any rate.'

'She didn't really get in the car with them, did she?' said Gin, looming over him.

'She got in the boot. It was open, and she jumped in,' said William.

'That is not getting in with them, idiot,' said Fingers. 'That's called stowin' away.'

'Only one place they could be going, and that's Hamwell,' said Ida. 'At least we know where to look for her now.'

'Are we going, then? To find her?' said Fingers, standing up. Her chair toppled as she dashed for the door.

'Stop!' said Gin, putting herself between Fingers and the door. 'Hamwell's miles away and Baby might not even still be there.'

'But she might be,' said Ida, 'and as luck would have it, I have a thing that's really good at going miles away. And for once, I don't have to steal it!' She reached into her pocket and dangled a set of keys.

'Now Ida, are you sure? It's late and I'm busy all day tomorrow,' said Gin.

'Do you want to stay behind, then?' said Ida.

'Not on your nelly!' Gin threw off her gown, to reveal a different smart day dress. She shooed William out of the way and slipped her feet into some shoes under the coat rack. And swooshing a silky scarf around her neck, she said, 'Are you coming too, Veronica?'

'Sure,' said Veronica, feeling as at home with these girls as she did with Arnold.

'Isn't under cover of darkness the best time to do anything?' said Ida gleefully, as she followed Fingers through The Lillie's door into the little moonlit glade outside.

'What shall we do with him?' said Gin, pointing to William, still hugging his knees under the coats.

'Leave 'im 'ere,' said Fingers, hitching her skirt up and heading for the bushy tunnel.

'No,' said Brian. 'He can help me peel tomorrow's spuds.'

'How about gas? Will you have enough?' asked Veronica.

'Gas?' said Ida. 'Oh, you mean petrol. I expect so. Come on!' She disappeared through the bushes after Fingers, with Gin hot on their heels.

Brian switched off all the lights and dragged William out of The Lillie. It was a bit like a pony dragging a giraffe. She closed the door carefully after Veronica and, with William in tow, Brian followed Ida, Gin and Fingers through the tunnel. Veronica was glad that spud peeling was one job she wouldn't have to do the next day.

'Be a bit careful,' said Brian to the girls, waving them off as she led William across the street to the orphanage.

Ida and the others were already halfway down the street, lit with the green, gassy glow of the streetlights.

Veronica did wonder if this was more about Ida driving a car than rescuing the small brown girl called Baby. But because she was definitely ready for the adventure, she picked up speed.

Veronica caught up with them outside the Courier, dark and locked up for the night. But the girls weren't stopping there. They only paused for half a moment outside a pharmacy for Ida to say, 'I always like to give Uncle Arthur's a wide berth,' before they all dashed across the street, thankfully avoiding the alley to Mrs Tatler's, to head down a small road off West Street, to a garage with two gas pumps outside.

Ida pulled the garage doors open.

Veronica smelled oil and gas and some kind of cleaning solution that she couldn't quite place.

Ida proudly clicked on an electric light bulb dangling from the garage ceiling to show off the sleekest, most elegant but quirkiest vehicle Veronica had ever seen. The panels were all different colours.

'We were going to paint them all the same, but actually I like them like this. It makes the car stand out.'

'Will you always want it to stand out?' asked Veronica, thinking this current mission should be a bit more covert.

'It's dark,' said Ida simply, sitting herself in the driver's seat. She beckoned Veronica into the passenger seat before placing her hands reverently on the steering wheel.

Fingers, her skirt rolled into something of a donut round her middle, closed the garage doors and climbed into the back with Gin elegantly getting in beside her. Ida manoeuvred the car out of the garage, off the forecourt, and into the road. The engine purred like a very contented cat.

Ida certainly knew how to drive, something Veronica hadn't yet tried.

The car hiccupped a bit as it passed the church. 'Nothing to worry about!' said Ida, fiddling with the gear lever.

Outside the orphanage, someone was flagging them to stop.

'Dad was awake,' said Brian, opening the back door and getting in. 'He said I should come along. He said I should have adventures too, especially "kicking Nazi scum" adventures.'

Everyone cheered, and Veronica cheered with them.

And so they drove into the night. Five girls out to challenge fascism. It was incredible. At that moment, Veronica felt more British than American—and she loved it.

They hadn't gone far out of Nettlefield when they were in the English countryside, under a moonlit star-sparkling sky. It was a bit like how Veronica imagined the Midwest.

Ida's hands gripped the wheel. Veronica spotted a tear forming in the corning of her eye. 'How are you doing?' she asked.

'Me? Oh, I'm fine,' Ida sniffed, and the tear rolled over her cheek. 'I just always thought that my first trip in my own car would be with my mum and my sister... but never mind. My friends are as good as family.'

Veronica felt extra warm inside. Although they hadn't known each other long, she really felt that 'friends as good as family' included her.

21
BABY IN THE BOOT
Two Days Earlier, Wednesday 30th March

IF THERE WAS ONE THING that Baby could wish into the world at that very moment, it would be better drivers. Leonard Cook, Constable Spencer, even fellow Wonder Girl, Ida Barnes; none of 'em cared about their passengers. It was just the thrill of the open road. And this old Blackshirt driver, whoever they were, was no better. Though, of course, of this particular passenger, they were unaware.

To be fair, the boot wasn't the best place to hitch a ride, but it was safer than hanging onto the outside, which she'd done before. And Baby was well used to small spaces, having grown up sleeping in a barrel with Fingers.

The blanket was itchy and smelled weird—toff weird. She pulled it off. Her finger caught in a small hole. She yanked her finger out and hit something hard. It was a box, smooth and square and not a typewriter, nor an Enigma machine. She felt for the lid, but when she found the catch, she also felt a small padlock. She was curious but she couldn't look inside because she didn't have Fingers, and when she thought of her sister with the new American, that pang of jealousy gripped her heart again. She curled herself up even tighter.

With every bump that joggled her against the boot lid or the side of the car, she reasoned Hamwell couldn't be far. They'd come on the train, hadn't they? If it was far, they'd have stayed on the train. Did Hamwell have a station? She hadn't thought of that. She hadn't thought of much when she jumped into this boot. Was she catching something off that act-before-you-think Ida Barnes? Though sometimes that was what you had to be—impulsive, seizing the opportunity. That was the sort of thing Brian's old dad would say.

But perhaps one big thing she should have thought of before she jumped inside this car was how she was going to get out. Because it was one thing shutting the boot lid without looking at what was inside, but opening it? You couldn't avoid whatever surprise was waiting for you.

In the darkness, she could hear muffled laughter coming from inside the car: talking; haw-haw voices; the odd shriek, too.

The car stopped. Doors slammed.

A woman's voice whined about the mud, 'Give me something to walk on, someone. I'll ruin my shoes.'

Another announced, 'Darlings, I'm staying in the car.'

Baby wriggled round onto her hands and knees, arched her back and tried to push the boot open. She didn't have enough push, so she wriggled onto her back and tried again with her feet.

But it wouldn't budge. More doors slammed. And the car started again.

She was stuck.

And stuck with more terrible driving. Worse driving. The bumps got bumpier and the bounces bouncier. With every bump and bounce and joggle, Baby tried to focus on the fact that she was going to Hamwell. Probably. The viper's nest, the root of all the Blackshirt evil in Nettlefield. If she could just sort them all out, her job would be done.

But with every *other* bump and bounce and joggle, the thought of that viper's nest brought a football-sized lump to her throat and turned her legs to jelly. She was hungry, and hot, too. As nice as her new blue jacket was, it wasn't as flexible or as cool as her old silk one, designed for warmer places like car boots.

But she was Baby. And as sick as she felt about the people who wanted her dead, or gone at least, she felt powerful. What was she, but a small-ish brown girl who threatened all their schemes and plans, who had done so before and would do again? And they knew it.

The car went over an enormous bump, which bashed her elbow into the side of the boot and sent a horrible tingling all the way along her arm. Then the car slowed, and Baby heard a familiar crunch of stones. The field at the Basque Children's Camp was littered with them. She wasn't back there, was she? But inside the boot, as tight as the space was, Baby was sliding downhill.

The car stopped again.

Doors slammed as feet landed with the crunch of stones, and the shrieks of the women that were less, well, shrieky.

All Baby's muscles tightened as if she could shrink herself because the footsteps outside were crunching louder and coming closer to her boot. She reached for the tartan blanket, found the hole, and pulled the itchy stuff over her legs and up to her head.

A key turned in the boot lid. The metal hinges cracked as the boot opened.

Through the tiny hole in the blanket, Baby saw a hand with rings and painted nails grab the little box.

Baby heard some 'Thank you, darling's, and a 'Do mind my jewellery box,' and the lid was closing again with an 'Is that everything, Pamela?' and an 'I think so, Teddy. What about this blanket? No, leave that there...'

Baby's heart was beating so fast she barely noticed the tickle of the old blanket against her nose. Even through the wool, the light made her squint. The tickle turned to a sneezy feeling and went right up her nostril.

But the boot lid was going down. She'd still be stuck in the car, but she wouldn't be caught. Maybe they wouldn't lock it and she could get out when it was dark?

But the sneezy feeling had reached her eyes, and they were watering with the holding in of it.

Until she couldn't.

Baby sneezed with all the power of a small explosion.

The boot lid flew up again, and the blanket was snatched away like a magician's silk scarf.

Baby squinted at the person holding the lid open.

'I say, what have we here?' said a youngish man with a black shirt and a well-oiled haircut.

She scrambled over the edge of the car. The fresh air on her face felt lovely. Hands clawed at her, but Baby was slippery. She wriggled out of their clutches and barged through some other Blackshirts running to join them. A rough gravel road led up and away through a dark tunnel of trees. Her way out! Head down, elbows elbowing, she pushed her way through into...

Thud.

A large solid blockage.

She smelled cigar smoke and looked up into the stony, hard face of Sir Malcolm Taggart. Of course.

'Well, well, what have we here? A stowaway. It's third time lucky for me, isn't it? I've got you this time, you little savage.'

No sooner had Baby enjoyed that welcome rush of fresh air than the grabbing hands had her. She was locked between Taggart and a stampede of Blackshirt devils.

Baby wriggled and squirmed, but there were too many of them. 'Whatever it is you're really up to, we'll find out and we'll get you!' she blurted.

At this, the gathering crowd burst into raucous laughter.

'What? You, a street urchin, are going to stop the greatest movement of our time?' said a black-shirted, grey-skirted woman on Taggart's arm.

'You think you can stop the march of fascism? That is just too funny!' said another on Taggart's other arm.

What else could Baby say? 'Yes.'

Sir Malcolm threw his head back and guffawed.

'Oh, this is too much,' said one of the Blackshirt women.

The laughter spread through the crowd.

Like a clown at the circus, Baby was surrounded.

'Chuck her in the cellar,' said Sir Malcolm, releasing an arm to wipe his eyes. 'We'll decide how to dispose of her later.'

Baby kicked and wriggled and squirmed, but two Blackshirts from the crowd, thick as tree trunks, clamped themselves on either side of her. She was outnumbered. Even if Fingers were here, she'd be outnumbered. They both would. Even if the whole gang were here with her, they'd be outnumbered.

But the Wonder Girls were clever. They could have done something.

But they weren't here, and they didn't even know where 'here' was.

Then she had a horrible, jealous little thought. It was mostly a very sad thought that made her want to cry as she was being hauled away, her feet making little channels in the dirt. That thought was that Fingers would be alright. She'd be fine without Baby because Fingers now had a real live American to be with. Fingers could go to America as soon as she liked because there would be no Baby to stop her.

Baby flumped inside and out and let herself be dragged away. What had happened to her? This wasn't like Baby at all. And that made her feel even worse.

The two Blackshirt henchman hauled Baby past a tall post where a pub sign creaked in a fresh breeze. She tried twisting to read its name, but they'd already pulled her past it. Did the ordinary drinkers know what was going on under the noses? Perhaps they did and just didn't care. Perhaps this place was worse than Nettlefield, much worse, and there were no ordinary drinkers? Did the ordinary people even know this place was here? The road wasn't a proper road and the tunnel of trees covering it made her think of the dear old Lillie...

This really was their hidey-hole! Like The Lillie had been for her and the other girls. But this was no friendly little glade at the end of a tunnel. It was a nest; an evil nest of Blackshirts, hidden from the world.

The black-shirted oafs dragged her to the pub; a mansion of a pub, white-walled and criss-crossed with black timbers. One of them opened a wooden trapdoor in the gravel, while the other held her firmly in his grip. She was cemented to him like Liberty's torch. Until he flung her into the hole like a bit of rubbish.

All her bones juddered with a thud on the stone; cold, damp and smelling of beer.

Three faces stared down at her, in shadow against the bright blue afternoon sky. The largest cigar-smoking face nodding approval before the trapdoor fell shut again and with it, from behind her, a smack around her head, so hard it turned Baby's world to night.

22
THE BLACKSHIRTS' NEST
Friday 1st April

BABY WANTED TO RUB HER EYES, but her arms were bound to her sides with old ropes. And her head hurt; a pain so thick, it was like someone had stuffed it with wire wool. Her neck creaked when she held it upright. All she could see, in the dimmest of lights, were dark, curved shapes, boxes with round bellies, and above her, a few thin sketchy lines of brightness. Where was she? Thinking was like turning a rusty crank, but she tried. She willed some sense back into her brain and, bit by bit, she remembered.

What she couldn't remember, though, was how she got to be tied to a post in the middle of the Blackshirt pub cellar and how long she had been like that.

Her legs didn't belong to her anymore. Could she stand up? She couldn't tell until she'd got rid of the ropes tying her to the post. Her belly hurt, too. She was sure she was hungry, but she was also sure she needed the lav. How was that going to work?

Baby smelled beer and reached for one of the boxes surrounding her. Her fingertips stroked the splintery curve of a barrel. Despite her situation, it comforted her, reminding her of Moll and their days by the Thames.

But there was another smell, a sweet smell. Very faint, but it was there, and didn't belong in a pub cellar. At her side was an empty teacup, old and chipped. She reached it, but could see some milky dregs in the bottom, the source of the sweet smell. She stuck her nose in the cup and knew immediately what it was.

Malty, sweet Ovaltine.

Exactly what Arthur Underwood used to drug the children he kidnapped.

She had to get out of there.

Baby found her superpower. She wriggled her shoulders, her middle, and she jiggled on her bottom.

She had to warn June.

Again.

But she needed more evidence, and this was the place to get it. She still wasn't sure what Taggart was really up to. Could it get any worse?

The ropes loosened. She squirmed some more and soon she had the use of her lower arms. More wriggling, and she had wormed her way out of the coil of ropes, slipping them over her head like a jersey.

She tried to stand, but her legs wouldn't hold her, like her bones had dissolved. How long had she been like this? She pulled herself up on the post, hugging it for balance.

When she'd worked out that she could still walk, she took a few practice steps and began to feel something like normal again.

Time to explore.

In the little light from the gaps in the trapdoor, she could make out even more barrels, lots of them in a disorganised fashion in the large underground room. She felt her way between them.

Baby was cross with herself. She had done an Ida Barnes and not told anyone where she was running off to. It was worse than an Ida Barnes because at least it was obvious where Ida had run off to when she tried to rescue her sister from the clutches of her evil Uncle Arthur.

Would the girls work out where Baby was without Baby to help them? Oh gawd, this was not how it was meant to happen at all.

Her belly ached and she couldn't hold on much longer. Her skirt was twisted and pinched round her middle. What was wrong with it? It had been like that ever since she left The Lillie with Fingers to have another look at the island.

She undid the top button and found a bucket with a smelly mop inside to relieve herself into. The pain in her belly didn't go away, but now it was just hunger. And she still had no idea how long she'd been down here. It was daylight when they threw her in, and it seemed to be daylight still. Was it the same day? Or the next? Or the next?

There must be a way out somewhere. She could do with a secret door like the orphanage used to have before it got burned down. But she was underground – a tunnel perhaps? No, they'd have to come down here to get new barrels, so where was their door?

The barrels, their smell, their perfect curves, the wood and the rusty metal bands all made her think of Moll. *Oh, Moll, what would you think of us, still not in America?* A wave of hopelessness about Moll and the Blackshirt devils swarming about this pub threatened to overwhelm Baby. How come, in spite of all their efforts, hers and the girls, the Blackshirts seemed to be multiplying?

Being hungry didn't help. But she'd been hungry before and she hadn't given in. She'd gone out and done something about it. She could do that again and she knew now: these Blackshirts were scared of her, no matter how much they boasted and guffawed. Scared of a little brown girl with twice... ten... a hundred times as many wits as them.

So, despite the hunger and the pain in her head, Baby shook the hopelessness away and remembered Moll, and how she taught her and Fingers to survive. Well, Baby was doing more than that. She was not just surviving; she was going to win, and before long she'd be blasting all these Blackshirts out of Nettlefield. And, as soon as someone invented a rocket big enough, blasting them into outer space.

The hopeless Baby, the Baby those Blackshirts chucked through the trapdoor, was gone. She had recovered her steel, her determination, her brain. She was going to find out what that newspaper monster was really up to and put a stop to it.

Logic told her she had woken up because they had stopped drugging her. So, they must have wanted her to wake up, which meant that something about her situation was going to change. Baby had to be in control of that.

She could see her way in. The trapdoor and its cracks of light, too high for her to reach, taunted her. But where was her way out? Not outside 'out' though; out into that pub. There had to be another door.

To find a door, you had to find a wall.

In the darkness, even darker the further she moved away from the trapdoor, she squeezed between beer-sloshing barrels, heaving and rolling them out of the way, reaching for a wall. She found another pillar like the one she'd been tied to, or was it the same pillar? It was hard to tell. But all her fingers felt was a dark nothing. Or more barrels. The frustration was like last summer at the camp. Running around to find the right white tent amongst hundreds of identical white tents. She couldn't let her wits fail her now.

And then it came to her. Oh, how could she be so stupid?

All she had to do was wait.

She perched on a barrel.

It was hard to stay awake in the dark. She clenched as many muscles as she could find, but Baby still felt herself dropping off to sleep...

She woke with a start. Rigid, alert. Had somebody been in and she'd missed them? But the faint jangle of keys had woken her.

She slid off her barrel, squatted on the beer-damp floor and listened to a door opening and an electric light switch flicking.

The cellar flickered with light.

A barman trotted down some stairs, hoisted a barrel onto his shoulders and trotted back up. Did he know she was here? Baby thought about barging past him but had no idea what she'd be barging into. She wasn't making that mistake again.

Baby fixed the position of the door in her mind and wove her way through the barrels towards it. She crept up the steps. With her ear to the door, she listened to the hubbub of the pub's drinkers. Were they really all in on it, all part of the Blackshirt nest?

They had to be.

Baby felt the wall for the light switch, a cold brass thing with a little knob. She flicked it. The cellar was not exactly filled with light, but enough to see how far the underground room went.

It looked like the room went as far as the pub did. And between the pillars holding the pub up were barrels and barrels.

Winding her way between them, Baby discovered that in some places, she could hear conversations from the floor above, muffled as if through carpet. But not clear enough to hear what people were saying.

Where was her sister when she needed her?

But did she need her? The thought had threatened the return of hopeless Baby, until she realised that Fingers was with her, sort of.

There was a reason Baby's skirt was too tight.

The many pocketed skirts that she and Fingers wore were something from their previous life on the streets of London. Neither of them wanted to stop wearing them...

Baby may not have Fingers in person, but she did have her skirt on!

Fingers wasn't meant to have it, but Baby knew her sister still kept her special universal key and a lock-picking wire in one of the pockets. She felt through the layers.

Success! With the key and the wire in her hand, she wove her way between the pillars and barrels back to the door into the pub.

She wiggled both the key and wire in the lock in turn, the way Fingers had showed her, and listened for the clicks.

It wasn't easy and Baby was worried that the barman would be getting another barrel before she managed to pick the lock.

Just as she was about to give up, she felt a resistance inside the lock and the bolt slide across.

She took a deep breath, turned the doorknob, and peeped through.

The door opened onto a short corridor and, at the end, another door. Baby hoped that one wasn't locked too. She could hear voices with the clatters of a kitchen. A woman with a tray appeared. The woman was concentrating hard on the tray; a plate of steak and kidney pudding, by the smell. She leaned her back against the door at the end. The noisy hubbub of the pub increased for a moment before the door swung shut behind her.

Baby made a dash for it, past the open kitchen and slipped through the swing door into the pub.

It was busy and bigger than the Bonnet in Nettlefield. All sorts of folk, many in their black shirts, sloshing glasses, deep in conversation and laughing at each other's jokes.

Baby's skin tingled with the awful thrill of being in the heart of the nest. Nobody was looking down at her.

Through the bodies, she saw something she thought she recognised.

Sitting on top of a large table in the corner, surrounded by one round, padded seat, almost like a throne, was Taggart's briefcase, with a roll of paper beside it.

The woman with the tray was coming back.

Willing herself invisible—how would that work?—Baby slipped between the drinkers. Before the Blackshirts knew what was happening, she'd dived under the round table with the one hefty table leg in the middle.

Panting with the thrill, all her aches and pains forgotten, she pushed her brain into thinking out a plan. She needed that briefcase. It had to contain all the answers.

But stockinged, elegant legs were sliding round one side of the bench. Ladies' legs; four of them. They were joined by the humphs of a much larger person. Their sharply creased trousers, baggy Oxford Bags in fine expensive cloth, slid in from the other side.

Baby clung for her life to the one table leg and listened.

'This is what you've been waiting for, my dears,' said Sir Malcolm Taggart. 'I thought I'd show you the layout of our new HQ so you can think of some modern design ideas that will impress our guests. I'm expecting to be informed of a date any day now.'

Baby could see the briefcase, now sitting next to him on the plush bench. So close.

'Oh, do you mean...' and then a woman, a young impressionable woman by the sound of it, hissed a name that Baby couldn't quite hear.

Sir Malcolm, who, it seemed, couldn't whisper to save his life, replied huskily, 'No, not the Führer. Herr Himmler.'

'Himmler?' Where had she heard that name? Obviously, he was a Nazi and Baby had read about him in the Courier, but she had overheard somebody else say that name a long time ago...

'Now, ladies. These will be your quarters. They do look out over the railway line, but I'm told that in the reconstruction they were soundproofed so your beauty sleep will not be disturbed.'

He was showing them the plans of the new orphanage!

Was he planning to take it over? Though for the life of her, Baby couldn't see him as another Mrs Bullar. What would happen to the orphans?

'Off you go, my dears. I need to talk to the rest of the team.'

With squeaky giggles, the ladies' legs slid out from under the table.

Sir Malcolm's legs stretched.

Baby tucked in Fingers's skirts and clung tighter to the table.

Her instinct was to make a run for it, but had she heard everything? The mention of Himmler troubled her, and not just because it sounded like Hitler.

And then, like a boulder in the belly, it hit her. When she was still in London, trying to stop Underwood kidnapping Sophie, her guardian angel, Underwood had said, *'My contact has the ear of Herr Himmler'*.

Sir Malcolm Taggart was Arthur Underwood's contact!

Taggart was how Arthur Underwood thought he was going to get in with the top Nazis! Taggart had wanted kids from Underwood to give to Himmler for the Lebensborn programme. And Ida's little sister Bonnie would have been the cherry on the cake; the perfect flower girl for Hitler himself! That was until Baby and the other Wonder Girls had put a stop to their evil plans and got Arthur Underwood sent to jail.

So, Baby knew *exactly* why Taggart wanted revenge. But what she couldn't work out was what he could want with the island in the creek. Unless that was where he wanted to put the children? But that didn't sound right. The kids would probably like it, just like in *Swallows and Amazons*. Just like how they'd liked the idea of going to Germany, 'It being always Christmas there,' so Arthur Underwood had told them.

But Baby knew what would really have happened to the orphans. Or what would have happened to the orphans who passed their 'test', who met their requirements for *Lebensborn*, choosing the right sort of blond kids to be part of their Aryan master race? What would have happened to the orphans who failed the test was too dreadful to think about.

Oh, goodness! Where Underwood had failed, Taggart wouldn't! And Himmler here in Britain? Was Taggart expecting the Nazis to invade and take over like they just had in Austria? None of the countries surrounding Germany were safe from him.

But Baby had learned a lot from reading the paper. Britain had the English Channel in the way. Britain had boats to defend it. Britain had the Royal Navy.

What other ambitions did Taggart have?

These whats and whys whizzed round in Baby's brain like the clackers on a football rattle. She could feel panic rising in her chest.

But right at that moment, the whys didn't matter. What was certain, because she had just heard it, was that Taggart had his eye on the orphanage and the orphans. Would they never be safe?

While she'd been clinging, trousered and booted legs had lined up round the table, imprisoning her. Taggart's voice boomed out, 'Do it now. I'm not taking any chances with the little runt. The savage ruined my plans the last time. So, I'm going to ruin hers for *all* time.'

Baby knew enough. It was time to go. Now.

If there was one thing these people did, it was underestimating the likes of Baby and Fingers. Even with the knowledge that two London street urchins—former urchins—had foiled Taggart's and Underwood's plans last time, they were still none the wiser!

Baby reached up, pulled the briefcase off the bench, grabbed a wodge of paper, and shot out from under the table.

'What the dickens...' harrumphed Taggart from above.

She would have laughed if she wasn't on the run again.

Baby toppled pub chairs, dodged tables, and headed for the door.

From behind Baby, Target barked orders, 'Get her, fools!'

You're the fool, Sir Malcolm Taggart.

The black-shirted oafs behind her weren't as nimble as Baby. They crashed into the furniture, spreadeagled over tables, flailing their fat grabby hands.

Baby burst out into the daylight, the paper in her hand fluttering in the fresh breeze and the orange light of a setting sun.

She ran across the gravel, past the Blackshirt cars, to the rough, unmade road through the trees.

One way was the sea. The other was where the car had come from, the tree tunnel back to the good people, the orphanage, and The Lillie. Baby didn't have a boat and she couldn't swim...

Could she outrun Taggart and his Blackshirts all the way to Nettlefield?

23

ON THE ROAD
Friday 1st April, Even Later

VERONICA WAS GLAD of her pullover, motoring along the open road with the windows open and Ida at the wheel. She saw something of herself in Ida. She watched the girl with black-lined fingernails and motor-oil-smudged overalls bear over the steering wheel, racing-driver style, foot pressed on the pedal.

Impulsiveness, that was what it was. It was what made Veronica scatter all those flyers outside City Hall. It was what got her on that boat and made her write her first report for the *Courier* without thinking of the consequences. If Archie had been there, he would have stopped her. Instead, Arnold had to rescue her. She needed to do a lot more listening before she went and laid all her cards on the table like that again.

On a stretch of road with fields on either side, Veronica felt the car slowing down.

'No!' said Ida, her leg working the foot pedal like it was a pump. 'No, no, no!' She leaned even lower over the steering wheel as the engine spluttered, then stopped.

Ida hid her face in her hands. 'I'm so sorry.'

'Oh darling, have we run out of fuel, by any chance?' said Gin from the back.

'I know where we are,' said Brian.

'How do you know?' said Fingers sharply.

'Look!' said Brian, 'Look at that tree!' She pointed through the back window to a single tree standing in the middle of the field under the full moon.

'Gosh, so it is,' said Gin. 'Oh dear, it's fate, isn't it?'

Brian explained how nearly two years ago they'd crashed into that very tree, trying to get to Southampton before a boat sailed with kidnapped orphans on board. 'But that time, Ida came to the rescue.'

Ida slammed open the driver's door and lifted the bonnet. The others got out too and joined her, peering at the car engine.

'Did we pass any gas stations our way?' Veronica seriously doubted any would be open in this little country this late.

'Well,' said Ida, closing the flap, 'we can either go on foot to Hamwell, which will take us a couple of hours, or go back to Nettlefield.'

'Which will take ages too,' said Fingers. 'Why didn't you check there was enough petrol? You... you... twit!'

Ida turned her back on Fingers and started pacing along the weedy grass verge.

'It's weird without Baby,' said Brian. 'She would know what to do.'

While realising more and more how wrong she'd been about Baby, Veronica was also growing in sympathy with Ida. Veronica wanted to put an arm round Ida's shoulder and tell her that she knew exactly what it was like to act without thinking and then feel terrible about the consequences. But a voice in Veronica's head told her that an arm round Ida's shoulder would not be a good idea at that moment. And for once, Veronica listened.

While they were dithering, Veronica heard the engine of another vehicle. 'Somebody's coming.'

'Run!' said Fingers.

'But the car,' said Ida, 'I can't leave it.'

'They've probably seen us now, anyway. Perhaps they can help?' Gin strode out into the middle of the road, waving her scarf.

Fingers pulled her back. 'Don't you see who that is?'

'No, I can't, Fingers, darling. It's dark,' said Gin, continuing to wave her scarf at the rapidly approaching van. 'Oh my, I see what you mean!' She dashed off the road and joined the others hiding behind Ida's car.

At the wheel of a dark van was the silhouette of a grown man.

'If that's Bill Teasdale, I can take him,' said Gin.

'So can I,' said Fingers.

'Me too,' said Brian.

'I'm sure I can as well,' said Veronica, joining in.

The van stopped a few yards behind them. They heard the wrench of the handbrake and a man, older than the paper thief, got out and walked towards them.

'We thought you were Mr Underwood, back in his van!' said Brian.

Ida looked very sheepish. 'I'm sorry, Mr Rogers, really I am. But it was an emergency.'

'Did you forget?' said the man in overalls like Ida's.

'I was just so... excited,' said Ida.

'That young Alf has set your heart all a flutter, hasn't he?'

'No, no, he hasn't, not at all,' spluttered Ida.

Veronica whispered in Gin's ear, 'Who's Alf?'

'Ida's beau, not that she'll admit to him, of course,' said Gin, not bothering to whisper at all.

Ida flashed a thunderous frown in return.

'Well,' continued Mr Rogers, 'I nipped back to the garage for a spanner—bit of a blockage in one of the pipes at home—and I saw you drive out. Seriously, Ida, this was a bit of a risk. It was lucky that I had that laundry van in for a service.'

'I know, and I'm sorry. But it's Baby. She's gone missing.'

'Has she now? Well, If I remember rightly, Baby could get an Olympic gold medal for getting out of awkward fixes. I'm not saying that's not concerning, but there's not a lot you can do about it with this motor. Did you even know where you were going?'

'We had a fair idea,' said Ida defensively. 'Hamwell.'

'Yes, I've heard about that lot. Trouble is, a lot of the town are in with them. Look, I've got to get back to the wife and kids. I'm going to take you all back. No arguments.'

Reluctantly, they all piled into the van and made themselves as comfortable as they could among sacks of dirty washing, while Mr Rogers hooked Ida's car to the back.

It wasn't long before they were in Nettlefield again, most of them reassured by Mr Rogers's confidence in Baby. But Veronica wasn't sure. Baby was one smallish girl against what sounded like half a town's worth of Nazis. While she heavily regretted implying that Baby was somehow in sympathy with them, Veronica was beginning to feel a bit better about at least trying to expose them in the *Courier*. None of their activities sounded very secretive.

'I'd better let you all out here, hadn't I?' called Mr Rogers from the front, as they were driving under the railway bridge by the orphanage. 'I'll take care of the Austin, Ida.'

But Ida was already halfway out of the back door. She shot across the street and instead of heading for the slope up to the station, she launched herself at the weedy bank—the most direct route to the ticket booth.

'Where are you going?' called Fingers.

'Southampton! I should just make the last train!' she shouted from the top. 'I've got an idea!'

'That's our Ida,' said Gin. 'Not always a team player, you might say.'

'Ida, it's late!' called Veronica. 'Shouldn't we just go back to The Lillie and work out what to do in the morning?'

But Ida was already out of sight.

'Look,' said Brian, pointing towards the orphanage's impressive front door. 'Is she alright?'

Pacing up and down outside in the dim light shining through the stained glass above, was June Lovelock in her dressing gown.

'Well, let's go find out,' said Gin. 'Keep Baby to yourselves.'

June Lovelock looked up as they approached. 'Oh, I'm so glad you're all here. I'm really not sure what to do.'

24
FRANCES
Friday 1st April, Later Still

'WHAT'S HAPPENED?' said Veronica, stepping in June Lovelock's way.

But June simply continued to pace around her. This was not the calm, capable woman Veronica had been getting to know over the last few days.

Gin kindly took hold of June's hand. 'Darling, stop. Tell us what's the matter.'

'It's just like the Spanish children all over again,' said June, 'but worse. Not, of course, that the Spanish children were at fault. Not at all. They were innocent victims. But I'm not sure these people are victims in any way...'

'Who are these people? Reporters? Photographers?' said Gin.

'I don't think all these people can be reporters or photographers. Just how many people do you need for a short series of articles about the modern orphanage in a small town like Nettlefield? They all arrived this evening while you were out. Apparently, this is the second tranche and more are expected, from what Mrs Tatler said.' June pulled away from Gin and started pacing again, waving her hands in desperation. 'I have to say, I was immediately suspicious that Mrs Tatler was with them. Oh, I should have listened to Baby! No amount of money is worth this upheaval. And I've had to top and tail the children again…'

'We'll be there to help, won't we, Brian?' said Veronica, pacing with June. 'Arnold has given me a few days off, so I can do extra shifts.' She was trying to sound confident; that her few days off were just that, rather than a consequence of making Arnold reprint almost an entire edition of the *Courier*.

'Oh dear, Veronica, I shall have to ask you to give up your room.' June paused momentarily in the dim light. The moon was round and bright above them, but its light didn't reach the orphanage front porch. The darkness added to June's hopelessness.

'No matter, I'm pretty much sorted out in The Lillie,' said Veronica, trying to sound positive.

But June had stopped listening and was already onto her next worry. 'And Sir Malcolm will be back tomorrow morning and he's invited the school over too "to get an all-round view on life for children in a small town." How on earth will we cope? I really don't know what he'll be expecting to see.'

The mention of Sir Malcolm's imminent return concerned Veronica, too. She was desperate to interrogate the man—about his activities, the *Beacon*, and, not least of all, the parents that she still couldn't remember—but couldn't risk it. He already knew that 'Veronica Park' was trying to pass herself off as a boy. Surely he would recognise her.

Gin, Fingers, and Brian were busy trying to reassure June that it would all be fine. Veronica noticed that they didn't mention Baby, and probably because June was so distracted, *she* didn't notice Baby's absence either.

'Thank you, girls. I'm so glad you're here.' June rubbed her arms. 'I am getting a bit chilly now. And I think you all will need a good night's sleep. What there is left of it! I'm so sorry I can't offer you your usual beds, but at least our guests haven't invaded The Lillie.'

'Not yet,' said Fingers under her breath.

'Could you be here, bright and early for a six am start for breakfast? Is that all right with you, Brian? Veronica?'

'We'll be there too, won't we, Fingers?' said Gin, nudging the girl's shoulder.

'Yeah,' said Fingers, a heavy frown bearing down on her face.

While Brian remained her usual calm and placid self, Veronica's head was spinning with possibilities.

As the church clock was chiming eleven, June wished them all goodnight and went inside, closing the door behind her. The one light shining through the stained glass over the door went out, leaving the four of them under a starry sky in the orphanage playground.

'He can't see me, not like this,' Veronica said aloud.

'What? Who can't see you?' said Fingers, sitting on one of the playground swings.

Now was the time to tell them.

'Sir Malcolm Taggart. I've been wanting to tell you. I think we're related. And I think he may not wish me well, but I'm not sure why yet.' That was probably a gross understatement.

Veronica was surprised no one reacted to this revelation, but Gin and Fingers looked half asleep already.

'None of them like us very much,' said Brian. 'So you'll need a disguise.' She tugged on Veronica's sleeve, surveying her jacket and pants. 'Another one. Dad will still be up. Let's get it now.'

'Another disguise?' Surely no stores would be open at this time of night? Or was Brian going to make her wear one of her father's weird outfits?

But Brian was tugging on Veronica's sleeve.

'Do you mind if I just go to bed?' said Gin. 'I'm bushed and we have a hellishly early start.' She trudged across the playground, heading for the gates.

Fingers followed, muttering, 'If it was one of you lot, she wouldn't rest till you was back safe and sound...'

Brian pulled Veronica towards the rather scraggy hedge that separated the orphanage from the strange cottage next door. She hauled Veronica through the widest gap in the bushes. These girls loved bushes. Maybe it was a British thing, hedgerows and all that?

They wound down a path like creeping ivy through the overgrown garden. Without knocking, Brian pushed the cottage door open.

Inside, Mr Shaw was sitting under a bright electric light, at a little table, in a kitchen bursting with an assortment of kitchen implements, tools, and wired bits of machinery. Miss Oswald from the library was sitting with him. An ornate china teapot sat on the table between them with two cups and saucers.

'Hello, Brenda my dear. Olivia and I were just sorting out a particularly challenging philosophical problem. Would you like to join us? You so often have brilliant insight.'

'Oh, Dad...' said *Brenda*. Brian sounded a bit embarrassed at the compliment. 'You're always saying things like that.'

'Is that the young American lady with you?' said Miss Oswald. 'How fortunate.'

Veronica wanted to ask exactly why 'fortunate'? It was a strange choice of words, but already Brian was taking charge.

'I'll go and get the case,' she said as she climbed a rickety ladder in the corner of the kitchen. 'You sit there with Dad and Miss O.'

There wasn't anywhere else to sit.

'Take my chair,' said Miss Oswald, getting up. 'Time does fly when you're having fun, doesn't it, Alexander?' She took her hat from the dresser and, once she had positioned it on her head to her satisfaction, stabbed it with her giant daisy pin.

That hatpin was as a good as a lethal weapon.

Miss Oswald reached under the table and produced her carpet bag. 'Same time next week, Alexander?'

'Of course, my dear Olivia,' he said, getting up.

'No, don't stir...'

'But, ma'am, will you be safe? It's nearly midnight,' said Veronica.

'Of course I will,' Miss Oswald patted her daisy hatpin. 'You met Mister, didn't you?' She gently pulled the top of the bag open and one paw with a very sharp set of claws stretched through it. 'Now don't forget to have a chat with Arnold, will you?' With that, she slipped out the door.

A chat with Arnold? They had 'chats' all the time.

As the door closed, a shower of scarves and hats and dresses tumbled down the ladder from the hole in the ceiling. Brian climbed down after them.

As Mr Shaw cleared away the teapot and cups, Brian scooped up an armful of the clothes and dumped them on top of the clutter on the table. 'There you are,' she said. 'These don't fit Gin anymore, so you can choose anything.'

Veronica took off her jacket, slung it over the back of the chair and rummaged through the strangely perfumed pile. She found a plain black, slightly old-fashioned dress that would pass for a servant's clothing.

'Excellent choice, my dear,' said Mr Shaw. 'It is a well-known fact that the working classes are invisible to the aristocracy. I'm guessing that it's our newspaper baron visitor you wish to avoid?'

'How did you know, sir?' said Veronica, but her question was muffled by Brian standing on a stool, trying to remove Veronica's pullover.

'Dad, can you turn around, please? Veronica needs to try this on.'

'Oh yes, of course,' said Mr Shaw, dutifully.

The dress fitted well enough. It was strange wearing one after being in a pants suit for such a long time.

'You'll need something on your legs,' said Brian, pulling out a stretchy black stocking from the tangle of clothes on the table.

If a dress felt unnatural, stockings were even more so, but Veronica gave in to Brian's attentions. She found an apron and a cap with a wig attached—useful. After another trip up the ladder, a pair of stout shoes fell from the hatch in the ceiling and landed with two clumps on the flagstone floor.

'How do I look?' said Veronica. She had to admit she was enjoying the little heels on the shoes.

'Unrecognisable,' said Mr Shaw.

'Almost perfect,' said Brian, rummaging again in the pile of clothing. She produced a pair of wire spectacles from the pocket of a blue jacket. 'Elsie left these behind last year. Dad has fixed them.'

Veronica wondered who Elsie was, but she was tired and decided to save that story for later. 'Brian, while I'm dressed like this, do you think you could call me by my middle name? It's Frances.'

'Oh yes. I can do that. Gin turns into *Aunt Constance* and you turn into *Frances*. I'm good at remembering that. It's Dad that gets in a muddle with names, isn't that right, Dad?'

'Oh yes, I'm a proper old duffer when it comes to names,' said Mr Shaw. 'Now as you two young ladies don't have a murderous cat to protect you, I'll walk you over to the good old Lillie Langtry.'

Veronica gathered her own clothes. It really was time to sleep now. She was surprised that she hadn't noticed it before, but on the chair where Miss Oswald had been sitting, Veronica spotted a neatly folded sheet of newspaper, showing uppermost a very familiar photograph.

Because the image of her supposed family was now printed indelibly on her mind, rummaging inside the bundle of her own clothes for Archie's clipping was not really necessary.

But she did rummage.

And, of course, the photographs and captions in both clippings were exactly the same.

But Miss Oswald's had the whole story as well.

Veronica snatched Miss Oswald's folded clipping off the chair and quickly slipped it into her jacket pocket with Archie's.

'Let's go,' said Mr Shaw. 'Even you, my dear Brenda, need a few hours' sleep.'

Veronica bundled her jacket with the rest of her clothes and followed Brian and her father out of the little cottage and across to the station. She had no idea how she was going to sleep now that she had the full clipping. She lurched between wanting to save it for *never* and reading it there and then.

What was the story Archie had not wanted her to read?

25

INTERVIEWS

Saturday 2nd April, Breakfast-time

VERONICA WOKE in a tangle of quilts and legs. Just a few hours earlier, Gin and Fingers had fallen asleep where they fell and Veronica, dressed as 'Frances,' had joined them. She supposed Brian had, too.

Gin and Fingers dozed on. Brian, however, was wide awake and banging a pan with a wooden spoon. 'Time to get up, everyone! June needs our help!'

'Don't you ever sleep?' said Fingers, hauling herself awake across the mattresses.

Gin sat up. A curl flopped over her face. She blew it away and groaned. 'Why do these people come into our lives just when everything was working out so swimmingly?'

'What was working out? She's still lost, or had you forgotten?' said Fingers.

'Of course. No. Nothing. Ignore me,' said Gin, slipping her feet into her shoes.

Veronica forced herself off the mattresses too and smoothed some of the creases out of the black servant's outfit she was wearing. She was aware of her own clothes heaped in the corner. She was especially aware of the contents of her jacket pocket, but she had no time to look at the two clippings now. She was winding the arms of the wire spectacles round her ears when she noticed both Gin and Fingers gawping at her.

'Well, you look different,' said Fingers. 'It is you, ain't it?'

'Frances. Oi'm Frances now.' Veronica used her best British accent.

Fingers covered her ears. 'Ow, that was terrible. You'd best keep quiet.'

'Definitely. Frances the Silent,' said Gin. 'We'd better get going.'

The orphanage heaved with all the extra adult bodies. Sophisticated young women and smart young men swanned about in silk dressing gowns demanding breakfast.

There was no sign of Sir Malcolm Taggart.

On her way to the kitchen, Veronica, as 'Frances', passed a frazzled June in conversation with a young woman in an elegantly long nightgown.

'It really is the best we could do in such quantity and at such short notice,' said June. 'As it is, the children are on short rations.' She indicated the stack of well-scraped bowls that Veronica was carrying.

'Really?' was all the young woman could say in reply. She grimaced at the tray of barely touched porridge bowls, rejected by the adult 'guests' that Gin was at that moment returning to the kitchen.

The young woman then appeared to float upstairs as Gin gazed longingly at the rippling silk showing off the woman's bare back. 'I'm pretty sure that's a Léron...'

A small queue of timid orphans was forming at the front door.

'Yes children, go out to play. We'll call you in when we need you. Thank goodness most of the school cried off.' She followed Veronica and Gin to the kitchen. 'Parents weren't keen, what with it being a Saturday. Though the caretaker did come by and deliver another rather large parcel that he wasn't happy about leaving at the school over the weekend.'

In the kitchen, Mr Shaw's arms were plunged in a sink full of dirty dishes. Fingers stood beside him, flapping a tea towel. Brian was buttering slices of bread at the table. 'Has everyone eaten some breakfast now?' she asked. 'There is a little bit of porridge left.'

'Just ourselves, I think,' said June, inspecting Gin's tray. 'Perhaps one of these will be cool enough for Mother...'

'I'll start on the floor,' said Veronica, collecting a mop and bucket from the broom cupboard.

'Don't forget to eat, will you, Veronica dear?' said June.

'And don't forget to keep quiet,' said Fingers, dashing over from the sink with her tea towel to whisper in Veronica's ear.

'Don't you worry,' said Veronica, whispering in reply to both. She had no room for food. Her belly had nervous knots at the prospect of coming face to face with Sir Malcolm Taggart. He was expected at any moment for 'the interviews.' Was it the maid costume making her feel this way? Was she getting too far into her role? Where was her chutzpah?

In the corner of the living room, there was indeed a second, rather large triangular parcel near the fireplace. The wildflowers in the grate were limp, but the parcel reminded her of something she couldn't quite put her finger on. Though fingers were somehow important...

She heard a car arrive outside. On tiptoe, peering through the window, she saw Sir Malcolm Taggart get out of his Daimler, a British limousine. At the sight of the man, the Nazi sympathiser, Veronica forgot her role. With some relief, she felt her fury return to what he represented.

Seconds later, the living room doors flew open as if he had just shown up in a Wild West saloon. Sir Malcolm Taggart entered, an entourage of young people in his wake. 'We'll see them in here, and you can be quick about it.' Taggart made himself comfortable in June Lovelock's story chair in the library corner of the living room. He dwarfed it.

As Mr Shaw predicted, Veronica, on the other side of the room, was invisible as 'Frances.' The clattering of her mop only drew the slightest of raised eyebrows from one of the young men organising himself at the table with a brand-new notepad and a perfectly sharp pencil. Veronica doubted he had ever written so much as a small ad.

Veronica finished with her mop, clattered out, and in the kitchen found a dustpan and brush to busy herself in the living room fireplace while getting a closer look at Taggart.

When she returned, children were already filing in from the playground outside. This time, the young woman admitting the children turned her away. 'Later, skivvy,' she said with a sneer and a limp wave of her hand.

Veronica tried to see what was going on, but Taggart's people blocked the view through the windows in the doors.

A little white dog hared out of the front door, his tail between his legs, followed by his young master, Robert Perkins. 'Wait for me, Frank!' called Robert.

Veronica followed them both through the big yellow front door.

Robert jumped on the roundabout and sat hugging his knees as it turned. Frank leapt up to join him.

'What did they want to know in there?' asked Veronica, grabbing a bar and pulling the roundabout to a stop. She whispered, in case any of Taggart's people were within earshot.

Robert wrapped his arms around his head.

Aggie, Robert's best friend, a scrawny girl in a pinafore dress, belonging more to the nineteenth century than the twentieth, appeared at the open front door. She ran across the playground and leapt onto the roundabout next to Robert, putting her arm around him. 'These questions they always ask, they get 'im all upset.'

'The questions they *always* ask?' said Veronica.

But Aggie was too busy comforting her friend.

From the outside, the orphanage's living room windows were too high to see in, but one was open. Veronica heard the pop of flashbulbs.

More children were set free and soon the playground was busy. Saturday morning busy. Some of the children were playing around Taggart's car under the sneering gaze of the driver standing guard. Veronica didn't recognise him.

She heard the orphanage telephone ring in the entrance hall and Gin answer it. 'Oh good-oh,' she said. 'We're on our way.'

June appeared, pushing old Mrs Lovelock in her wheelchair. 'Sir Malcolm and his team have finished the interviews, so I thought we'd take the children to the park for a picnic. Brian's made the sandwiches.'

On hearing the word 'picnic,' the children's cheers spread.

Piled on Mrs Lovelock's lap was a basket filled with Brian's sandwiches, wrapped in paper. June carried another shopping basket containing bottles of soda. 'Sir Malcolm has kindly donated some lemonade. The children don't often have lemonade.'

'I ain't touching that,' said Robert.

'Me neither,' said Aggie.

'You can stay here with Brian and Mr Shaw if you really don't want to come on the picnic,' said June. 'Perhaps one of you could let Baby know where we are? She loves a picnic,' she added to whoever was listening.

Still, nobody had told her that Baby was missing.

Where the other children were gathering into a line, Robert, Aggie and Frank sat resolutely on the roundabout.

June beckoned Veronica. 'Ver... Frances, perhaps you could accompany us. Gin is coming too.'

'Did somebody say my name?' Gin ran round the corner from the kitchen and took the handles on Mrs Lovelock's wheelchair. 'I think this is a job for me,' she said. 'All that keeping fit Dad made me do in Berlin is paying off. Shall we get going?'

'I'd like to go to the pictures,' said Mrs Lovelock in her wheelchair. '*Snow White*'s on at The Embassy, I'm told. Much nicer than a picnic in the rain.' She pointed to a dark cloud overhead.

A ripple of whispers travelled along the children's line. 'Ooh, *Snow White*!'

'We'll see,' said June. 'But we don't want anyone to miss out. Robert! Aggie!'

But at that moment, Sir Malcolm Taggart appeared at the front door. He had a cigar in his mouth and paused on the step for a moment. He looked like a man standing outside his own piece of real estate.

Robert and Aggie clung to each other on the roundabout. Frank, the little white dog, who until then had been keeping them company, leapt to the ground. He bolted across the playground and, as if the dog knew the man was somewhere he shouldn't be, he yapped and snarled at Taggart's ankles.

'Oh dear, I am sorry, Sir Malcolm,' said June, rushing over, lemonade bottles clinking. She shooed Frank away.

'No matter, June. One or two more of our people will be arriving this evening...'

'More?' said June, her knees buckling, probably not only from the weight of the basket of soda bottles.

'Yes, just one or two. If you could accommodate them and maybe rustle up some supper?' He flicked ash onto the orphanage front step, took the few steps to the car and waited while his driver opened the Daimler's door.

Now was her chance. Veronica's disguise was her shield, her protection. So, while June was still apologising, Veronica dashed across the playground to the front step and brushed Taggart's ash into her pan, as he was easing himself into the car.

With the door shut and the driver having installed himself in his own seat, Taggart looked up through the car window. He waved at June, and with the engine running, shifted his gaze to Veronica.

It turned out that her disguise was no shield at all.

Taggart's eyes aimed like gun barrels at the heart of her, ready to fire through her, to blast her to who knew where...

In that moment, she knew that *he* knew. And she knew he believed he knew everything.

But Archie always said, thinking you know everything is *always* a mistake.

26

Truth

Same Day, Saturday 2nd April, Morning

VERONICA FELT as if an electric current had passed between her and Sir Malcolm Taggart. It didn't scare her. His confidence enraged her, and she tingled with it.

She asked June for some time to change into her regular clothes, ready for more of that knowledge. Now was the time to compare Miss Oswald's sheet of newspaper with Archie's clipping. Both waiting for her in her jacket pocket back at The Lillie.

'Yes, of course, you know the way to Tub Lane Recreation Ground, don't you?' said June, perspiring slightly with the effort of carrying her basket.

Veronica didn't, but she had a tongue in her head. 'Yes, I'll be with you all real soon.' She dashed across the road, up the slope and past the station.

It had to be a good sign. Because, for the first time, she found her way through the bushes that hid The Lillie from general view without help.

The Lillie's door was unlocked but no one would be in. Should she be worried about that? No mind.

Inside, she threw the cap wig into the room-bed—it was itchy anyway—and grabbed her pile of clothes. She changed back into her pants and shirt. She didn't bother with the pullover, but just tied her turquoise scarf at a jaunty angle round her neck. She put on her jacket and sat down at the table by the window. The morning light was shining through it, like a spotlight on a Broadway stage. She was ready.

Veronica reached into her jacket pocket.

She found Archie's clipping and placed it on the table. The sheet must be in the other pocket.

Nothing.

A shadow passed across the window. Branches blown about by the breeze, she assumed.

She must have dropped it somewhere. She'd been so close. She was ready for the truth, but it was still just out of reach. She'd have to go look for it.

The Lillie's door opened.

'I think you might be looking for this,' said Mr Shaw, offering her the still folded sheet of newspaper.

'Oh, thank you! You picked it up.'

'Brenda did. You were all half asleep, except for dear Brenda. Sometimes I think she runs on nuclear fusion! There was no opportunity to return it in all the kerfuffle this morning.'

The newspaper trembled in Veronica's hand. 'Why are you here? Weren't you meant to stay with Robert and Aggie?'

'They're here. I thought it was safer for them. Listen.' Laughter, shrieks from the kids, woofs from Frank, all came from the trees surrounding the railway car. 'Brenda's out there too. The trees are such fun to climb.'

'No Fingers?'

'No,' he said. 'May I come in?'

For the first time, Veronica saw a look of concern on the old man's bearded face. 'Of course.'

'Fingers finished the drying up after breakfast, then slipped out before we had a chance to tell her about the picnic.'

'Where did she go?'

'I'm not certain, but like all the girls, she's very resourceful. Now would you like me to stay while you read?' He indicated the folded sheet of newspaper in her hand.

Now that the time had come, Veronica was less sure about wanting to know the truth. But Brian's father, for all his eccentricity, seemed to be the most solid and sure person she had met in Nettlefield, which helped.

'Yes, please.'

Mr Shaw drew out a chair at the table and sat down. He looked very at home.

Veronica sat down less comfortably, facing him.

To the muffled sound of children playing, and in the sunlight shining through the window, Veronica peeled open the folds of the yellowing sheet of newspaper and spread it out on the table. Her breathing became shallow as the 'trying not to look' and the 'desperately wanting to know' competed in her heart. But she was a muckraker, a journalist. She had to know.

The date at the top matched that on the clipping, November 5th 1929. Most of the text was about the man and the woman, her parents, whom she still felt nothing for. Was she adopted? Kept in a cellar? She knew that sort of thing happened. But nothing resonated with her.

But the biggest photograph on the page, however, was of someone she knew very well indeed. She could see it, but she was trying not to look until she had to.

The picture was of Archie.

She felt her heart breaking all over again. He was younger in the picture, no eyeglasses, not even a trace of white in his hair, and he was clean-shaven. His expression was harder, sterner, too; one that Veronica had only seen in response to some terrible cruelty they'd uncovered as muckrakers. As her finger traced the face that she loved, she came to the caption:

'Archibald Coombes wanted in connection with the disappearance of Miss Euphemia, known as 'Veronica', Campbell-Taggart, seven years of age.'

No.

Then she read the paragraph underneath:

'Coombes has a history of violence and the family fear for the safety of the child.'

NO.

And why Coombes? Archie's name was Parker.

But what did Miss Oswald say? 'Don't forget to have a chat with Arnold,' she'd said. Arnold *Coombes*? Veronica was struggling to understand. She knew Arnold's name was Coombes. Why had the paper attached it to Archie? It had to be a coincidence that the wrong name they gave him just happened to be 'Coombes'. Arnold's name.

She stood up. 'The paper is wrong. The *Beacon* does what papers like that always do. They lie!'

Mr Shaw remained seated. 'They are certainly creative with the truth, Veronica. They write according to their own agendas, and any research they may or may not do is to support that agenda. But isn't that the case for all journalists? Isn't that the case for *you*, Veronica?' He put that week's copy of the *Courier* on the table and opened it to the ad pages.

Arnold didn't catch them all. Oh, no! How many papers with her terrible report were still out there?

She flumped back down on the chair. 'But that was a mistake. I was wrong.'

'You didn't intend to mislead, but your lack of knowledge caused you to.' He laid his hand with a reverence on Archie's photo. 'And yes, whether this is a genuine mistake through lack of research or a deliberate attempt to accuse an innocent person because their politics are not in line with the newspaper's agenda, I don't know. But there is one person who can shed some light.'

'Really? You don't mean Arnold, do you? Isn't it just a coincidence about the name? Archie's surname was Parker. It's partly why he and I chose Park for me.'

She gasped—a snatch for breath that sent her heart racing—as it occurred to her that maybe Archie chose his name, too.

'Dad, shall I make our sandwiches now?' said Brian from the door.

'Jolly good idea, Brenda! We'll just clear the table.' He carefully folded the piece of newsprint and handed it to Veronica. 'Go and see Arnold. He'll have a story to tell.'

Did she *want* to see Arnold? What was he going to tell her? 'But June and the children...'

'They'll be fine.' He glanced through the window. 'It looks like rain.'

A cloud had indeed hidden the sun.

Frank bounded through the open door, past Brian, and leapt onto Mr Shaw's lap and licked his beard enthusiastically. Robert and Aggie tumbled in after him. They were both looking a lot happier than earlier, but Robert especially. 'When I'm twelve, I'm going to be a Wonder Girl and live here with Aggie,' he said.

So that was what these girls were. Only a few hours before, Veronica had felt like one of them. She wasn't so sure now.

Mr Shaw gave Veronica the directions for the park, where the children were picnicking. It was quite easy. Past the Courier there was a street called Tub Lane, turning right off West Street. It would take her straight there. 'Go *after* you've heard from Arnold,' he insisted.

West Street seemed busy for Nettlefield. Children were grumpily following their mothers with baskets of shopping. The sun was out from behind the clouds. At that moment, it didn't look like rain at all. Awnings were out and shop displays were all paying homage to the approaching Easter holiday with toy chicks and rabbits and foil-wrapped chocolate eggs. It all looked very pretty. That is until she reached the Courier.

In front of her, on the sidewalk, was a typewriter; an upside-down typewriter surrounded by broken glass.

She looked up. The largest of Arnold's remaining office windows was shattered.

A black-shirted thug, his sleeves rolled up ready for a fight, swaggered out of the shop door. Ignoring Veronica, he barged away through the shoppers.

The thug was followed sheepishly by the man from Betty Marie's, the ferry, and Mrs Tatler's. 'Miss

Taggart,' he said, touching the rim of his fedora with a wad of paper, which he then stuffed inside his coat.

'Yes,' she replied defiantly. 'So, you've found me. What do you want?'

But the man from Betty Marie's ignored her reply, continued walking and was soon lost in the busyness of West Street's Saturday morning.

How she hated that name. 'Taggart.' Was her cover now completely blown? Why didn't he arrest her or something?

A mother trailing a small boy stepped neatly round the typewriter. 'Can I take it home, Mum? Pleeeeease?'

'Not now, George,' said the mother, walking him briskly away.

The boy whined, but his whines were drowned out by the urgent squawking, 'READ ALL ABOUT IT! READ ALL ABOUT IT!' coming through the broken window.

She tore through the shop and up the stairs. 'Arnold! Arnold! Where are you? What's happened?'

The office door was open. The place was a tip. Everything that could be emptied was emptied onto the floor: papers, files, books. Arnold's camera was smashed; its lens broken, its film ripped out and curled amongst the mess.

On a pile of old newspapers under his cage lay Houdini's silk cover. He was still urgently screeching and rattling his cage. 'READ ALL ABOUT IT! READ ALL ABOUT IT!'

'That's enough, Houdini,' said Veronica, replacing the silk cover. She couldn't think with that racket.

A groan came from behind the desk.

She found Arnold slumped against the wall under the pinboard. 'That's it. I've lost. They've got it.'

'They've got what?'

'The proof. The evidence. Though it wouldn't count for much, even if I had it. Half of Nettlefield Police are in on it. I'm done.'

He was reaching for something behind his back.

'It's up to you now, Veronica. At least you'll get your inheritance, though I suspect there'll only be a fraction of it left. Just don't let them change you...'

He found what he was reaching for.

From behind his back, across the floor, Arnold slid a gun.

His finger was hooked round the trigger.

27
Baby's Boat Trip
Friday 1st to Saturday 2nd April

UNDER A DARKENING EVENING SKY, made darker by the tunnel of trees, a solid wall of Blackshirts blocked Baby's escape. From hedge to hedge, they stretched across the country road that wound up and away from the pub, the Blackshirts' nest.

She dodged side to side like she'd seen Fingers do when she was playing football. Baby thought she could burrow through the bushes. She'd done that often enough.

But the line was curling round her, trapping her.

There were too many of them. Before Baby could turn tail and head for the sea, hoping for a boat or a very quick swimming lesson, the Blackshirts had wrapped round her completely.

'Have you got the slippery little rat?' Taggart's voice boomed from behind, followed by the creak and crunch of his smart shoes on the gravel road. 'No mistakes this time, or you'll suffer the same fate as this savage.' He was dressed for an evening out; a short cloak round his shoulders and spats covering his shiny shoes. In one hand he clutched a matching pair of gloves, and in the other, that cane.

'Get off me! You're the savages! You evil Blackshirt Nazis!' Baby wriggled, squirmed, kicked, and bit, but the two huge men who held her, an arm each, were hard as rock, and their hands like clamps.

'Get the jacket!' shouted Taggart to the rest of the waiting Blackshirts, who all raced off in competition to be the first.

Baby was still gripping the paper she'd snatched from Taggart's briefcase, all screwed up now.

He tucked the cane under his arm and snatched the paper back. 'As you're so interested, I will be delighted to show you this *in situ.*'

Baby had no idea what he was talking about. She'd only had the briefest of glances at the top piece of paper, which was a drawing of something, mostly lines, angles, and tiny writing.

The fastest Blackshirt was none other than Bill Teasdale, again, brother of William, wearing his black shirt, sleeves rolled up and big boots under trousers with sharply pressed creases. He was carrying a stiff canvas with leather straps.

'Put it on her, then,' barked Taggart.

Baby struggled but Bill and the other Blackshirts were too strong. They held her while Bill pushed her arms into a back-to-front jacket, a straitjacket, like they made the poor confused folks wear at the asylum.

'You 'old still, you little rat,' said Bill. 'You put me inside and you ain't getting away with that.' Bill's bristles scoured her ear. 'You're vermin. You're a little piece of...'

All Baby heard was hate.

She struggled, of course she did, but Bill and his Blackshirt friends were each like four of her. Three times four; twelve Babys to one!

Bill pulled on the sleeves that were far too long. He tugged at straps and buckles round her body and between her legs.

Fingers's skirt bunched round her thighs and very soon, Baby was as trussed up like the cat in *Samuel Whiskers*, Fingers's favourite book in the orphanage library. The more Baby struggled, the tighter he pulled.

Blackshirt Bill grabbed the straps and dragged Baby across the gravel. Her poor shoes scuffed the stones again.

With the other thugs, Taggart strolled behind Bill and Baby. They passed the pub and its sign. Now in the still evening air, she could read it: *The Black Shirt*. Was that actually what the pub was called? How could it be as brazen as that and people not notice?

Hopelessness overwhelmed Baby. After all their efforts to rid Nettlefield of the Blackshirt menaces, twice as many were taking their place. A tiny voice hissed in her ear: *Give up, you can't win...*

But that was exactly what Baby needed to hear!

Because she was *Baby*! And anyone who knew her—truly knew her—would know she was never giving up! What did these people always do? Underestimate, that's what. They never learned, not properly. Taggart knew she was slippery, but he didn't know how slippery!

They were heading towards the sea. Was he going to drop her in it? After all those years living by Old Father Thames, why hadn't she learned to swim? But just swimming in the river would kill you, Moll always said, so Baby never learned. If he really was going to drop her in, she'd just have to learn quickly. Were arms needed to swim? Did eels have arms? No, and neither did Baby at that moment.

Against a scattering of clouds and a sliver of orange light from the setting sun, a jetty stuck out into the water, where a smart new motorboat was waiting. Smoke was puffing from its funnel and a sailor in uniform with gold braid round his cap was waiting with it. He looked like the captain of a much bigger boat.

Bill stopped. Was he just waiting for the order?

'I thought you always wanted a trip on a boat?' said Taggart, sauntering towards the jetty. 'You may wonder how I know that. But I know everything there is to know about you.' Taggart strode towards her along the jetty. It bounced with his weight. 'I've made you my research project over the last eighteen months. I have my agents all over the world.'

He ordered the other thugs away. 'Go back to the pub and tell them to put the champagne on ice. The plan is finally coming together.'

There was no way Taggart knew everything about Baby. 'Oh yeah?' she said. 'Then who's me ma?'

'I'm *so* glad you asked that!' He stopped and leaned on his cane. 'Your mother is Mukta Devi, though how much longer she'll live is anybody's guess. She sells second-, third-, and fourth-hand sarees at the side of the road in Bombay. Her children, her other surviving children, beg for rupees near The Gate of India.'

Had he just punched her with that information? It felt like it. 'You... you just made that up. You don't know,' said Baby, her confidence shrinking.

'How do *you* know for sure?' said Taggart, a self-satisfied smile growing on his face. 'You can, of course, believe what you want to believe. Though sometimes, it pleases me to tell the truth, the whole truth, and nothing but the truth.'

He'd properly caught her off guard, unbalanced her.

'That's enough with the questions.' Turning to Bill, who still had her in his grip, Taggart said, 'Get her on board and gag the little runt. Because that was what she was, the runt of the litter, offered to whoever was passing. I'm now doing what your sorry excuse for a mother should have done at birth. Though she could never have done it in quite such a spectacular way.'

Spectacular? What did that mean? Baby didn't like the way he said it. A good word turned sour. It turned her insides.

'Weigh anchor in the channel,' boomed Taggart to the heavily braided sailor on the boat. 'She can ponder her fate for the night, and we'll sail on the morning tide.'

'But sir,' said Bill, 'what if she escapes again?'

'She's in a straitjacket, you fool!' Taggart whacked Bill's head with his cane. Bill's lip quivered. Despite his bulk and tough words, Bill was a coward.

'Get her on board. And you can tie her up as well *and* stay on guard. Her fate will be yours if you lose her.' The jetty bounced as Bill dragged Baby onto the boat and dropped her on a bench at the back.

Bill followed his orders and picked up a coil of rope from the boat's floor and wound it round and round Baby. Then he wound it round himself. 'You ain't going nowhere without me. Well, not till the, you know... I ain't doing that.'

'What's the "you know?"' asked Baby.

'You just wait and see.' From his pocket, Bill took a dirty rag and tied it round her mouth. It smelled of mould and tasted salty. Baby's stomach churned again.

The boat's engine started with a quiet chug, chug, chug and manoeuvred away from the jetty, away from an easy escape.

Taggart's boat was new, smart, and shiny. Polished wood and gleaming metal surrounded her. The sailor disappeared through the cabin door in front of her. She glimpsed the luxurious inside, as posh as any toff's place she and Fingers had seen in their burgling days.

The sun had properly set now, and stars were popping out in tiny points of light above her. Baby tried to think. Strapped inside a straitjacket and tied to Blackshirt Bill, thinking was all she could do.

Where was Taggart going to take her? That was an obvious question, but all she had in her head was that name. *Mukta Devi*. Was that really her ma? Or had he just said that to torture her? How could he have found that out? That was the trouble when people said a thing. When it was spoken and out there, it became a thing to consider, true or not. Especially when spoken by people like him: people with 'Sir' before their names; people who owned newspapers; people that everyone knew.

Whether it was true or not, even people with brains in their head couldn't help wondering. It was how newspapers worked. Newspapers should tell the truth about people, but they didn't. But the trouble was, when the person spoken about could be your ma, and what was spoken fitted with what the woman who last summer *pretended* to be your ma said, Baby couldn't help wondering. And the more she wondered, the more the thought hooked into her brain. And it wound round her heart tighter than the straps and ropes wrapping her arms to her body.

She looked up at the stupid oaf beside her, his bristly head, short neck and muscles bulging under his black shirt. She watched his eyelids droop, and she did the only thing she could; she pulled her legs up to her chest and slept until morning.

When Baby awoke, it was just light, a hard morning light. She was aware that she'd been dreaming of someone warm and kind but couldn't put a face to them. Was it a memory or her imagination? Because, although Moll was gone, she did have friends, sisters, who gave her that feeling; who, in lots of different measures, gave her that love.

Questions about whoever it was soon dissolved when Baby remembered where she was.

The boat was back by the jetty and Taggart, in a tweed jacket with breeches and boots, was being helped on board by the captain.

With the bobbing of the boat, Bill sat bolt upright.

'Oh, dear me, I forgot to order the condemned rat's last meal,' said Taggart, glancing down his nose at Baby before he made himself comfortable inside the cabin, chuckling to himself.

Baby wriggled and tried to tell him that he was wrong; wrong about everything, and that he was for it, and she would get him in the end. But the gag was still tight round her mouth, and her brave defiant words just came out as a series of grunts.

The engine started, and the boat once again pulled away from the jetty and The Black Shirt pub. Baby smelled the salt. She closed her eyes, and, for a moment at least, tried to forget everything.

This was Baby's first boat trip. Whatever lay at the end of it, Baby thought she might as well enjoy it as best she could. She tilted her head back and let the sea breeze clear her mind. Across the sky, dark clouds were rolling in, which seemed appropriate.

Soon, they were out into a wider river. Was it a river at all? The land was further away, and waves rocked the boat. The swell of the water, saltier than before, did strange things to Baby's empty insides. She opened her eyes and above her, saw a black cloud, and birds, mostly white and squawky, circling.

Baby worked out that the land she could see must be The Isle of Wight, so she was on The Solent, not The Atlantic Ocean, not even The English Channel. But ships came along here to go up Southampton Water, so it must be deep. Baby didn't fancy her chances if this was where he planned to chuck her overboard.

They were nearing a place bigger than Hamwell, bigger than Nettlefield even. The shoreline broke like a gateway and they were heading for it. It couldn't be Southampton, so it must be Portsmouth Harbour. Baby's reading was paying off.

Taggart, with a whisky glass in his hand, leaned out of the cabin door and addressed Bill. 'Untie yourself and chuck a tarpaulin over the ship's rat, will you? Don't want the Navy getting unnecessarily curious.'

It was good to be rid, if only by an inch, of the stupid Blackshirt, Bill Teasdale.

Bill lifted a lid on a box fixed to the middle of the deck, pulled out a large canvas tarpaulin and threw it over Baby.

The tarpaulin was heavy and stiff. It had a musty smell and felt damp. In the dark, all Baby had to go on was the swell of the sea. How it rose and dropped when another boat passed. The bigger the swell, the closer or the bigger the boat that had passed them. She heard raindrops, fat sploshy ones, land on the tarpaulin and so she was glad of the shelter.

The boat motored on and, even under her musty old covering, an unmistakable stink was reaching her nostrils.

Mud.

Creek mud.

The boat's engine had stopped, as had the rain. Baby heard the cabin door open. She felt somebody tug at the tarpaulin. As soon as her eyes got used to the light again, she saw the person was Taggart. 'Your time has come, savage. You have been a thorn in my side for too long. I am not letting you impede the march of history.'

Baby could impede the 'march of history'? She guessed that impede meant something like 'stop,' and couldn't help but think, *Wow! This villain thinks that much of me.*

Bill, on the other hand, was leaning over the side of the boat, being sick. Despite his muscles, he could barely impede anything. His wet black shirt stuck to his back.

Taggart was perfectly dry, though there was a little puddle of rainwater in the floor of the boat. His boots, a new shiny leather that covered his legs to his knees, were more than enough protection. He wore matching leather gloves, too.

'We've arrived,' he said. 'I knew you wanted to see Hewett Island, and now you're going to. For a short while, you may even have a bird's-eye view.' He laughed at his remark as though it were a joke. Though it didn't sound like a joke to Baby.

The boat bobbed in a narrow channel of water with mud flats on both sides. Baby recognised the grounds of the big house on one side. On the other side, another short jetty led to what Baby had until then only seen at a distance from the shore opposite. The island in the creek.

Hewett Island.

Of course, that was where they were going! If her head hadn't been so full of her ma, she would have guessed in an instant.

The jetty's new planks, wet from the rain, were mostly clean. They looked like hardly anyone had walked on them yet. And no wonder. Fixed to the end of the jetty was a board on a post. In large unfriendly writing, it said, *'Keep Out by Royal Command',* and in the corner a squiggle of a signature.

Baby could only read the capitals, *'E... R...'*

28

History
Saturday 2nd April

'STOP! YOU CAN'T DO THAT,' said Veronica Arnold was pointing the gun at himself. Any sudden movement could be fatal.

'I can.' The gun trembled in Arnold's hand.

'No. You. Can't.' Veronica unfolded the sheet of newspaper left for her by Miss Oswald. 'Not before you've explained this.' She waved the sheet in front of his face.

Arnold peered at the newspaper, his gun hand dangerously near his head. 'I need my glasses.'

Veronica looked and found them under the desk; bent, and with one lens broken.

Arnold held the good lens to his eye as he scanned the sheet. He lowered the gun and placed it on the floor next to him.

Veronica pushed it away with her foot and let out a long sigh; he hadn't realised she'd been holding her breath.

Arnold took the paper, and a tear slid across his cheek. 'My brother.'

'What? What are you saying?'

'I knew he was dead the minute I saw you.'

'No. What are you saying about Archie? Did you know him? It makes sense, you're both newspapermen.' Veronica crouched in front of Arnold. 'Was Archie *like* a brother to you? Where did you meet?'

'No, he wasn't like anything. That was the trouble. He was my brother. My twin brother.'

'But...'

'Yes, I know. I am white and he is... was black. It was hard. Hard on the whole family. But hardest on Mother. A black child to two white parents was unheard of, unless, of course, Archie's father was not my father. People said she lied about us being twins and accused her of adultery. But not just adultery, adultery with a black man, which, to their small minds, was a hundred times worse.' Arnold dragged his hand across his face.

He continued, 'Mother tried not to listen. She said that Archie was her gift from God, her Messiah, and that was what sent her to the asylum.' Arnold's gaze drifted away from Veronica to the typewriter-sized broken window. 'Then Arch left, and Dad carried on as long as he could. People thought he was better off.' Arnold patted the floor beside him.

Was he feeling for the gun again?

'But Arnold...' said Veronica, calling him back. So many questions buzzed round her brain, but she had to stop Arnold reaching for that trigger. 'Why did Archie go to New York? Why America?'

'He had help. After the war, he thought it would be easier there, easier to fit in, but you know what it's like. From the frying pan into the fire.'

Veronica could imagine the disappointment of thinking he was in the land of the free, only to discover that, as a black man, it was anything but.

'Of course, it wasn't so bad in the North. No Jim Crow laws. Even so, if you were black, you were always going to be the first suspect for any wrongdoing. Then Taggart wanted him to do this job, probably offered him a lot of money. I suppose Archie thought he'd be protected... But at the last minute, whatever he was meant to do, he didn't. And somehow you, the lost girl, came into his life.'

Veronica sat on the floor amongst the paper and the mess and tried to process what she had just heard. Not so much that Archie had a brother who was a white man and that here she was, sitting in his newspaper office in a small town in England. But that Archie was hired to do 'a job' by Taggart; the same Taggart, Uncle Taggart, who seemed to be taking over this small town in England.

'You know what Taggart wanted him to do, don't you? Tell me.'

Did Veronica really want Arnold to put it into words? She had a fair idea what 'wanted in connection with the disappearance of' implied. But yes, now she was ready to know for sure. 'Tell me. I can handle it.'

Arnold turned again to the typewriter-sized hole in the window. It was raining. At that moment, West Street, like the rest of the world, looked grey and depressing.

'He was hired to kill you, Veronica.'

Another punch, another blow. But before it could land, it stopped mid-air.

Archie was hired to kill her. But he didn't.

Archie saved her, like she always knew.

But Taggart, Uncle Taggart... 'Why did my great uncle want me dead?'

'Money and power, I expect,' said Arnold, as if they were the reasons for all evil doing.

'And why Archie?' she found it impossible to imagine her Archie, the only father she could remember, doing anything bad.

'It all goes back to the war... well, before the war. A long time before. Taggart isn't really a Scot. The stories he tells about himself are like those in his paper, lies. He actually grew up not far from here, in Hamwell...'

'Hamwell?' said Veronica, wondering what this had to do with her beloved Archie.

'Yes.'

'Hamwell keeps coming up.'

'Taggart, *Malcolm*, and Dad were boys together there. They were different classes. Taggart's family had money—a lot of money—but him and Dad were childhood friends. But growing up, they drifted apart in every possible way.'

Veronica remembered what she'd read in the library. 'Taggart had twin sons too, didn't he?'

'Yes, and he lost them in the last weeks of the war. We were under their command. It was one of those quirks of fate that happen in wartime. We survived...'

'And his boys died.'

'Yes. As far as Taggart was concerned, that was the wrong way round.'

'So, trying to use Archie as a hired killer was Taggart's revenge on your dad? But why did he want *me* dead? Does he still? He's had opportunities...' She felt a sob in her throat and swallowed it back. 'He killed Archie, didn't he?'

'Had him killed, undoubtedly,' said Arnold, nodding his head.

The last butterfly of worry about Archie had finally dropped dead. He was hired to kill her. But he didn't. He chose to hide her in boy's clothes in a newspaper office.

'What surprises me,' said Arnold, 'is how long he took to get round to it. Taggart must have known Archie didn't do the job he was paid for. The man has people everywhere.'

'My parents, Howard and Sylvia. Do you know what really happened to them?' She still felt nothing; her memory was a blank page. It was as if she had no life at all before Archie.

'It wasn't an alien abduction, that's for sure.'

Veronica couldn't help laughing at the ridiculousness of some of the newspaper reports. At least that brought a smile to Arnold's face. 'Archie didn't write to you about that?'

'No, not a word.'

Veronica thought that was strange, as he had done his best to communicate everything else important, one way or another. He must have known what really happened to them.

But this was all history, and whatever Taggart was doing at the orphanage was more pressing. Veronica was sure that it was not for the welfare of those children. 'Was this—Taggart, and the paper, and the children—was this why Archie wanted me here? To report on it? To blow the whistle?'

'I think, if he'd had any sense, Nettlefield would have been the last place he wanted you.'

'But he wrote "Nettlefield" on the paper? Like a clue; an instruction.'

'I don't know.' Arnold peered over the frames of his glasses. 'Are you sure it was Archie who left you that paper?'

'Yes, I'm sure.' Why would Betty Marie have lied?

'Was it Archie's handwriting?'

Veronica had always assumed it was scribbled hurriedly. She was beginning to feel stupid. Had she walked herself into a trap?

Arnold sat up and surveyed the damage in the office. 'Archie wrote that Taggart had been seen in Brooklyn, and that Taggart had someone looking for you and, therefore, him. It's not just Hamwell where Taggart has history. You know about Underwood?'

'Yes, I read your special feature.' Veronica's head was buzzing, but she didn't want to distract Arnold...

He went on, 'Well, I didn't publish everything. There was a lot of stuff I kept back should I need any "insurance." When you accuse people like Sir Malcolm Taggart, you need a *lot* of evidence.'

'So, the evidence is what they—Taggart's people—have taken?'

Arnold picked up a manila folder and shook it upside down. 'Pictures, letters, the lot. And look...' He pointed to the broken camera and the spoiled reel of film strewn across the floor.

'What about the photos on the board?'

'Oh, they came for those months ago. Pictures of the '36 march, and many of Nettlefield's so-called finest citizens, waving flags, supporting Hitler.'

Veronica studied the pinboard above Arnold's head. There was no order to it. Pictures and clippings overlapped, many had to share the same thumb tack.

Yes, there were less-faded patches uncovered by the previous thief, but had that thief taken everything? Veronica took off her jacket, hung it over Arnold's chair and cleared a space on his desk. She started pulling thumb tacks from the pinboard.

'What are you doing? I told you, they've got everything.' He was reaching for the gun again.

'I just want to make sure.' She positioned herself between Arnold and his gun. 'I could use your help.'

'It's hopeless,' said Arnold, not moving from the floor.

Every picture and clipping she took off the board, she laid on the desk. Occasionally, from the floor, Arnold would glance at a picture and say things like 'That marrow fed the Rogers family for a week,' while Veronica sorted between photographs and other bits of paper, from the flimsiest scraps to even a portrait of a kindly looking old man in a card mount that should have had a frame, 'Dear old Abel.'

'Move along a bit,' she said, forcing Arnold to move further from the gun.

'You won't find anything.'

'Humor me.'

Veronica was beginning to lose hope herself as the two little piles grew taller and in danger of being blown about by the breeze from the broken window. She looked for a paperweight. 'Oh, that'll do,' she said and picked up the gun and laid it across the two little piles on the desk, pushing them, and the gun, completely out of Arnold's reach.

Veronica removed the last photo from the board, a picture of a proud mum and a round-faced baby showing off its first tooth. *'Little Peter Carr, Nettlefield's Bonniest Baby, 1932. His mother says he's a terror on a trike, nowadays.'*

Arnold heaved himself up against the wall and picked up the gun. 'It's alright, I'm not going to do anything. You're right, it's the coward's way out.'

'I didn't say that.'

'No, but you looked it. I'm going to put it away.'

Just then, the wind whistled through the broken window, scattering the photos, clippings, and once-interesting scraps over the mess already on the floor.

'Well, we shall just have to gather more evidence,' said Veronica. 'I'm supposed to be with the orphans in the park, but I'll help you tidy up first.'

Arnold was on his way downstairs with the old gun.

Veronica picked up the empty manila folder and put each scattered photo and scrap of paper inside. When she came to the picture of the kindly looking old man, she noticed it was slipping out of its mount.

But it wasn't the picture of the old man that was slipping out.

Veronica pulled, and from between the layers of card and photograph, she pulled another photograph and a letter.

'What's that you've got there?' said Arnold from the door, now mercifully unarmed.

Veronica showed him a photograph taken from the office window. A picture of another window; the window over the street, on the first floor of the undertakers' shop, belonging to Ida's infamous Uncle Arthur.

Three men were standing at the window. The photograph captured a moment when all three were looking up, their faces clearly identifiable.

Arnold snatched the photograph and gasped, his face all joy. 'Clever girl, you found it! How could I have forgotten?' He read from the back: *'Arthur Underwood, Malcom Taggart, Heinrich Himmler, November 1936.'*

29

RETURN TO HEWETT ISLAND
Saturday 2nd April

BABY WATCHED the gold-braided sailor throw a rope around a post at the end of the jetty with the unfriendly 'Royal' sign. Was the King a Blackshirt too? But didn't the King's name begin with a G, not an E?

'Hurry up, man. We'll be running aground if you can't get your act together,' said Taggart, waiting by the steps in the boat.

Bill finished being sick over the side, dragged the back of his hand across his mouth and hauled Baby up to standing. Her bottom was numb after a night on the hard bench, strait-jacketed and gagged. She couldn't kick or even shout out.

On the jetty, the sailor nervously finished securing the rope. He straightened his cap and stood to attention. 'Ready to disembark, sir.'

With one foot on the first step, Taggart turned his attention to Bill, who was still guarding Baby, bound like a suet pudding by his side. 'Bag her up man, you don't think she's walking there of her own accord, do you? And the evidence, don't forget the evidence.'

'No, sir. Yes, sir.'

Evidence? What evidence? What would Taggart do with evidence?

From the box on the deck, Bill pulled out an old army bag, which he slung over his shoulder. It didn't appear to have much in it. He then pulled a rough sack from the same box on the deck and threw it over Baby's head.

As Bill twisted the top of the sack and grabbed it in his fist, Baby lost her balance and fell inside. The next thing she knew, she was upside down, itchy, and all she could smell was mould.

Slung in the bag over Bill's shoulder like a sack of potatoes—or one very big potato—Baby joggled against his back. She felt the bounce of the new jetty and wondered how deep the mud was. But before she could decide on a plan of action, she heard the mud squelch and Baby was on her feet again, her feet sinking into it.

Bill pulled the rough sack off, over Baby's head, grabbed the straitjacket straps and, leaving the jetty and the sack behind, dragged Baby across the mud. It was caking her shoes.

On firmer ground, the grass was wet. Her feet were now soaked, heavy with wet mud.

The island looked a lot bigger up close, more like a football field, but with swishy grass and clumps of brambles here and there. It *would* have been a nice place for a picnic, especially under a warm sun in a big blue sky with the gentle lap of the water. When the tide was properly in, of course.

'That is where we're going,' said Taggart. He waved his stick at the wooden shed in the middle of the island field. The same shed she saw that day with Fingers. It felt like an age ago.

Bill pulled her on through the grass and between the brambles. The wet grass cleaned most of the mud off her shoes. They were probably ruined but, at that moment, they were the least of her worries.

The hut had no windows, just that same unfriendly notice on a door padlocked with a shiny new lock. Taggart handed Bill a ring of keys.

Was this it? Were they just going to leave her here locked up in this island prison? What about the King?

Bill was still trying to find the right key.

'Hurry up, man,' barked Taggart. 'And pull that thing off. No one can hear her out here, anyway.'

'Yes, sir. Right, sir,' said Bill, dropping the keys and flinching as if he expected a whack from Taggart's cane.

Baby almost felt sorry for him as his fat fingers fumbled with the knot at the back of Baby's head.

Taggart hit the wall of the hut. 'Nothing,' he said, 'not you, nor your little band of communist friends, is going to stop me this time. I am making sure of it. Come on, man! Open up.' This time he did whack Bill.

Free at last of the horrible gag, Baby said, 'Why don't you do it yourself, then?'

'You think you're so clever, don't you?' said Taggart. 'But you're not. The irony is, by throwing a spanner in the works in '36, you'll need one ten times as big today. I have all the bases covered, as my misguided American niece might say.'

Who was he talking about? The only American Baby knew of, and very much wished she didn't, was that bossy know-it-all in Arnold Coombes's paper shop, now Brian's right-hand girl in the orphanage kitchen *and* Fingers's favourite person.

'Oh, you didn't know?' said Taggart. 'That young woman with no talent for disguise is my long-lost great-niece. You've met her, I'm sure. She's working for the lovely June Lovelock *and* the local rag. But when she knows how much money is involved, I'll bring her back on board. If there's one thing Americans prize above all else, it's hard cash.'

Bill finally opened the hut door, his rolled shirtsleeves showing off his muscle-bound arms as sweat trickled down his forehead.

With his gloved hands, Taggart grabbed the straps at Baby's back and threw her inside.

Baby landed on the wet grass and saw why the hut didn't need windows. It didn't have a roof.

His shirt untucked, but with his army bag still over his shoulder, Bill followed them inside.

'Bolt it,' ordered Taggart.

'Yes, sir,' said Bill, sliding a bolt across the top of the door, like the one in Underwood's yard on Queenie's stable. It was well out of Baby's reach.

The sun, like a spotlight, peeped through the grey clouds overhead. And in that spotlight, in the middle of the shed, wet from the rain, was a huge frame that, at the orphanage, could have been the beginnings of some interesting playground equipment. Except for the box fixed to its side and connected by wires.

And balanced on the frame, pointing in opposite directions, like a gigantic lopsided letter 'V', two rockets.

Bill pulled a pair of handcuffs from his trouser pocket.

'Good luck with those,' said Baby. Her arms were still wrapped inside the straitjacket, practically pasted to her body.

'You think you're so clever, don't you?' said Bill, parroting his master. He hooked the cuffs through the straps at her back and locked her to the frame—the rockets' launcher.

One rocket was huge; as big as Baby. The other was ENORMOUS; three, maybe four times as big as Baby.

Both rockets looked like something out of *Flash Gordon*, except that, on the ENORMOUS rocket, leather straps and buckles, thicker and heavier than those on her horrible straitjacket, were draped across the metal casing.

Taggart took a small black notebook from his inside pocket. Then he unclipped the lid of the box fixed to the rockets' launcher, which revealed the panel of dials, switches, and knobs that Baby last saw inside Queenie's stable. 'Ah, here we are,' he said, seeming to compare the switches, knobs, and dials with whatever was written in his notebook.

'What a magnificent display I'm preparing in your name!' He clicked his fingers at Bill. 'The evidence? Where is it?'

'Here, sir.' Bill struggled to open the flap on his bag, but when he did, he pulled out something that Baby knew very well indeed.

Her old green silk jacket.

'Where did you get that? You stole it, didn't you?' said Baby, frustrated that she couldn't accuse him with a poking finger.

'You be quiet, vermin.' But the old jacket slipped through Bill's clumsy fingers to the grassy floor, for which he felt another whack of Taggart's stick.

'In there, man. And quickly, we have a tide to catch. We, not you, of course,' said Taggart to Baby. He then lifted a small section of the huge rocket's metal casing for Bill to stuff it inside.

'What are you doing that for?' said Baby.

But with a horrible realisation, she knew.

Evidence. Planted evidence.

Taggart leaned on his stick. 'I'm going to tell you, because until Britain is part of the Third Reich, we are saved from war, and *I* have prevented any more young men needlessly sacrificing themselves, who else can I tell?'

'There's that lot at the pub,' said Baby. Her chest heaved at the injustice of the false evidence.

Taggart ignored Baby's helpful remark and went on. 'This rocket, with your famous green rag of a jacket to be found in the wreckage,' continued Taggart as if he were talking to a much larger audience, 'is destined for Nettlefield. The idea is that it will land on the Town Hall steps, but one can never be certain with these smaller missiles.'

'So, you want to save the men from war but not from being blown up when they're doing their normal jobs?' Baby ground her teeth.

Taggart wasn't interested in the obvious flaw in his thinking. 'Wherever it lands, the town council will be in disarray, so my team will be able to take over in that lovely new orphanage building while they sort themselves out. They never will, by the way. The orphans, those that meet the Aryan standards, will be re-homed with families sympathetic to the cause, either here or in Germany, as per our original plan.'

'But this one...' Taggart sauntered past Baby. With a flourish, he pointed his stick at the ENORMOUS rocket pointing the other way. '... calibrated to take account of its particularly troublesome load, this is what we've come for: the main show; the finale; the Royal Command Performance if you like, because at least one Royal is sympathetic to our cause. This beast will light up Portsmouth Dockyard for miles around and put paid to any naval defences that might hamper our German friends' arrival on these shores. And *you're* going to see it happen—the best view in town! Well, not quite, but that's a detail.'

He waved his stick at Bill, who'd been hanging on his every word. 'You know what to do.'

Bill fumbled again for the right key and unlocked the handcuffs tying Baby to the launcher.

Baby wriggled and squirmed, but without her arms to push and shove, her wriggling and squirming could only get her as far as the door, which was bolted out of her reach, if she had a reach.

Bill clamped his fat hands to her sides.

She kicked him anyway.

He picked her up and dumped her against the rocket's metal casing with a force that banged her head so hard the world spun for a few seconds.

Bill worked quickly, strapping Baby to the ENORMOUS rocket and buckling the straps so tight that Baby struggled to breathe.

Taggart watched approvingly.

'All done, sir,' said Bill, a horrible grin widening on his face.

Taggart opened a flap on the side of the box containing the control panel. Baby was strapped to the rocket too tightly to see, but heard him flick two switches, followed by a quiet but insistent and regular quiet tick, loud tick, quiet tick, loud tick... coming from the box. 'You have one hour before the British Navy and your reputation are blown to smithereens. Now we can't stand here chatting all day.'

Baby heard the bolt slide, the shed door open, the shed door shut, and the padlock on the outside click as it was locked.

And they were gone.

She was alone.

Alone, apart from the *tick tick* of the timer counting down her last hour on earth.

30

MEMORY
Saturday 2nd April

VERONICA LEFT ARNOLD tidying the office. Arnold's evidence had been safely tucked away where no one would dare look. The rain had stopped, so she hadn't bothered with her jacket. She ran along West Street in her shirtsleeves, dodging the puddles, and took the right turn down Tub Lane, just before the council offices Arnold had shown her.

All the while, she couldn't help wondering about what Archie had left her. The clipping, the passport, the copy of the *Beacon*. Had it really all been left by him or by somebody else? Why did it take Uncle Taggart so long to get around to finding Archie, and what was his plan for her now? Let alone what he was really doing here in Nettlefield, with the orphans and the Blackshirts. And then there was the girl she'd so terribly maligned, whom she'd actually accused of being a Nazi sympathiser. Where was she? Where was Baby? Veronica hoped to God she was safe.

As Veronica followed the road, the houses in Tub Lane got smaller and more squashed together. The road came to a dead end and only the sidewalk continued through a tunnel under the railway embankment into the park.

The park was wide enough to play baseball, or 'rounders', as the Brits called it. A path with railings ran along one edge of the field, separating it from the 'creek,' which was far more than the dribble of water that she was expecting and at that moment not smelling too bad.

Veronica headed across the wet grass towards a children's playground. Damp seeped up the leg of her pants. Beyond two watchful gulls, perched on the railings, she saw boats moored in an expanse of water that wound away into the distance.

Below the railings, water lapped on a small muddy 'beach.' She couldn't see the island that the girls spoke about back in The Lillie.

Behind her, across the field, a steep bank rose to the railway line which, just outside the park, connected with a tall arched bridge, a viaduct. She saw workmen with shovels on the viaduct. She had a very strong urge to climb the bank and bring the workmen down to safety. But told herself not to be silly, that was their job. They probably did it every day. She turned her attention to the creek water lapping gently onto the mud beneath the viaduct. All was well.

She looked for the children. She would welcome one of Brian's sandwiches, or something to drink at least.

The grass was too damp to sit down for a picnic, but she could hear the happy sound of play. One kid was being pushed on the roundabout by a woman in a jaunty hat and a tightly belted raincoat, probably the kid's mother. The small boy gripping the roundabout handles was shrieking with delight, making enough noise for half a dozen children. This boy was not one of the orphans. So where were they?

Veronica left the little family and trudged over the grass, looking for any sign of June, the orphans, or Gin pushing Mrs Lovelock in her wheelchair. She scanned the grass for crusts or crumbs from the picnic, but they had probably been enjoyed by the seagulls watching her from the railings.

Then Veronica spotted something the birds couldn't enjoy. By a bench at the foot of the embankment, a small bottle of Uncle Taggart's gifted lemonade soda was rolling about on the gravel path. So, the orphans had definitely been there.

She remembered the talk about the 'pictures'—the movie theatre in the middle of the main street. It was the alternative plan if it rained, and it had rained.

The bottle was still full of lemonade. It had a greenish tinge—a bit unusual for lemonade soda. But Veronica was thirsty, so she pulled out the stopper, anyway. It smelled like lemonade, but there was another smell that was quite heady, pleasant even. It gave her a lovely, woozy feeling.

Thirstily, she drank the whole bottle.

The men were still up there on the railway line, nearer to the viaduct now. Had she been here before, alone, looking up at a bridge? Where was that? When was that?

It was getting harder to focus.

She didn't like those people being up there, so near the edge. They could fall. Somebody was coming... another man... He was bad. She knew it! She wanted to warn them: *'Come down before you fall!'* Because they *were* going to fall. But her head was so heavy and when she opened her mouth, no sound came.

No, not fall. They were going to be pushed. The third man was going to push them off. She'd seen it before! Mama and Papa were on a bridge. They should be with her. But they had left her with Nanny. But Nanny had gone too. And Mama and Papa did fall. She watched them fall, down and down, coats flapping, like sails, not wings. She heard her name, tiny and far away: *'Veronicaaaaa!'* Mama and Papa couldn't fly away. They fell into the water. One, two splashes and they were gone. The third man was still on the bridge. Almost gone, walking away like nothing had happened.

She remembered. She'd run to the edge. She'd tried to find them. Where were they? But as hard as she looked at the river, she couldn't see them at all. Not even ripples. She could only see the water that closed them in.

Then somebody grabbed her arm. 'Veronica!' they said, then picked her up and carried her away from the water.

After that, she slept. A long sleep in a new bed. And then woke up with nothing in her head, nothing at all. Just a warm fire and cocoa, and a kind man.

Sleep was what Veronica wanted now. She laid down in the grass and weeds behind the park bench and hoped to dream of Archie.

31
BABY'S LAST HOUR
Meanwhile, Saturday 2nd April, Hewett Island

SHOULD BABY RISK trying to move? Risk pulling the straps loose? Risk dislodging the rocket and setting it off? She knew some exploding things didn't like movement. What would happen if she knocked the clock? Would that launch the rocket sooner? A thousand butterflies had made their home in her chest, wings fluttering with the *tick tick* of the countdown, and Baby had no idea what to do.

But she couldn't just wait there to be fired off like a rocket on fireworks night; a rocket more powerful than thousands of fireworks put together!

She was beginning to feel hot. The sun was shining directly on her. A drop of sweat from her forehead dripped into her eye.

The shed door rattled. Had they come back? Did they forget something? Maybe they didn't trust the timer and were going to send her off there and then? If that was the case, she was wriggling for her life.

A whisper came from the other side of the door. 'Baby, are you there?'

'Ida?' Baby was always pleased to hear Ida's voice, but never more so than now.

'Yes! I'm here with Alf. We followed Taggart's boat from Hamwell.'

'How? In the tugboat?'

'No, in Alf's boat!'

'Our boat!' said Alf's voice. 'How do we get in, Baby?'

'Over the top. The door's bolted!'

A moment later, Ida's head was blocking the sunlight. 'Oh, my word! What is that?'

'Ten thousand fireworks nights all at once,' said Baby. 'One huge rocket for Nettlefield Town Hall, he said, and an ENORMOUS one for Portsmouth Dockyard.'

Ida heaved herself over the shed wall and landed with a clanking of the spanners on her tool belt. 'Oh Baby, we've got to get you off there.'

The shed boards creaked as Alf heaved himself over after Ida. 'Hello Baby. We'll get you out, don't worry.' Sandy-haired and sun-brown from all his outdoor work on the tugboats at Southampton Docks, his big smile gave Baby confidence and the fluttering in her chest calmed down a bit.

'And stop these things from going off?' said Baby.

'We're going to do our best.' Alf had grown at least a foot and a half since she last saw him. Baby could see why Ida liked him. He was just like Mr Rogers from the garage; unflappable.

In matching overalls, Ida and Alf examined the control panel and the clocks beneath Baby, counting down the hour.

Over the regular, insistent *tick tick-ing* Baby could hear Ida and Alf whispering to each other. But she couldn't turn any further to see what they were doing. The straps were too tight.

Ida stood up and moved to where Baby could see her. 'It's not good,' said Ida. 'The two rockets are connected. Defusing one locks the other into its countdown. If we try to stop it, it launches immediately. Stop the clocks for both rockets, and they both launch immediately. Are you sure that Taggart said it was aimed at the Town Hall?'

'Yes,' said Baby. 'I'm sure 'e said that.' She didn't think it would help to say that Taggart wasn't sure how accurate that was and that he didn't care.

Alf towered over Ida. 'The best thing we can do is save you, Baby, and then go like the clappers to warn everyone. At least it's a Saturday and the Town Hall will be empty.'

'But West Street won't be!' said Ida.

Alf took a knife out of the top pocket of his overalls and sliced through all the straps on the rocket and the horrible jacket. With his powerful arms, he helped Baby onto her feet on the grassy shed floor.

She shook off the straitjacket and was free at last. Her own new blue jacket, like Letitia's, was creased and crumpled, but no matter. She patted the emergency pocket; it was intact. Though her back was sore from the straps and the ridges in the rocket's metal casing, with her arms freed, Baby felt like she could fly. She stamped Taggart's horrible straitjacket into the wet grass.

She tried to see what Ida was doing with her spanner, but Alf was in the way, seeming to help Ida lift a bit of the contraption away.

The loud ticks stopped. Baby gasped. She'd been holding her breath again. She swallowed back some more of the flutters in her chest. But the tick... tick of the other clock remained.

'There, the Royal Navy is safe,' announced Ida, dragging her hand across her forehead.

It was a relief to know that Portsmouth Dockyard and the Navy would be safe, but Nettlefield—where was everyone? Where were the orphans?

'By the time on the clock, we have forty minutes to warn Nettlefield,' said Ida.

'Well done,' said Alf gently squeezing Ida's shoulder.

Baby was sure he wanted to give her a kiss, but after gathering up her tools, Ida was on her feet and ready to go.

'Forty minutes,' said Ida.

'Right,' said Alf, locking his fingers together. 'You first, Baby.'

Baby put a foot in the step Alf made.

'Hold on.' And lifting her to his chest, he said, 'On my shoulders.'

Baby clung to the top of the shed wall. From Alf's shoulders, she hauled herself over the top and landed in long grass on the other side.

Ida landed beside her with the clanking of her tool belt.

'Where's your boat?' asked Baby.

Ida grabbed Baby's sleeve, now ripped from the shed's splintery new wood. 'This way,' she said, dodging brambles, heading for the other side of the island.

Baby heard a thump and rattle of the shed wall as Alf clambered over.

'This is *our* boat,' she said, proudly pointing to a small boat freshly painted blue and yellow, with a little cabin, and the name *The Wonder* painted on the side in fancy black letters. 'I helped him with the motor.'

'Thirty-two minutes,' said Alf running past them, his long strides worth two of Baby's. 'I'll get her started. The tide's nearly out!'

The Wonder was bobbing in a narrow channel of water in the middle of the mud.

'How are we going to get across?' said Baby. If she ran really quick, like scarpering-from-the-coppers-quick, maybe she'd barely touch the mud and not sink at all?

But Ida and Alf were already lugging a load of fence slats onto the muddiest bit.

'What are you doing?' said Baby.

'Making a bridge!' said Ida.

They were and all! The slats stayed on top of the mud without sinking and she remembered the old cockle digger telling her and Fingers about his bits of board.

'Got to be quick,' said Alf. 'We're down to twenty-five minutes. The mud bridge will last just long enough for us to get to the boat. I'll go first, so I can give you two a leg up on board.'

'Aye, aye, Cap'n,' said Ida. No sooner said than done, all three were in the boat motoring through the channel to Nettlefield and Tub Lane Recreation Ground.

'Twenty minutes!' said Ida over the noise of the motor. 'D'you think we'll make it?'

But Alf was busy steering *The Wonder* through the creek's narrow channel, getting narrower the further they went.

'Twenty minutes—that's half the time gone!' said Baby. But they'd done so much already, stopping the big rocket, escaping from Taggart's secret shed, getting to the boat across a mud bridge... So there had to be enough time to save Nettlefield too, didn't there?

She hadn't told Ida and Alf how Taggart was trying to frame her. She had to get there and find her old jacket before any more Blackshirts tried to use it against her. It didn't matter that it was ridiculous that she, Baby, would never have set the rocket off. How could she have possibly done that? But they and their old Blackshirt paper would twist it so folk would believe whatever Taggart and his lot wanted them to believe, no matter how stupid.

Ida checked her watch. 'Seventeen minutes.' She sat on the edge of the seat, tapping her hand nervously against her leg.

'It's just round this bend. You'll see the Tub Lane Rec in a minute,' said Alf, at the helm, steering *The Wonder* through the shrinking channel.

And sure enough, there was the park, 'The Rec.' Baby could see the railway line above and the viaduct rising up out of the mud.

The little boat chugged along. If they weren't under such pressure, Baby would be loving this boat trip; the comfy seats painted in bright yellow and blue stripes to match the boat. There were even matching cushions. And the lovely view. From this angle, Nettlefield didn't look so bad. The creek, however, was turning to its horrible, stinking mud. Just the narrowest channel of water remained.

'Sophie helped with the decorating,' explained Ida, her hands nervously clenched into fists. Both girls were training in Bournemouth; Ida doing mechanics, and Sophie tailoring and sewing. 'Did you meet Veronica? She's marvellous. She knows she can come across a bit strong sometimes, but it's because she's as keen to stop the fascists as you are, Baby. She's just like us, one of the gang.'

If Baby was honest with herself, she knew that. How could she be jealous of another sister? Well, that was easy, but it didn't make it right.

'Oh no,' said Ida. 'Twelve minutes! If we run really fast...'

But at that moment, they heard a scraping sound, and the boat juddered to a halt.

Ida gripped the sides, her face a mixture of terror and determination. 'Noooo!'

'Oo-ooh,' said Alf. 'I knew we were cutting it fine with the tide.'

Baby could see the park railings. She was pretty sure that if her arms were about ten times longer and she had the strength of ten Alfs, she could reach the railings and pull the boat across the mud. If only.

They were going to be too late. Would it be all her fault? No.

'I've got to go.' Baby had one leg on the step.

Ida climbed onto the bench, ready to leap over the side with Baby. The boat was leaning with their weight when they all heard a whistling sound over their heads.

Baby, Ida and Alf together looked up, shading their eyes against the sun.

On target for a busy Saturday afternoon in Nettlefield's West Street was Taggart's rocket.

32

WHERE ARE THE ORPHANS?
Saturday 2nd April, Afternoon

'Veronica! Veronica! Wake up! Where are the kids?' A voice was coming from somewhere. Was it inside or outside her head? She couldn't decide.

Veronica felt a hand gripping her shoulder, shouting in her ear. Something terrible had just happened. She felt it in her dream, the earth beneath her shaking.

The sun was shining in her eyes and the creek smell was making them water. She squinted at three heads in shadow against the brightness.

'Where are they? Gin said they'd be here! Who's taken them? Who's taken Bonnie?' Ida was shaking her awake with a muddy wet hand.

A man, a young man, was with her. And so was that poor girl, Baby. Where did they come from? They all looked and smelled like creatures from the swamp. Mud dripped from their sodden clothes. And yes, where were the kids?

She sat up. Apart from the three muddy young people, the rest of the park was deserted. She had a memory of something; the smell of the bottle, and yes... that memory. Her mother and father, murdered. She couldn't find an answer to Ida's question. 'I don't know...' She searched past that one monstrous memory for where the orphans should be... and found it. 'The movies! They said they might go to the movies if it rained!'

Ida clapped a muddy hand over her mouth. 'No!'

'What's happened?' Fear gripped Veronica like a finger pressing into her throat.

'I can't believe it didn't wake you up!' said Baby, muddy water dripping from her skirt as she paced backwards and forwards behind the young man.

'What didn't wake me up?' Veronica's throat was so tight she could barely speak.

'A rocket,' explained the young man calmly. 'A bomb has landed somewhere in West Street. We've stopped the biggest one that was going for all the navy's battleships over in Portsmouth. But we couldn't stop the other. We need to go and help.'

It was bad, very bad, but the young man's calmness restored her. This was not the time to be paralysed by fear.

'We can't hang about 'ere. Come on, MOVE!' said Baby.

'It's Taggart, Uncle Taggart, isn't it? It's all him,' said Veronica, heaving herself up. Whatever was in that lemonade was still trying to drag her down. 'The lemonade the kids had was drugged...'

'What?' said Ida, flinging her arms up. 'That means they could be anywhere! It's happening again! How could we let it happen again?'

'Look!' said Baby, pointing to the road just outside the park turnstile, where two black vans were parked. A man in a black shirt was leaning against one of them, smoking a cigarette. 'That's Underwood's van.'

'They're in there!' said Ida. 'Bonnie!' She hared across the damp field to the park turnstile.

Baby ran after her and grabbed Ida's arm.

Veronica caught up with them both as the black-shirted man was stubbing out his cigarette with his heel.

'Shhh,' said Baby. '*Think*, Ida. What's 'e doing hanging around outside if there's a load of kids inside? Wouldn't those Blackshirts have left already, if they had 'em?'

'That's a really good point, Ida,' said Veronica.

Baby flashed Veronica a glance that had none of the resentment of a few days ago in the orphanage kitchen.

The driver of the other van was sitting in the driver's seat. Veronica could just see a newspaper, undoubtedly the *Beacon*, spread out on the steering wheel.

'But what if they are, and we're just letting them go?' said Ida, still pulling away.

The Blackshirt checked his watch, then glanced in their direction.

Baby hid behind Veronica. 'Just look normal,' she whispered. 'I don't recognise 'im, so 'e might not know us.'

Veronica wondered how Baby and Ida, caked in drying mud, could possibly look normal. 'I'm sorry...' she whispered over her shoulder as she and Baby edged closer to the waiting Blackshirts. 'We hit it off on the wrong foot. I was wrong. We're on the same side, aren't we?'

'You're right, we are. And I'm sorry too,' said Baby. Veronica wanted to say, *What for?* What could Baby have to be sorry for? But more than that, Veronica wanted to know if she could be forgiven for her misjudged *Courier* report? Did Baby even know about it, and could Veronica confess to it if Baby didn't?

But Veronica couldn't ask any of these things because the Blackshirt who'd been smoking was climbing into his van, signalling to the other driver, and starting the engine. Ida threw up her hands, and all three watched in dismay as the two Blackshirt vans drove away.

Alf was running to join them. 'It's alright, sort of,' he said. 'The park keeper said the nippers definitely went to the pictures. He said that June Lovelock left him with a message for you, Veronica, but he was sorry that it being a Saturday, he had a longer than usual tea break.'

'What! Saturday's his busiest day,' said Ida.

'Yes,' said Alf, 'I think that's why he had a long tea break. Hadn't we better get up West Street, find Bonnie, and see how we can help?'

'What are we waiting for? Come on!' said Baby, heading for the turnstile.

'No, Tub Lane's better,' said Alf, beckoning them in the opposite direction.

Ida sprinted after Alf and in no time had caught up with him.

Baby grabbed Veronica's hand. 'This way I'll show you,'

With Baby's hand round hers, in the lingering aroma of creek mud, Veronica knew that she and Baby were probably going to be okay.

Somewhere between the tunnel under the railroad and the centre of town, Veronica lost Baby. People were milling about all over West Street, craning their necks to see what was going on at the Town Hall. A dust cloud hung over their heads. Veronica tasted soot and smelled burning. A tram was stuck as far back as the church. She had completely lost sight of Ida and Alf, too. They had all disappeared into the crowd.

Men and women in new tin hats with ARP painted in white were trying to bring some order to the chaos. She heard a policeman's whistle, but nobody was taking any notice.

A white van with a big red cross painted on the doors was trying to get through the crowd. The driver stuck his head out of the window. He was honking the horn and cussing at anybody within hailing distance. 'Get outta the way, you idiots! This is an emergency!'

Veronica felt sick at the thought of the casualties. She put her thumb and first finger to her lips and whistled as hard as she did when Archie took her to see the Yankees beat the Boston Red Sox 4-1. As it did back in '35, the crowd turned as one to see where the eardrum-piercing shrill had come from.

'What is the matter with you people?' said Veronica at the top of her voice. 'Can't you see?' She pointed to the ambulance. 'He needs to get through.'

As the crowd parted like the Red Sea in the Bible, she saw what had happened.

The Town Hall was rubble. Only half of one column remained. Standing on the top step was Mrs Allemby, the council cleaning lady. Her hair made a halo of shock around her face. She looked very confused, holding a ring of keys in one hand and a new mop in the other; its price tag flapped from the handle like a little flag.

Veronica wished she had Arnold's camera, but then remembered what had happened to it. Where was Arnold? Was he alright?

From the other end of the street, a fire truck was trying to make its way past a trolley bus, and at last a siren somewhere blasted out a warning, which sent a wave of panic through the crowd. 'A bit late, but we'll get the hang of it,' said an ARP man. 'Now move yourselves along here.'

Arnold, though, was more than alright. He was crouching on the steps with a very old-fashioned camera taking a picture of Mrs Allemby, who he'd just posed to look like The Statue of Liberty. That was until the ambulance driver moved him on. But the lady was beginning to look like she was enjoying the attention.

'Veronica!' Arnold ran down the bottom few steps with the energy of someone half his age. 'They forgot about this one,' he said, showing her the camera, which was little more than a small, scruffy box. 'Father's Box Brownie, Arch and I had fun with it when we were boys. I think I've got one or two good shots.'

'Arnold, I've remembered what happened to my parents. You can guess, can't you? And Archie did save me.'

'Thank you.' Arnold squeezed Veronica's arm. 'Yes, I can guess your Uncle Taggart had a hand or two in it. We'll talk later. I'm going to get a few more shots and some eyewitness accounts—always good for sales. People love seeing their names in the paper.'

'Was anyone hurt?' It was a positive sign that she hadn't seen anyone on stretchers.

'No, thank heavens. Saturday, so none of the council was at work, though if it had been a minute earlier, Mrs Allemby would have been a goner...'

And as if on cue, Mrs Allemby—Lady Liberty with her mop—was being guided past them by another ARP man. It was the kind man that Veronica recognised as Mr Rogers from the garage who rescued them all the other night.

'I hope you got my good side, Mr Coombes,' said Mrs Allemby.

'No doubt about that, Mrs A.'

'Arnold, can you take this for me and keep it safe?' said Mr Rogers, passing him a bundle of charred green rags from inside his jacket. 'Could be misleading for the police when they get round to sorting through the rubble.'

'Ah, Baby's famous jacket. I see what you mean. I know a good place for it,' said Arnold.

Mr Rogers offered Mrs Allemby his arm. 'Let's get you a nice hot cup of sweet tea, Mrs A.'

Veronica felt like she'd caught some of Alf's calmness when she realised all that had been blown up was the empty Town Hall. Empty of people anyway. She guessed it would be inconvenient for a while, but whenever she'd walked past the Town Hall, it looked like it had been falling down, anyway.

The crowd was dispersing, though some folks were taking the opportunity to get a closer look at the rubble. Veronica had seen enough for now. It was time to find Ida, Baby, Alf and the rest of the gang, so she made her way through the crowd of spectators, towards The Embassy cinema.

She was just passing the alley to Mrs Tatler's and The Blue Bonnet pub, when a hand clamped over her shoulder. Another locked her arms behind her back.

A sweet heady smell, but sharp like lemonade, made her eyes prick and her head swim.

Oh no, not again, was her last thought before everything went black.

33

REUNION, ALMOST
Saturday 2nd April

WEST STREET WAS THICK WITH PEOPLE; Cable Street all over again. Except that some people, those that had them, mostly kids, were wearing their gas masks. Baby hunched her shoulders, ready to barge through the crowd. The others were behind her somewhere.

She tugged on the sleeve of a street-sweeper, leaning on his cart. 'What's happened?'

'Someone's gone and blown up the council!' he said with a chuckle.

'Is anybody hurt?'

'No, they all get Saturday off, don't they? Not like the rest of us.'

Most of the knots of worry inside Baby loosened, but there was still her old green jacket. Maybe it was destroyed by the explosion? Maybe Taggart wasn't as clever as he thought he was. She had no idea how she was going to find it. All she could see were peoples' backs, right in the way of where she wanted to go.

She climbed a lamp post outside the police station. At last, she could see what was going on. Mr Coombes was on the council steps, taking pictures of Mrs Allemby, the council charlady, of all people. The steps and half a post seemed to be all that was left. Mrs Allemby looked in a bit of a state, and behind her was Mr Rogers, who spotted Baby and gave her the thumbs up. What did that mean?

A siren blasted. Was another rocket on its way? One that she didn't know about? But an ARP man running by, his gas mask bouncing on his chest, told everyone not to panic.

Baby wasn't panicking. She thought she'd done enough of that for the day. Until she saw something that gave her heart a flutter and nearly made her lose her grip on the lamp post.

Fingers was weaving her way through the crowd, dragging a person that looked like the person Fingers would become in another twenty years or so. The person had the same ginger bird's nest curly head of hair; very easy to spot in a crowd, but unlike Fingers, she was fashionably and smartly dressed. The two of them were heading away from the bomb site.

Was that why Fingers hadn't come to look for her? Because Baby was sure that if Fingers had made up her mind to look for Baby, Fingers, by hook or by crook, would have found her. Had she found someone new instead? Or not just someone...

The jealousy that had been directed at Veronica was now looking for another home, but Baby batted it away. She was done with that. She knew this would happen sometime, no matter how far her and Fingers ran. All she had to do was make sure the woman wasn't a Blackshirt too.

'Baby.' Mr Rogers was looking up at her. A dazed Mrs Allemby was leaning on his arm. 'I was trying to tell you. I found your jacket. It's safe. And don't worry, of course I know this is nothing to do with you.'

'Thanks,' said Baby, climbing down the lamp post. 'Have you seen...?' She was going to ask him if he'd seen any of the others, but he was already pressing his way through the crowd with Mrs Allemby.

What did Veronica say? They were going to the pictures, and that looked like the direction that Fingers and grown-up Fingers were going, anyway. So, Baby climbed down and barged through with her elbows, ignoring the protests of the crowd.

But that was when Baby caught sight of Veronica's flashy turquoise scarf and her muddy grass-stained white shirt.

And two black-sleeved arms dragging Veronica into the pub alley.

'Veronica!' Just as she shouted, the crowd suddenly surged with excitement.

'Have you heard about the five-pound notes in the rubble?' someone said.

'Five-pound notes?'

'You bet! A small fortune's going begging.'

The crowd rushed forward, pushing Baby with it. She'd lost sight of Veronica and Fingers already. Had the Blackshirts got them both?

The only way was to go with the crowd. She surged with it, past Doswells' Department Store. Round the corner into High Street, a lot of the Town Hall was still standing, propped up by the scaffolding. She scooted past it and up the old street until she could turn off for the back of the shops and the other end of the pub alley.

The Blue Bonnet was deserted; the door open and chairs kicked over in the rush for five-pound notes, probably. Where was Veronica? Where was Fingers? Where was anyone?

Along the alley, outside Mrs Tatler's door, she heard the booming voice of Sir Malcolm Taggart, making a victory speech, followed by foot-stomping applause. Baby wanted to barge through that door and challenge the whole lot of them, but for once, caution stopped her. Because she had a better idea. She had learned from Ida Barnes's impulsiveness.

Veronica was in Tatler's with them, that was for sure. Was one little brown girl going to get her out and put the whole damn lot of Blackshirts in jail where they belong?

Yes, by using her brain.

And her contacts.

Baby zipped down the alley. Against the shop fronts, she pressed through the crowd to the Courier. She tried the handle, but it was locked for once. She knocked and rattled the door.

Mr Clarence was grabbing the last of his outside display. 'Arnold's out with his camera,' he said, before he closed the door and flipped the sign to '*Closed*'.

It was no good. She had to do it. Baby could have really used one of Mr Clarence's brooms. There had to be one in there. Then she remembered—she was still wearing Fingers's skirt! She riffled through all the pockets and found the wire.

She was wiggling the wire around, the way Fingers taught her, when she felt a hand on her shoulder.

'It would be easier with this,' said Arnold Coombes, reaching over her and putting his key in the lock.

'They've got Veronica.'

'Where?'

'Tatler's.'

He thrust the ancient box camera he was carrying at her. 'Look after this.'

Baby grabbed his arm. 'Stop, I've got a much better idea. You have got a telephone, haven't you?'

'I have, and I've moved it back upstairs. Follow me.' Arnold took Baby through the shop, up the stairs to the office where the floor was covered in rubbish.

Houdini the parrot was screeching, 'READ ALL ABOUT IT! READ ALL ABOUT IT!'

Arnold threw a tattered piece of green silk over the cage.

'My jacket!' said Baby.

'Syd Rogers found it in the rubble. I didn't think you'd want it back.' Arnold picked his way through piles of paper on the floor. 'I was clearing up when the rocket hit. It was a rocket, wasn't it? I've read about the V2s. There's the phone.' He pointed to a telephone on his desk, acting as a paperweight on two piles of newspaper cuttings and old photos. 'It's old, but it works.'

'Thank you,' said Baby and reached inside her jacket. Some of the creek mud had now dried. Shame about the rip, but Baby was pleased the mud brushed off at least. She undid the emergency button on the emergency pocket. It was tight. She hadn't used it before. She had, of course, had the direst of emergencies in the last few days, but no access to a telephone.

Baby unfolded the neat little piece of paper and smoothed out the creases in a space on the desk. She knew the code but was sworn to secrecy. So, after asking Arnold to turn away, she decoded Letitia's neat hand.

To the sound of what could only be Blackshirt jeers from the street, she lifted the receiver off its stand and dialled.

34
TAGGART'S PERSUASION
Saturday 2nd April

THE SMALL CROWD of black-shirted fascists Uncle Taggart had been addressing stomped out of Mrs Tatler's boarding house under the impression they'd blown up the British Navy. With her arms tied to the back of the chair in the front parlour, Veronica now sat under the gazes of forbidding long-dead Victorians framed on the old Blackshirt woman's damp walls. She remembered what Alf had told her and wanted so badly to tell Uncle Taggart that his plan had failed. But perhaps he should believe in his victory? For a little while, at least.

He sat in front of Veronica, leaning on a cane in his Fifth Avenue suit, a silk handkerchief flopping lazily out of the top pocket. He occupied the space more densely that anyone had the right to, so out of place in the budget boarding house.

The fascist old lady bobbed around Uncle Taggart with a sickly smile for him, and a sneer for Veronica. She opened her mouth to speak.

But he silenced her with a white-gloved finger to his lips and then addressed Veronica, his remaining captive audience. 'Here we are at last, Veronica. Or should I say *Euphemia*? Because that is your name.'

'I prefer Veronica.'

'Well, *Veronica*, I am hoping to persuade you to see sense.' He beckoned Mrs Tatler. 'Give me the paper.'

Mrs Tatler handed him a folded copy of not the *Beacon*, but the *Courier*. Veronica recognised the front-page headline. It was this week's edition. She felt a flutter of worry.

Taggart, he was no uncle to her, opened the paper to the ad pages, then held them for her to see. There it was; her story. How many more unedited copies were out there?

'You've proved yourself. This is the sort of creative journalism we want,' said Taggart, pushing Veronica's report about Baby in her face. 'Though perhaps with a different angle.'

'How did you get that? It was a mistake, unresearched. I was wrong.'

Taggart laughed. 'You say that, but isn't this the real Veronica?'

'No.' She rocked the chair and tried to stand, tried to pull her hands out of the ropes, but the black-shirted oaf in the corridor had tied them to the chair and each other. Her rocking only brought her closer to the man she despised. Now in his face so she could see every bristle on his chin, she added, 'And I would never ever, ever, EVER, work for you.'

'We'll see,' said Taggart, a smile curling the corners of his mouth. 'Would you believe that your ridiculous parents made me your godfather?'

'Is that why you had them killed? Because they were ridiculous? Because you did have them killed, didn't you?' She mimicked his occasional mock-Scottish accent.

'In a word, yes. Their notions were ridiculous. Your father, my nephew, wanted to *donate*...' he spat out the word like sour milk, '... *all* their money. The family fortune that should have been mine, for *my* boys...' He clenched his gloved hand round the top of the cane. 'Had I been born minutes earlier... Howard and his fool of a wife were so naïve. They thought that propping up one bank would prevent the '29 crash. They were just like their father, my elder by minutes, my *brother*.' Another sour word in his mouth. 'They had to be stopped.'

So, not two, but three sets of twins, in this story. Archie and Arnold, Taggart's sons, and now Taggart and his own twin brother. People said twins had a special connection. Was there also a weird universal force that drew *sets* of twins together for ill as well as good?

'But there's you,' continued Taggart. 'Although that ne'er-do-well Coombes, Parker, whatever he wanted to call himself, thwarted my rescue mission.'

'Rescue? What rescue?'

'Rescuing a fortune, of course.'

'You killed him too.' She blinked back the tears stinging her eyes. She must not show this man her weakness.

'A consequence of insubordination. He'd finally fulfilled his purpose.'

'And what was that?'

'When he didn't do what he was paid to do, I thought his punishment,' he gestured the inappropriateness of the word, 'could be babysitting you. I decided to wait and see if you turned out to be as stupid as your parents. After all, I would need an heir.'

Veronica tugged at the ropes behind her back. She could feel her anger churning inside her again. How Archie was used. How he was manipulated. Although she could now remember her parents and the terrible thing that happened to them, it was Archie who inhabited their place in her heart.

'You may have followed my trail of crumbs, but you are not as wet as those parents of yours. They couldn't do a damn thing right and that included raising you. In the end, Coombes did me some good.' Taggart leaned back in his own stiffly upholstered chair as if there was not another word to say on the matter.

Though rage clawed at her insides, Veronica realised that being aggressive was not helping her situation. Taggart had tried to kill her before, and here she was, tied up at his mercy. *And* she'd just told him in no uncertain terms that she'd *never ever* work for him... What choice did he have, but finally to get rid of her? Could she keep him talking until she could think of a way out? She changed tack. 'Your sons died, didn't they? In the last weeks of the war?'

'Yes, my sons died.'

Veronica was surprised to see his eyes glistening as he leaned forward again, this time more heavily on his cane.

'Their mother too.'

Mrs Tatler had silently entered the room and now stood behind him, her hand hovering over his shoulder as if to comfort him.

But in an instant, his expression turned to anger. Any tears he might have had were soaked into the lines on his face. His eyes narrowed and his lips pressed together like a clamp. After a long breath out through his nostrils that might have snorted fire in a different story, he spoke again. 'Yes, they died, and it is now my mission to prevent war at all costs.' He spoke as if he were addressing a rally, not one captive girl and a sycophantic old lady. 'I will not go through another.'

'But you've blown up the British Navy!' she lied. 'How is that not an act of war?'

'To *prevent* a war. Without a navy, Britannia won't be able to defend herself and there will be a transition of power to Herr Hitler and peace will reign. And the warmongers who run this country, who sent hundreds of thousands of young men to their deaths, will get their just desserts. So, as I was saying, you, Veronica, are now my heir.'

'Wouldn't I have inherited, anyway?'

'Under normal circumstances, yes. But the legalities over your disappearance, time lapses, and your age meant that the fortune came to me. But as I have since had much success making my own considerable fortune, it is not as necessary to me as it once was. And as you are such an aspiring young journalist, I want you on board. Don't waste yourself on provincial rags like the *Courier*.' He flapped Arnold's paper in her face before tossing it across the room.

Mrs Tatler scurried over and picked it up.

'Coombes,' said Taggart, 'is a hack, with no ambition. You could make a real, lasting difference at the *Beacon*. You could turn this country around. We have barely scratched the surface of the power that we, in the media, can wield. You could help me be the agent of peace. What do you say?'

The agent of peace. That sounded good to Veronica.

For one microsecond. Perhaps only half a microsecond.

This was how newspapers worked, newspapers like the Beacon. Their power was not in truth, but in persuasion. Manipulation. And she knew enough truth that a Nazi peace would not mean peace at all. Certainly not for anyone who didn't match their Aryan standards or who disagreed with their ideas.

'What about the children? What's happening to them?'

'What children?'

'The orphans. You don't really want their stories for the paper, do you?'

'Oh, those children. On the contrary, I want the stories their lives will write once they are happily placed with families committed to the cause. They are orphans. How can finding them families be bad? To succeed, I need the ear of Nazi High Command, and children are a very important part of that ultimate solution to the world's ills. Providing Herr Himmler, and so the Führer, with a steady supply of the right sort of children from Britain, will ensure my and, if you want it, your place in history.'

The *right sort* of children.

'What about the wrong sort of children? The wrong sort of people?'

'Every successful scheme to make the world better will come with collateral damage.'

She'd heard the rumours, knew what that meant. Not war, but death. The thought that, even for a microsecond, Taggart's words had found a place in her consideration made Veronica want to vomit. She hated the man, the monster sitting opposite her.

She used the only weapon left to her, her voice. She couldn't help herself. Wisely or not, she screamed, 'Never! Never! Never! NEVER!', until her throat was hoarse. And then she screamed some more. She felt Mrs Tatler's cold, bony hand over her mouth. Veronica bit it and screamed again, for her life, for the lives of everyone who didn't fit that Aryan ideal.

She was sure Mrs Tatler wailed, but Veronica didn't hear it as the old woman disappeared to the kitchen, nursing her hand.

Veronica watched Taggart stand silently, put his cane under his arm and leave the room.

In a moment of silence between screams, she heard him say to the oaf on guard at the door, 'Kill her. Do it now.'

35

Too Late

Saturday 2nd April

THE TATLER FRONT DOOR was on the latch. Baby slipped through and ran on tiptoes through the old cabbage-smelling hall to the kitchen and found Mrs Tatler at the kitchen table trying to bandage her hand with a tea cloth.

'Get out, vermin!' she screeched.

But Baby took no notice. 'Where is she?'

'Who? That filthy girl? You're too late.'

Baby's heart leapt to her throat. She couldn't be too late! She hadn't explained why she was jealous. She hadn't asked her about America. She hadn't told her story!

Baby heard the front door slam. Somewhere on the ground floor of the house, she heard Veronica, her accent unmistakable. 'Go on then, do it. Though if you fire it like that, it'll blow your hand off and everyone will hear. You haven't fired a gun before, have you? And I should know, I come from the land of cowboys and gunslingers. For all your big guy act, you're just a lily-livered coward.'

Baby couldn't help smiling; the girl really was a Wonder-and-a-half! Baby grabbed the nearest thing off Mrs Tatler's hall stand—a horrible old jug with an ugly face—and burst into the old lady's front parlour. She leapt onto the would-be murderer's back and bashed the jug against his own ugly head.

With a noise like a raspberry jelly would sound if it could speak, Bill Teasdale toppled to the ground, and the gun fell out of his hand.

'We meet again!' said Baby. 'You have been busy today.'

But Bill was nursing his head and groaning on the floor.

Baby dropped the jug.

It smashed into pieces on the hard parquet floor.

'Oops,' said Baby.

'Thanks,' said Veronica. 'The safety catch was still on, anyway,' and kicked the gun across the floor out of Bill's reach. 'I'm sure glad to see you, Baby!'

'Likewise,' said Baby, sitting astride the would-be murderer, now face down on the floor. She yanked on his arm and twisted it behind his back. 'Bill Teasdale, you're as feeble as your brother. How did you get here so quick, eh? Don't bother, I don't care. They're coming for you now and it won't be no few months' holiday in jail. You're for it!'

'Oh yeah?' said Bill, trying to sound tough but sounding exactly like his brother William. 'The coppers do what 'is lordship says in Nettlefield.'

'The coppers might, but the SOE don't,' said Baby. 'Special Operations Executive,' she explained for Veronica.

Veronica's mouth was open but the only words she could find were, 'Hh... how do you...?'

Then the front door crashed open and boots stomped inside.

'In 'ere!' shouted Baby.

'Hello, Wonder-in-chief!' came a familiar voice from the hall.

'Harry!' said Baby, feeling extra-warm inside.

Harry Miller, beau to June Lovelock, and long-time friend to the Wonders, as he called them, was standing there in uniform.

'How did you know?' said Baby.

'The call came through and a load of us were at the dockyard already for some training. Fleet Air Arm. That's me, nowadays.' He tapped his nose in a hush hush way. 'The British Navy's air force, if you like,' he explained for Veronica, whose mouth was still wide open. 'Here, let me.' Harry grabbed Bill's arms, slapped a pair of cuffs round his wrists, and hauled him up.

Bill whimpered like, in Veronica's words, the 'lily-livered coward' that he was.

Through the open door, Baby saw Mrs Tatler being led away by a woman in a similar uniform to Harry's.

Harry tossed Baby a penknife. 'Can you do the honours while I keep hold of this one?'

Baby flicked the knife open and cut through the rope binding Veronica.

'Thank you, sir,' said Veronica, and introduced herself. She rubbed her wrists before offering Harry her hand. 'My Uncle Taggart skedaddled only about ten minutes ago.'

'Yes, we've got him,' said Harry. 'You've done it again, girls! Well done! And not letting on that he missed the dockyard meant he wasn't expecting us. Genius move!' Harry finally let go of Veronica's hand. 'By my estimations, the rest of us should be turning up at the orphanage in about twenty minutes.' With Bill still in his grip, Harry beckoned Baby and Veronica out of Tatler's front parlour. 'And there's another platoon on their way to Hamwell. I vote we catch the end of Snow White at The Embassy. There's more than enough of us to deal with the interlopers at Nettlefield Grange.'

'Where?' asked Veronica, who looked a bit dazed and unsteady.

'Nettlefield Grange is the proper name for the orphanage,' said Baby. 'Are you alright?'

'I'm sure I'll be fine,' said Veronica, swaying a little. 'Really. Let's just get out of here.'

Baby, with her eye on Veronica, followed Harry and the captive Bill out of old lady Tatler's horrible boarding house and into West Street, where another crowd had gathered. This time not gawping at the rubble of the Town Hall but at Harry's favourite and, it seemed, quickest way of getting about.

'What. Is. That?' said Veronica.

36

Rendezvous
Saturday 2nd April, Afternoon

VERONICA WAS VERY IMPRESSED at the forces Baby could command when necessary. The arrest and detainment of Uncle Taggart and his minions, thugs, reporters, fanatics, hangers-on, whatever they were, was a full-scale military operation. All she could think was that this was going to make a great story, if she'd ever be allowed to tell it, because she gathered that the SOE—the Special Operations Executive—was all spies and secret agents; serious stuff. And if she was allowed to tell it, when and which paper would it be for?

She'd been wondering how the military—the *spies*—got here so quickly. The thing in West Street looked so flimsy, a cross between a bicycle, a baby's pram and a windmill. 'Does it actually fly?'

'It's called a gyrocopter and yes, it certainly does,' said Harry. 'You just ask Ida. You know Ida? Do you want a go? Rog and Lillian came in one a little bigger. It's down the street, on the church green.'

Veronica really like the idea of flying, *in theory*. But she thought she'd check that out with Ida first.

'I ain't going in, that!' said Bill the Blackshirt oaf, which raised lots of laughs and jeers from the many bystanders gathered round the gyrocopter, and generally milling about in the street. *Ha! Told you your big mouth would get you into trouble, Bill Teasdale! Lock 'im up and throw away the key! Down with The Blackshirts!*

With a firm grip on Blackshirt Bill's arm, Harry marched him through the parting crowds to where the jolly police officer Veronica met over a week ago was waiting under the blue police light. 'You'll go where you're put,' said Harry. 'And I wouldn't have your dirty Blackshirt behind in my 'copter, anyway.'

The jolly police sergeant cheerfully took custody of the prisoner.

'Here you are, Ted, you know what to do with this one.'

'I most certainly do,' said Sergeant 'Ted', grabbing Prisoner Teasdale by the collar.

So, the cops couldn't all be bad.

A woman in a similar military uniform to Harry's delivered Prisoner Tatler, handcuffed and cursing, which prompted a few more jeers from the crowd. *Save your breath for the judge, Doris Tatler! Good job you ain't wearing your old hat; there ain't a cell big enough! It's not fair, she'll get better grub inside!* All of which made the jolly policeman even jollier.

'*Snow White*, then the orphanage for a debrief, I think,' said Harry.

Evidently, it was alright to leave the gyrocopter in the street under police and ARP guard, 'the good ones' according to Harry.

'And I just need to fetch something,' said Veronica.

The Courier's office was in much the same state as it had been when she left it earlier in the day. It was also deserted. The cloth had fallen off Houdini's cage again, but the bird was quietly perching, probably worn out with all the excitement. 'Arnold! Are you in?' she called.

'Yes, down here!' came a muffled voice from downstairs.

Veronica followed the voice.

'I'm in the darkroom, hang on a mo,' said Arnold.

Veronica waited patiently by the silent printing press. Her head was

aching, and she felt quite nauseous. It had to be the effect of being drugged twice in one day. But she wasn't going to let on to Arnold.

Arnold popped his head out of the darkroom door. 'I'm all done in here,' he said, rubbing his hands with an uncharacteristic glee. 'Next week's edition is going to be a bumper,' he said. 'Come in and have a look.'

Pegged on a line of string over the various developing trays were pictures of the Town Hall's rubble and Mrs Allemby, the cleaning lady. Arnold even caught a shot, blurred maybe, of the rocket missile in flight. There was one of Harry's gyrocopter landing too.

'Now, you've seen all that.' He gently pulled her to the other end of the washing line of developed photos. 'What you haven't seen are these. I thought the reel was spoiled, but I'd forgotten I put a new roll of film in the camera just before Taggart's thugs broke in this morning.' He showed her pictures of Taggart threatening Baby. 'She'd gone before I could do anything to help.' Arnold also showed Veronica a picture of steel pipes and a frame-like contraption. 'It's the parts for a rocket-launcher stashed in Underwood's yard. See the Nazi stamp?' He pointed to a swastika, clearly visible on one of the pipes. He also had pictures of the so-called reporters arriving. 'I was so caught up in everything I didn't realise what Baby was doing. I could have stopped her. I'm that sorry.' His head drooped a little with the shame.

'But everything is fine now,' said Veronica, 'and I don't think it would have turned out so darn well if you had. We're all safe. Baby is amazing, and you've collected some damning and conclusive evidence!'

'Yeah, I think you're right. If I could just stop myself thinking about what could have happened...'

'What about these?' Veronica dragged him away from his melancholy to the first few pictures on the line. They turned out to be pictures of Taggart and Ida's Uncle Underwood.

Arnold brightened again. 'I forgot. That's the day I took the shot of the three of them in the window. It was another time I had to use the Brownie because I ran out of film on the other camera! These Brownie pictures are not great quality, but they're still evidence.' Arnold was so excited with all this new evidence he nearly forgot the picture Veronica had found on the noticeboard of Taggart and Underwood with Heinrich Himmler of Nazi High Command.

Houdini gave it up without a squawk as the world for Veronica, for the third time that day, faded to black.

37

Bravo, Bravo!
Saturday 2nd April, Teatime

As the closing credits were rolling and the lights were coming on, Baby scanned every row of seats in The Embassy cinema for Fingers and the older version of her. Where was she?

'Where's Fingers?' asked Baby when she found June and the orphans sitting in the front row. 'Didn't she come with you lot?'

'No,' said June, 'she said that she had something she had to do at school, which I thought was a bit strange, it being Saturday. But you know Fingers! Something of a law unto herself, and she was so definite. Is there something wrong?'

'You didn't hear it?'

'Hear what? The music was very loud…'

'And lovely,' added golden-haired Bonnie, clinging to her sister Ida.

'I haven't told them,' said Ida. 'They were having such a lovely time watching the film. I didn't want to spoil it.'

'Told us what?' asked June.

'Oh, you'll see,' said Ida. 'It was very good of them to let Alf and I in without paying, wasn't it? Especially as we're not really dressed for the pictures.' She indicated their creek-muddy overalls. Alf was standing very close to Ida. Something about how close told Baby that Alf and Ida hadn't been sitting with the rest of the children, Gin, June and her ma—or anywhere near them.

'Let's just go home,' said Baby. 'Ooh and there's someone to meet you outside. I'm sure he'll explain.'

The children filed out of their seats and followed June out of the cinema and down the steps. Gin joined them outside, pushing Mrs Lovelock along the pavement from her special place at the back of the cinema. 'Oh, I say what have we missed?' said Gin.

'World War Two, by the look of it,' said Mrs Lovelock.

They were all excited to see Harry waiting for them. June especially.

Baby looked away as June flung her arms around Harry's neck, forgetting she had charge of a dozen orphans and was in a public street, albeit in chaos from a rocket exploding on the Town Hall.

Compared to the rubble and the crowds still milling at the other end of the street, the orphanage appeared surprisingly calm, ordered, and quiet.

'Where is everyone?' said June, walking through the orphanage front door into the hall, where the stained glass above the door made pretty patterns on the new parquet floor. It was as if the reporters—Blackshirts, whoever they were—had never been.

Robert and Aggie ran into the entrance hall to meet them. 'They've all upped and gone,' said Robert, looking as if a huge weight had been lifted from his shoulders. A smile filled his face.

'We think it was sumfing to do with the rockit, don't we, Robit?' said Aggie.

'And Mr Shaw says he'll take us and Bri to the pictures on Monday to celebrate,' said Robert.

'Shall I sort out some tea?' said June. 'Lunch was such a long time ago.'

'No need,' said Mr Shaw, emerging from the kitchen. 'Brenda and I have made some tea and there's a little surprise for you all.'

'Well, I have to track Fingers down first,' said Baby. 'The little tyke's gone walkabout again.' Baby didn't like to mention the person she'd seen with her sister. She didn't want to worry anyone unnecessarily.

'No need,' repeated Mr Shaw, 'everything is under control. Now, if you'd all like to go into the living room and sit down...'

'Dad, I'm getting the sandwiches and the lemonade,' said Brian, heading for the kitchen.

'Stop!' said Veronica, who had just walked in the door, propped up by Arnold Coombes. 'Did someone say lemonade? Don't touch it! It was drugged.'

'I know,' said Brian. 'I fixed it before we left the park. Mr Taggart was thinking he was giving us something we didn't have, but we did. So, when it smelled wrong, I poured it away. It's happened before.'

'Not all of it,' said Veronica.

'I'm sorry,' said Brian, her eyebrows raised and her bottom lip giving the smallest tremble. 'Did I miss one?'

'That's alright, Brian,' said June, stroking Brian's arm. 'A lot was happening. The children wouldn't touch that bottle, anyway. The greenish tinge put them off.'

'But I did,' said Veronica.

Brian gasped. 'I'm very sorry, Veronica.'

'Brian, it's alright. You helped me remember my parents. Though it was strong stuff.'

'Are you feeling better, now?' asked Baby.

'Yeah, I think so. Arnold went to the pharmacy and got me some aspirin.'

'Come on, let's get you sat down,' said Arnold.

Brian's dad, Mr Shaw, wove through the small crowd in the entrance hall and opened one of the double doors to the orphanage living room. 'This way, everyone!'

'What's happening?' said Baby. But she knew. It was obvious. She just hadn't wanted to admit it. This was 'the end.' Hers and Fingers's lives were about to change again.

'Just go in and take your seats...' said Mr Shaw, ushering them all through.

The children, with June and Harry, filed in and took their seats on the pile of cushions, not arranged around June Lovelock's story chair, but in front of the mantlepiece, filled with daffodils. Brian followed with a trolley of sandwiches and glasses of fizzing lemonade—not green at all. Gin pushed Mrs Lovelock and parked her next to the row of comfy chairs from the dining tables lined up behind the cushions as Arnold helped a slightly unsteady Veronica sit down next to her.

'Shall we join them, Baby?' said Mr Shaw.

Baby stared at the scene. Maybe this wasn't the end, but a new beginning? She'd known what the triangular package was and, most obvious of all, she'd worked out fairly quickly who the grown-up Fingers was. What she didn't know now was what was this grown-up version of Fingers was doing here and whether or not they were any good. But how could they be a good person when they did what they did all those years ago?

In front of the fireplace sat not one, but two harps, one smaller than the other, each with an appropriately sized stool for the harpist to sit on.

When everyone was comfortable, Gin let out a squeal of glee and stood up. 'I will burst if I have to keep this secret much longer!' she said, clasping her hands together in delight. 'May I present, Miss Florence Violetta...'

A woman about the same age as June Lovelock walked in, in a stylish light blue silk gown with white wood anemones decorating her red curly hair. She sat down at the larger harp.

Gin clapped enthusiastically, and the audience followed suit.

As Miss Florence Violetta made herself comfortable on her stool and rested her long slim arms and long slim fingers gently against the harp strings, ready to play, Gin signalled for a hush.

'And please welcome to the stage, our very own Miss Florence Violetta Junior!'

Again, Gin clapped enthusiastically and, after a moment of silent surprise, the audience joined in. Robert and Aggie whistled and whooped.

Baby felt her jaw drop. Fingers, as Baby had never seen her before, was in a pretty, but not too frilly, light-blue frock with the same white flowers in her hair. Baby's street-sister, the one-time burglar, little Florrie Fingers, demurely sat down at the smaller harp.

After an unnatural hush, when the only sounds were the tiny gasps of amazement at the sight of this new Fingers, mother and daughter played.

The orphanage living room was filled with the most wonderful music. Baby had not heard music like that since the day in the theatre when Fingers showed Baby and Moll exactly what her long fingers were really for. The music was heavenly, angelic, divine even. It sounded as if all the Malcolm Taggarts, Arthur Underwoods, and Easton Fitzgeralds had never existed. It sounded happy and sad at the same time. It touched Baby's heart and made that sing too.

At the end, everyone stood and clapped until their hands were sore.

'Bravo! Bravo!' said Gin, clapping the loudest. 'Well done Fingers and her mama, the ethereal Miss Florence Violetta, whom I was so lucky to meet in Berlin!'

With tears in her eyes and an accent that didn't go with her elegance, Miss Florence Violetta, Fingers's Ma, said, 'Cor blimey, not' alf! I can't tell you 'ow 'appy I am to be back wiv little Florrie 'ere. I didn't want to give 'er up, but that's another story.' She pulled a large white lace-trimmed hankie out from the top of her dress and blew her nose for England.

Fingers got up to speak. When the clapping stopped, she said, 'Yes, this is me ma. I was scared of her comin' and changing things. Well, she 'as come now, and things will change.' She scanned the audience, all the children, and the adults; from Betsy, the youngest orphan, to old Mrs Lovelock in her wheelchair, all smiling and hands ready to clap and cheer some more.

Fingers's eyes locked on Baby's. 'That's alright, isn't it?'

Ever since they lost Moll, ever since they left London, Baby knew things were going to change, and everything Baby did was to try to stop them from changing. Stop them changing between her and Fingers, at least.

After Moll died, her only job was to look after her sister: take Moll's place; try to be like a mother; keep Fingers safe.

But here was Fingers announcing the changes. It was like Baby had been released, dismissed. No longer was she her sister's keeper. With the wrench that had been growing since Fingers started school, another feeling was growing.

Baby felt free.

She had her own mother to find.

38

Goodbye

Friday 22nd April 1938, Southampton Docks

Was Baby really free?

Did letting Fingers go mean that she didn't love her sister anymore?

No.

This. Was. Love.

Baby wanted the best for Fingers. And 'the best' was what Fingers wanted too; what Fingers had decided to do herself.

For Baby, it was being like a parent. If you love someone enough, a child, a sister, Moll… at some point, you'll have to let them go. And that was the love that Baby was feeling right at that moment. It hurt, but it was right. This parting was gentle, like the bread they break in church, but the separation was huge. But it was love. And at that moment, she was surrounded by it.

At Southampton Docks, everyone was there. June with Ida's sister Bonnie and all the other orphans, including, of course, Robert, with Frank in his arms and

Aggie clinging to his side. Harry pushed old Mrs Lovelock in her chair. Gin came with Brian and her dad. Mr Shaw had had a beard trim for the occasion and was wearing his very best shirt—a patchwork of all his favourite shirts from the past. Miss Oswald from the library was on his arm. Sophie, Letitia, and Veronica were there. Boy, did those three have a lot to talk about! Though their first meetings hadn't always gone so well, Baby now adored each one of them.

Arnold Coombes wove in and out of the crowd with his new camera—a cine camera, would you believe? A gift from Veronica. Mr Rogers from the garage brought Mrs Rogers and all their kids. Even Sergeant Ted Jackson showed up, driven by Constable Spencer in the Black Maria. And in the back of the Black Maria sat Mr Clarence with Leonard Cook, the boy-racer from the laundry, whose van had been very useful for getting them out of some very sticky situations in the past. He was in his Sunday best, no doubt hoping to catch Gin's eye. Baby hoped he took the opportunity to pick up a few driving tips too. When Baby watched Arnold's film back later, she even spotted William Teasdale lurking and trying to catch Fingers's eye as she boarded the ship with her ma. *The Queen Mary*, no less; her dream ship from ever since she arrived in Nettlefield. Though no one was stowing away today.

Fingers had known about her ma's arrival in Nettlefield since before Baby had shown her Hewett

Island in the creek on the day that Fingers didn't want to go to school. Her ma was playing for the schoolchildren that day and Fingers wasn't ready to see it.

Gin organised the whole thing, having met Miss Florence Violetta in Berlin by chance and made the connections. She had prepared Fingers for the meeting and had also been sworn to secrecy about it all.

Baby learned that everyone knew about Fingers's ma apart from her, Baby. She was a bit upset at being out of the loop at first, but came to understand the reason for not telling her was love; Fingers didn't know how to tell Baby without hurting her. As well as the fact that Fingers had to sort out her own thinking about her ma, whose return she'd dreaded for a long time.

Unfortunately, everyone knowing included Taggart, who didn't quite kidnap the famous harpist but did use his powers of persuasion to make her play for the Blackshirts in Hamwell after her visit to the school that day.

As it turned out, Miss Florence Violetta had her own power of persuasion. She *was* Fingers's mother. Their bond had never been broken, only stretched. And playing the harp was what Fingers was born for, her destiny.

So, hankies were waved, tears shed, kisses blown, and goodbyes hailed as the ship was manoeuvred away from the dockside and out into Southampton Water by Alf in his tugboat with Ida, of course.

For every wave, tear, and kiss for Fingers, there was a warm hug of reassurance for Baby. She need never be alone.

As far as The Blackshirt Menace was concerned, The Wonder Girls had proved that alone, you got into trouble, but together, you made a difference. In Nettlefield, at least, the Blackshirt grip on power was broken, and that was all down to the 'girls,' all of them, boys and girls, young and old, working together.

Together, they had stopped Arthur Underwood shipping Aryan kids out to Nazi families and worse. They'd stopped Easton Fitzgerald and his despicable use of young Spanish refugees as an undercover spy network. They'd put an end to Sir Malcolm Taggart picking up where Underwood left off, and stopped him taking over the whole town and setting it up as a centre for lies and propaganda. And not least of all, they had stopped him blowing up the Royal Navy and opening the gate for a Nazi Invasion. They all had a lot to be proud of.

The town wasn't entirely rid of Blackshirts, but those that were left were too frightened to stand up for their hateful beliefs since they'd learned the fate in store for Taggart, Tatler, Bill Teasdale, all those reporters, and the Blackshirts hiding out at Hamwell. They were all awaiting trial on charges of high treason.

It was well known the punishment for such a crime was *the* most awful.

The Wonder Girls and the good people of Nettlefield had resisted these Blackshirts and had overcome them together.

Baby was free.

But on this day of hope and excitement for the future, whatever it held, and in spite of all she'd learned, Baby was contemplating an adventure that should only be made alone...

39

INHERITANCE & RESPONSIBILITY
Easter, 1938

HOWEVER, VERONICA was only too pleased to help Baby.

Now that she had the means and the power.

Finding herself the owner of one of the biggest and most influential newspapers in Britain, as well as *The Maple Street Reporter* back in Brooklyn, and having made quite an investment in *The Nettlefield Courier*, Veronica was determined more than ever to do the right thing. She felt her responsibility keenly.

Taggart, so convinced of his influence and powers of persuasion, had already made Veronica his heir. With no regard for her youth, should anything happen to him to prevent him from running his publishing empire, his niece was to take over. She wondered how he could be so reckless? But this was the man who'd had her parents thrown off the Brooklyn Bridge in broad daylight. Recklessness and impulsivity seemed to run in the family.

There were, of course, the matters of his theft, deception, and conspiracy to murder that should be attended to, but the result would be the same. He was already charged with high treason, the worst crime that a person can commit, as far as the British establishment was concerned. And it carried the most dreadful punishment. So, what would be the point in pursuing the other crimes?

Truth and justice would be the point, of course. But at that moment in time, the world being in the state that it was in, Veronica felt that considering the bigger picture, far bigger than her own family, was more important. She had newspapers to run and publish for good.

She did, however, retain the services of a private detective; a man in an oversized gaberdine coat, with a scar cutting through his left eyebrow and an overfondness for the letter H. 'Ronald Lazenby, 'h'at your service, Miss.' And Miss Veronica Park, soon to be her official name by deed poll, *was* an investigative journalist.

Mr Lazenby, somewhat mercenary in his attitude, worked for whoever would pay. He prided himself on a thorough job and said he was pleased to be working for a less 'shall we say *bombastic*?' client.

Through Veronica's investigation, he checked out well enough and, most importantly, was not responsible for Archie's murder. Though—known only to Veronica and with many assurances regarding his safety, when the time came—he was prepared to testify as to who was.

But Mr Lazenby *was* guilty of providing 'the crumbs'; that copy of the *Beacon* at Betty Marie's that brought Veronica to Nettlefield.

'I thought I was doing the right thing,' Betty Marie had said a few days ago, over the crackly line of a transatlantic phone call from Arnold's telephone in the Courier's office. 'The Scotsman said it was for your good. He said there was money; family money. But because you were who you were, it had to be done right. He said you needed persuading, and this was the only way to do it.'

For a few moments, with the trundle of lorries clearing the town hall rubble in the background, all Veronica could hear on the line were the crackles. 'Betty? You still there?'

'I'm here,' said Betty, sounding even further away than she already was.

Veronica caught the hint of shame in Betty's voice. 'He also said, if I did it right, he'd book Maxine Sullivan for me. What could I say? She's a star, Veronica, honey.'

'Of course,' explained Mr Lazenby later, 'Miss Sullivan had no part in the transaction. H'as far as she was concerned, she was simply booked to sing in a Brooklyn bar.'

Veronica felt a little sad that Betty could be so persuaded and that she, Veronica, could be so deceived. But when she thought of all the wonderful things that came from that deception, she could only be happy.

Working for her, private investigator Lazenby lost much of that tired, drawn look he had on the other side of the Atlantic. And the advantage of a head start on Taggart put a spring in his step. 'Happy to spill h'all the beans to prevent any difficult h'association.'

One day, Veronica would write it all up, when a good stack of evidence would be handy, should the treason charges not take the expected course.

She'd taken a room at the orphanage with Fingers's mother. Arnold had been all for looking after Veronica just to make sure that all the knockout-drugs she took on that eventful day, Saturday 2nd April, had left her system. 'But Arnold, you have the *Courier* to get out,' said Veronica, over the whirr and flap of the press, busy on the fourth reprint of the first bumper edition after the demise of Taggart's *Beacon*.

The Nettlefield Courier, 7th April 1938, sold out within the hour. A queue had stretched almost to The Embassy cinema. 'Oh, Dad would have been so proud, and Arch too, God love him,' said Arnold, wearing his brother's old overall, and patting the faithful machine.

Veronica knew for sure that Archie would have burst with pride. Her investment in the *Courier* meant

Arnold could hire more staff and fill those empty desks in the office. He was all set to go daily by the summer.

'And we've learned something from the Beacon, haven't we?' said Veronica. 'Folk like sweeteners—or chips!—with their news. It can't be all bad. You've got to entertain them. They need hope.'

Which is why the following week's paper included an exclusive interview with famous harpist Miss Florence Violetta and her prodigy daughter, 'Little Florrie', the harpist formerly known as 'Fingers.'

She was, of course, still 'Fingers' to the all the Wonder Girls, young and old, female to male!

Veronica got the complete story of Florence being forced by her manager to leave 'Little Florrie' in the care of the old woman known as Moll, herself a one-time music hall performer, down on her luck.

'I was so young,' said Florence. 'I loved my baby, I swear I did. And 'er dad. We was gonna run away together. But 'e was a toff and his family wasn't having it and went and got 'im married off to some Lady thinygmajig overseas. And then me manager made me leave the baby behind. 'E was a bully but 'e was all I had left. It were so cruel on us... I admit it brought me down and I didn't fight for Little Florrie 'ere like I should 'ave.'

'It's alright, ma,' said Fingers back in her old skirt and boots. But when she turned to give her mother a reassuring pat on the hand, Veronica noticed a little blue bow nestled in her red curls.

The Violettas' story was front page, no need at all for it to be hidden amongst the ads.

Now it was Baby's turn.

Veronica learned that Taggart's investigation into Baby's mother was true. Veronica bought Baby's ticket to Mumbai, the proper name for the city the British called Bombay. Veronica then used the *Beacon's* resources to prepare Baby's mother for Baby's arrival.

Following Baby's strict instructions, Veronica told no one.

'Not until after the ship has sailed,' said Baby.

So Veronica helped her with this letter:

To my very dear Nettlefield Family and Friends,

I don't think you would have stopped me from leaving, but I think I may have stopped myself. Seeing you all there, waving me off like we did for Fingers and her ma, I would have run down those steps and waved with you!

So, with Veronica's help, I am leaving alone. My heart is breaking. But it is also yearning to know the woman I can truly call 'mother,' my own real ma. Veronica is sure she has found her, and I trust Veronica.

When I get there, I will write as best I can, though without Veronica to help me, the letters will be short, but they will have photographs. 'Pictures are worth a thousand words,' is what Veronica says, so she has got a photographer in India, because that's where I'm going, to come and snap them for you.

I am sure you will see me again. But it will be after I've tried out having a ma and seeing if I like it. I'll also see if there's anything over there that needs my help.

So, with love, far, far bigger than the ship I'm sailing on, I wish that you all stay very safe and very loved and very happy,

Your loving sister,

Baby

40
ONE YEAR LATER
May 1939, Mumbai, India

AWAY FROM THE SUNLIGHT spilling through the open door of her ma's corrugated tin hut, Baby sat at the charkha, a spinning wheel gifted by Ghandi himself. The floor was surprisingly cool. In her hand, she cradled a shrinking cloud of cotton joined to the wheel by a slubby, uneven thread.

After a few more turns and twists, the cloud was gone, and the spool was full. She knew it wouldn't pass her ma's test, but when it was woven into the khadi that would make her first saree, it would be there as a memory of their reunion.

'It will also,' her ma had said, 'remind you where you came from, Baby. And that you must always keep your mind open to learning new things.'

Her ma, so unlike the sad picture Taggart had painted of her, was full of wisdom.

It was true that she had sat at the side of the road selling old sarees surrounded by her children. She still did, though Baby's older brothers and sisters were all grown now, and some had their own children.

But Baby's ma was so much more than that. She was a Dalit woman, called 'untouchable' by some and had joined the Dalit Resistance. She fought against British rule and against the oppression of the Dalit people by those of higher castes.

'There is so much to do,' she said, cupping Baby's chin in her dark brown hand, 'and I am full of joy that you have come to help.'

Though Baby's ma only spoke Marathi and Baby only English, somehow, they understood each other. From that first moment of recognition in the heat and dust of the alleyway outside her ma's hut, their hearts were joined. Her mother's arms wrapped her in love, and Baby knew she was home.

Baby had travelled for weeks with the all the emotions—excitement, fear, sadness, hope, and everything in between—which, as a first-class passenger, she had time to indulge in. It wasn't the *Queen Mary*, but it was more luxurious than Baby could ever have imagined. 'And there's a ticket back if it doesn't work out,' Veronica had said. 'Just send me a wire.'

Well, it was working out very well indeed. She was just like her mother—or her mother was just like her! Baby couldn't decide.

The heat, however, was a struggle and was why Baby was at home, practising her spinning in as much shade as her mother's small Dharavi home could muster. Her ma, whose name really was Mukta, told Baby that, in the past, the British had helped the Dalit people especially, but it was time for Mother India to regain her independence. It was not right that they must give their cotton to the British to make into cloth, when it would be so much better that they spun and wove their cotton themselves. Especially as it grew in abundance here in India. 'And that is why', said Mukta, 'Ghandiji says that we must all learn to spin.'

Baby removed the full spool and closed the charkha. It would be in use again, much more efficiently, before the day was over. She felt in the pocket of her old skirt for the latest letter from Nettlefield. Though everyone wrote, June's letters were the most informative.

The neatly folded typewritten sheet included some cuttings from *The Nettlefield Courier* and *The New Beacon*. 'A beacon for truth and integrity,' Veronica had said about the newspaper she had inherited and reformed after her Uncle Taggart's arrest and imprisonment pending trial. Apparently, he had been persuaded to help the British government with information about Nazi activities, which would keep him away from the hangman's noose. Baby couldn't help feeling it was just toffs helping toffs.

But one of the cuttings was from neither the reformed *Beacon* nor the *Courier*. In *'The Maple Street Reporter,* 29th April 1939', Baby read a report, by 'Lorretta May,' about the first triumphant US tour of mother and daughter harpists The Violettas. Lorretta May was thrilled to report the tour delivered its finale performance in their own Betty Marie's Bar on Maple Street, Brooklyn. The report described how Miss Florence Violetta the younger, 'nicknamed Fingers' for her extraordinary reach across the strings, was using the harp to improvise in much the same way as Louis Armstrong did on the trumpet and, indeed, with his voice. Or like the celebrated jazz singer Maxine Sullivan, who had also performed at Betty Marie's. A new genre was born: Jazz Harp! The biggest photograph was of Fingers and her ma, almost like sisters, with their harps, in matching flowing dresses and their fingers blurred across the strings.

Baby felt a pang in her chest. She missed her sister. Ten years with a person did not fade so quickly. But she knew they were both home, and so lucky to have so many homes. With each other, with their mas, and with all the other Wonders!

Baby unfolded the sharp creases of June's letter and her heart almost burst with joy at the first paragraph. It was full of apologies, reasons, and excuses. But they weren't important, because June and Harry were married!

The rest of the letter was in Letitia's code, which Baby was now practised in reading.

June explained that their wedding was a hush-hush affair because Harry was going on a top–secret mission and he didn't know how long he'd be away. The wedding was at Sir Hugh Sinclair's new place somewhere up north—though almost everywhere was up north from Nettlefield. (It was Sir Hugh that Baby had rung from the Courier on the day of the Nettlefield rocket.) Letitia had been there for the wedding and so had Brian's dad, who was helping Sir Hugh with something 'hush-hush' again. Brian was there too. She'd gone along with her dad and was busy collecting lots of ideas for sandwich fillings. Mabel, the old orphanage cook, had returned to Nettlefield, having sadly lost her Bournemouth sister to tuberculosis. Mabel said that she was glad of the distraction from all her grieving. According to June, Mabel's every other word was 'luvaduck' at the innovations that had happened in her absence.

June also reported that Alf had bought Ida a very pretty ring, so they were now officially engaged, and to celebrate they'd ferried all the orphans to Hewett Island on *The Wonder* for a *Swallows and Amazons* picnic. Taggart's rocket launcher and its shed had all been well photographed and subsequently removed for evidence in the upcoming trials. Baby couldn't help thinking how jealous Fingers would be that they picnicked without her! For herself, Baby was in no hurry to see Hewett Island again.

The rebuilding of the council offices was well underway while the council was camped out, not at the orphanage as Taggart had planned for his puppet council, but at the big house on the other side of the creek. *'There is a rumour,'* June wrote, *'that the King himself will be coming to open the new Town Hall because he'd heard about everything that happened and there's talk of honours for all involved. Mother's not keen, though.'* Baby had often thought that old Mrs Lovelock, as well as being the oldest, was the most rebellious orphan of them all. Baby would love Mukta, her ma, to meet Mrs L. She was sure they'd get on like an orphanage on fire!

Catching up on all the news from her extended family made Baby feel happy and sad at the same time. She refolded the sheet and the newspaper cuttings to read again later. She needed to move. The sun had found its way through the door and was filling the small tin house.

Baby was carefully replacing June's letter in her skirt pocket when a shadow in the doorway brought some more welcome shade.

Her ma had returned home.

Baby knew her eyes were wet when she looked up to greet Mukta, her ma, and Baby knew that her ma, in her wisdom, knew why. She knelt beside Baby, holding her, shielding her, covering her, understanding her, loving her... And Baby, for a little while at least, could be something that in her fourteen years she could barely remember being at all.

She could be a child.

Epilogue
Many Years Later

BABY WAS AMAZED and so very grateful to whatever great being that watches over us, for how all the Wonders survived the war, when so many people didn't. Throughout her life, she marvelled with pride at how their adventures continued.

Ida and Alf rescued six extremely grateful servicemen off the beach at Dunkirk and sailed them across the English Channel to safety with the hundreds of other 'Little Ships.' Both Ida and Alf went on to fight. Ida worked on the tanks in the desert and Alf joined the Navy. They married on VE day in the registry office in the Nettlefield Town Hall, rebuilt and miraculously undamaged by the war.

Ida's sister Bonnie cut off her golden curls, sold them to a theatrical wigmaker and donated the money to the charities helping those made homeless by the Luftwaffe. Her friends mourned her lost beauty, but in the fifties her elfin hairstyle was all the rage and she found modelling provided a useful income to support her volunteering.

Sophie never did find her family. She supposed they had perished early on in one of Hitler's camps of horror. But she knew that although she didn't see her Nettlefield family that often, they were always there for her. And they were so proud of her achievements in couture and high fashion. At every opportunity, Bonnie Barnes modelled for her.

From time to time, Veronica would leave her newspapers in her trusted editors' capable hands to report on everyday life in occupied France, Holland, Belgium, and Greece. She travelled all over.

For years after the war was over, Letitia was still bound by the Official Secrets Act about her adventures. Though when Baby saw her in Mumbai, soon after Partition, when the British had finally and disastrously left India, she noticed how Letitia tried hard to disguise a limp and cover a long pale scar on her neck. Baby didn't remark on these, she just made sure that, despite the upheaval in India at that time, they had the most wonderful holiday together.

June and Harry's own children—twins, born in 1940—joined the orphans at Nettlefield Grange in one huge and very happy family that grew as the war progressed, with evacuees from London and other threatened cities. *'A few extra children were nothing after the hordes of fascists that demanded accommodating in the thirties,'* wrote June in her memoirs.

Gin found her fortune and her fame on the West End stage and danced her way through the London Blitz. She had many starring roles, not just because of her talent but her bravery too. She danced while the bombs fell. And being on the plumper side, she did so much for the millions of women that did not fit those pencil-thin waists of the forties and fifties!

Brian wrote a recipe book called *The Tasty Sandwich* with no help from her dad.

'The girl's a genius; I can't interfere with that!' Mr Shaw had said.

'But Dad, you did.'

'Just one or two ideas, my dear...'

'That's alright, Dad.'

Though she could make 'a nice English curry', sandwiches were always Brian's food of choice.

Robert Perkins, who always insisted that he was not an orphan, though his mum never came and got him, inherited The Lillie with his best friend Aggie. And years later Robert and Aggie had their own Wonder family of definitely not orphans, both human and dog!

Leonard Cook, farm labourer, laundryman, lorry driver, went on to a marry a surprising choice of wife; an artistic lady who loved to sing classical music, draw, and ride her bike just fast enough to keep upright. They went on to have two children, your author here and a tank driver for the British Army.

And Baby and Fingers? As apart geographically as they became, they never lost their sisterly love. And as communication across the globe became easier and easier, the two women grew even closer together and learned more and more about each other's lives, their achievements, their worries and hopes. Did they have families?

Yes, but I'll leave you to decide what type of families they had; who they were and what they did. Just know that Baby and Fingers never stopped being Wonders or wondering. Thinking, marvelling, resisting, rebelling, making a difference, being amazing!

Dear Reader,

I loved writing this story. I have tried hard to be respectful to those characters whose experience is different to mine. If you enjoyed their adventures, please do let me know. Just a sentence is enough. It makes such a difference to me. Here's my Amazon page –

Thank you so much,

Jan

About the Book

Here are some of the research rabbit holes I followed while writing **The Wonder Girls Rebel**. *Some of these topics may only have resulted in a sentence of story but they all influenced my telling of it.*

Harold Harmsworth, 1st Viscount Rothermere

After the general election in 2019 which made Boris Johnson the UK's prime minister, I knew that I wanted my next villain to be a newspaper baron. I was struck by how much power the media holds over popular opinion. It was not difficult to find a real-life example.

By the 1930's, Harold Harmsworth, 1st Viscount Rothermere owned multiple newspapers including *The Daily Mail* and *The Daily Mirror*. He was a very rich man whose fortune, even in 1922, amounted to £780 million, the equivalent of about £54 billion today. He was obsessed with his money, fearing its loss and regularly demanding that his staff check the state of his stocks and shares to make sure that his extreme wealth remained intact.

He despised democracy, firmly believing that only those in the upper classes, like himself, had the right to rule Britain. An enthusiast for fascism, he considered it a mistake to give the working classes and indeed, women, the vote and he used his newspapers to spread those beliefs.

Two of his three sons were killed in the First World War, which could have contributed to his desire to maintain a peace with Germany as Hitler took power. In 1934 he wrote his most famous *Daily Mail* editorial, headlined 'Hurrah for the Blackshirts', where he expressed his support for Oswald Mosley's British Union of Fascists. Though he withdrew this support following Blackshirt violence at a rally later that year, Viscount Rothermere did not waiver in his admiration for Hitler and the Nazis. He frequently either visited Hitler in Germany or socialized in London with Von Ribbentrop, the Nazi ambassador, throughout the 1930s.

After war was declared in 1939, Rothermere's pro-Nazi views, became deeply unpopular. Another press baron and minister for aircraft production, Lord Beaverbrook sent him to America, supposedly to inspect the aircraft industry there. Viscount Rothermere never returned to Britain, dying on holiday in Bermuda in 1940.

Frances Sweeney and Muckraking

Frances Sweeney, born in Boston around 1908, was a 'muckraker', an independent investigative journalist. In her twenties she founded her own paper *The Boston City Reporter*. At first, she focussed on corruption in politics but then turned her attention to fascist and anti-Semitic propaganda. As a Catholic herself she was especially appalled by the anti-Semitism she saw in the Catholic church.

In the 1930s, gangs of catholic youths would terrorise Jewish neighbourhoods assaulting residents and vandalising property. Boston at that time was one of the most anti-Semitic cities in the United States. She recruited a small team of mostly volunteer researchers and gave them one instruction *'What I want from you is facts.'* The only person allowed to have an opinion was Frances and then only if it was backed up by the facts.

During World War Two, Frances started a 'Rumour Clinic' with *The Boston Herald*. Each week the 'clinic' would take a rumour, trace it to its source which was usually Nazi Propaganda and soundly refute it. One such rumour was because a woman with permed hair went to work in a munitions factory, her head exploded!

As one young woman, working independently, her task was huge. It was likened by fellow muckraking journalist, Arthur Derounian, as *'digging at a mountain with a hand-spade'*. Frances died young, aged 36 in 1944 but posthumously succeeded in getting the pro-fascist magazine *Catholic International* banned from newsstands. Her work also raised awareness about anti-Semitism in the Boston police force. This led to the firing of the police commissioner and a sharp drop in violent crime against the Jewish community.

Irving Stone, an American Biographical writer said,

'Fran Sweeney could not be discouraged, could not be beaten down, could not be frightened, could not be put in her place. She was a one-man crusade. She burned with some of the hottest and most unextinguishable passion for social justice that I have ever seen.'

The Shortest History of Printing & Typesetting

Johannes Guttenberg invented the movable-type printing press in around 1440 and it is perhaps the most important invention in the history of the world. Previously books would have been individually and laboriously handwritten by monks. So there weren't many of them and but hardly anyone could read so that was ok But the printing press changed that. Reading matter could be copied and reproduced in a fraction of the time, so over time, more and more people learned to read and mass communication was born.

Although printing a book was now much quicker than writing one, preparing the press was still a laborious process. Each letter of each word was a single stamp—a single piece of type, which had to be positioned, set, in the block for that page. Once set, multiple pages could be printed very quickly. To do this for a book would be fine—it may be a year or more before you would have to print a new edition. But for a newspaper, a new edition needed to be printed, if not every day, every week at least. So in the 19th century, the race to devise a machine to do this more efficiently was on.

'The Unitype' invented by Joseph Thorne, who also worked for Singer Sewing Machines, was an early successful attempt to solve the typesetting problem. Metal type was stored in a cylinder. The operator, typing on a keyboard, would release the stored type sending it down a chute into a galley were it would be arranged into a block of text. This would then be transferred to the press for printing. Though advertised as a one man typesetter it took at least two and if you wanted a larger font for headlines for instance, you needed another machine. Notches cut into the type would enable it to be returned to its correct position in the cylinder after use.

An American school teacher called John R Rogers invented a **'The Rogers Typograph'**. It used letter moulds, 'matrices', to cast 'lines of type' in hot metal, which after cooling, could be set in a block of print similar to the Unitype. After use, these metal bars were melted down ready for remoulding. Although his machine was streamlined and efficient, in 1890 Mr Rogers' Typograph was 4 years too late.

'The Linotype' machine invented by a German immigrant to the US, Ottmar Mergenthaler, used the same hot metal 'line of type' principle. It went into production in 1886 and decisively won the typesetting race. In its heyday, the huge Mergenthaler factory in Brooklyn covered 12 acres of floor space over 9 floors and employed 2500 people.

By issuing patent infringements on other hot metal machines like the Rogers Typograph and offering a trade in on old Unitype machines, Mergenthaler cornered the markct. Nearly all the Unitypes were collected and destroyed by his agents. Though his Linotype looked quite different to the Typograph and another 'line of type' machine, the Ludlow, Mergenthaler accused other inventors of stealing his idea of 'a line of type'.

The Rogers Typograph, however, eventually found its way to Germany, into Europe, and Africa, where being a simpler machine and so less prone than the Lintotype to breaking down, it became the typesetter of choice for smaller publishers and printers.

Letterpress technology finally gave way to digital technology in the 1980s and these machines are now only curiosities, mostly in museums.

The First Daily Newspaper

The first daily newspaper in English was *The Daily Courant*, launched in 1702 and the first English Newspaper 'editor' (though the job title was yet to be invented) was E. Mallet. E. Mallet is referred to as the 'seller' of the newspaper and as a 'he'. But it is very likely that E stood for Elizabeth.

With her husband, Elizabeth was a printer and bookseller in London. *The Daily Courant.* (Au courant is French for 'current', as in current affairs.) was her most ambitious project. She published a digest of news from abroad, always referenced her sources and stated that her aim was to publish only facts to allow the reader to make up their own mind. Interestingly, she did not publish news from London because it could antagonise the government and be easily contradicted.

There is little written about Elizabeth, but she does appear in a list of 'honest (Mercurial) Women' by another bookseller/printer/author, John Dunton, in his 1705 memoir *'The Life and Errors of John Dunton'*.

Elizabeth died in 1706 having published 40 daily editions of the *Courant* before it was taken over by another bookseller/printer Samuel Buckley (also editor of *The Spectator*, still in circulation today). Elizabeth's *Courant* merged with *The Daily Gazetteer* in 1735 which continued in various forms until the end of the century when *The Times* was launched, and newspapers were firmly established.

Mukta Salve

Mukta Salve, born in India around 1841 was a Dalit woman. In India's caste system, a hierarchy that defines a person's place and value in society, a Dalit is the lowest. Dalits were often referred to as 'untouchable'. They were given the dirtiest jobs, dealing with rubbish, sewage and the dead. They had very little access, if any, to education or health care. They were even excluded from Hinduism, the religion that defined them. Crimes committed against Dalits went unpunished.

Mukta at fourteen years old, after only 3 years of education, wrote her essay *'About the Grief of the Mahar and the Mangs'*, the Mahar and the Mangs being subgroups within the Dalits.

She not only documented appalling atrocities committed against Dalits, and questioned Hinduism, she also analysed how the highest caste, the Brahmins, manipulated religion to maintain their influence over Indian society.

Mukta saw how her parents suffered under the caste system and in her essay, refers to the 'benevolent British government' who mitigated the pain of Mangs and Mahars. Under British influence, she writes how harassment and torture stopped and how some Brahmins even started schools for Mangs and Mahars. Her essay was published in the journal, *Dnyanodaya*, in 1855.

Though abolished on paper, videos from Indian commentators such as *Anneburg Media* show that even in the 21st century, the caste system remains entrenched in India.

The Charkha

The Charkha is a small portable spinning wheel in use since the 14th century but popularised by Ghandi, the leader of India's resistance against the British. It symbolises independence and self-sufficiency.

While under British rule, India was forced to send its cotton to Britain for spinning and weaving. The cloth was then sold back to India at a high cost. The Charkha enabled women, particularly, to change that. It gave them the means to set up and run their own cottage industries.

The Charkha is even represented on India's flag as a 24 spoke wheel.

The Partition of India

Britain finally gave India its independence in 1947. But done in such a hurry, 'Partition' was disastrous for the Indian people. Borders were drawn to make two nations India and Pakistan– to separate the two main religions. Though Pakistan was also divided into East and West, East Pakistan eventually becoming Bangladesh.

The Muslims were to be in in Pakistan, the Hindus in India but there were more than two religions in

India and people did not live so conveniently. This resulted in millions of people having to uproot, to leave villages where their families might have lived for hundreds of years and move to areas where they *thought* they might be safe.

Fears for the safety of women led to families being divided. Because the details about the new borders were not released until after Partition, there was much unrest and bloodshed. Kashmir in the north, in the 21st century, is still disputed.

Black and White Twins

Twins where one has much darker coloured skin than the other are rare, and rarer still when both parents are fairer-skinned. A person's skin colour results from a number of different genes that control the amount of 'melanin' produced in the skin. Usually, these genes come from parents, but it is not impossible that such a gene may pop up from a much earlier generation.

Jim Crow Laws

Jim Crow laws were the laws that allowed segregation of black and white people in the Southern states of America following the American Civil war. They were named after what is now an offensive music hall song called *Jumpin' Jim Crow* performed by a white singer made up in black face. The laws were a compensation to the South for losing the Civil War, which was fought over the abolition of slavery.

Maxine Sullivan & Dorothy Ashby

Maxine Sullivan was born in Pennsylvania in 1911 She performed as a jazz singer from the mid 1930s to shortly before her death in 1987. She sang and acted on stage and in films and was best known for her swing version of the Scottish folk song *Loch Lomond*.

Dorothy Ashby was the harpist from Detroit, born in 1932, who, in the 1950s, invented Jazz Harp. She established the harp as an instrument on which musicians could improvise as well as they could on the piano or saxophone. Dorothy also died in the 1980s.

Both black women triumphed despite the prejudices of their time.

Fareham Creek and Pewitt Island

Fareham, the town on the South coast of England where the author grew up, is the inspiration for 'Nettlefield'.

Fareham's creek, a large one by American standards is actually the upper reaches of Portsmouth Harbour and also has an island. Pewitt Island, visible at low *and* high tide is now a nature reserve, home to plant species such as sea lavender and golden samphire. Plans to build a fortification to protect Portsmouth were proposed in 1857 but improved artillery technology meant the fortification was never built.

In the 2020s, the creek doesn't smell nearly as bad as it did in the 1960s and 70s but it is just as muddy.

Rockets

In 1926, Robert H Goddard, an American scientist and inventor, built the first self-propelling liquid-fuelled rocket. His aim was to go into space. His work inspired a young German, Werner von Braun, also a space enthusiast. Throughout the 1930s, Werner developed his rocket technology, occasionally consulting with Robert Goddard. As early as 1934, von Braun's group had successfully launched two rockets that reached heights of 2.2 and 3.5 km. It was in 1944 that this rocket technology was fully adopted by the Nazis. And the V2 Rockets, the world's first guided ballistic missiles, were launched in their thousands in retaliation for the bombing of German cities by the allies. The V stood for 'vengeance'.

An estimated 2754 people were killed in London in V2 attacks. However, it could have been so much worse had British intelligence not sent false reports about how the rockets were missing their targets.

Again, I am indebted to Wikipedia as a great starting point to the research, which I am pleased to include here, rather than weigh the story down with it. If you like, I hope there is enough here for you check my research out for yourself.

Acknowledgements

Thank you to Crispin Keith and Jo King who read everything I write, as I write it and give me the encouragement to keep going.

Thank you to Sandra Horn, Valerie Bird, Lisa Conway, Penny Langford and Carol Cole, who listened so attentively and insightfully to my chapters as I was writing.

Thank you to my global zoom group, Adam Jarvis, Mark Hood, Lynne Clarke and especially Tara Waterman, who makes our zooming possible. Your feedback, excellent tips and all-round encouragement are brilliant.

Thank you to Morgan Delaney and Lynne Clarke, who are the most marvellous beta readers!

Thank you, too, to the excellent *Bestseller Experiment*, who through the podcast and Facebook group introduce me to so many wonderful writers from all over the world.

Thank you, again, to Anne Glenn for another outstanding cover design. Her covers give me such confidence to sell all three books.

Thank you to editor, Julian Barr, and proof-reader, Andy Hodge. The professional skills of both these gentlemen, I cannot recommend highly enough. Any errors left in the text are all mine as I am a compulsive fiddler and commas, like dog hair and pins, get everywhere!

Finally, as always and most importantly, thank you to my spectacular family—Daisy, Joel, Sam and Ruby and their wonderful partners—Phil, Becki, and Holly. I am so proud of you all. Everything I do is for you.

And Les, best husband, best dad, best tea-maker, best reader, best technical support and best-ever friend – you make me dinner and you make me laugh; I couldn't ask for more!

I love you all so very much.

ABOUT THE AUTHOR

J.M. Carr lives in Southampton UK, with her technical support. They share their home with a collie called Cindy, and anyone who needs a place to stay at the time. If you would like to find out more about the author, her other stories and the background to this book, head on over to **jmcarr.com.**

*In memory of a marvellous woman,
Pauline McWilliams,
the most amazing choir-leader and a brilliant friend.*

Printed in Great Britain
by Amazon